Two Feet Press

RUNAWAY

A RETRIEVAL, INC. NOVEL: *BOOK 1*

JB SCHROEDER

Two Feet Press

PO Box 351
Chatham, NJ 07928-9991

Runaway © 2015 by JB Schroeder, LLC

www.jbschroederauthor.com

Cover photographs ©mbot/Thinkstock,
©Akos Nagy/Shutterstock, and @Bruce Rolff/Thinkstock

Printed by CreateSpace
Print Edition 1.0

ISBN-10: 1-943561-01-X
ISBN-13: 978-1-943561-01-8

*As promised, the first book is dedicated
to my Gigi, Eddie Howard,
who always believed I'd succeed.*

CHAPTER 1

HIS FINGERS—CAUGHT MID-REACH between the upright bins of fruit and the plastic bag in his other hand—clenched around a kiwi, surely bruising the tender flesh hidden under the ugly skin as he stared at the stunning girl with the mahogany hair.

Her striped leggings led to tennis shoes that flashed with multicolored lights at every footfall. She skipped along the aisle. Eyes glued to the child, he threw the kiwi back toward the others, shoved the baggie in his basket, and followed. The girl and her mother stopped just ahead, so he halted too, at the bananas—though he hated their texture—and pretended to find a good bunch.

Turn. Turn around, he willed. He had to have another look at her face.

For it was like seeing an angel—or a ghost, depending on your perspective. Like seeing Laura fifteen years ago when he'd bought the house on Dale Drive. He hadn't realized then quite how their relationship would develop, and yet he'd known with the full force of his being that there'd been a reason he'd been brought into her circle, and she into his. He'd been beguiled by children before, although sexually he preferred his girls somewhat older. In the end, the craving he'd felt for Laura had proved something special. He'd stayed close, been patient, played the doting neighbor, watching in anticipation as she began to bud and bloom so early—and it had all paid off.

"Mackenzie, keep up, honey. Mackenzie!" the mother called, but the girl had her hand in a bag of grapes. Popped one in her mouth. She looked right at him then, all liquid brown eyes and rosy cheeks, and put her finger to her lips, including him in her secret. He managed to wink back before she turned and fled after her mother—but in truth, his brain stumbled as his heart raced. My god, she was a beauty. And indeed, uncannily similar to Laura. Just his type.

He wondered at her age. Perhaps six, or maybe seven and a bit small for her age?

The pair argued about something down the aisle. The mother was blond and blown out with angular features. The child must resemble her father, or perhaps some dead grandmother whose genes had finally achieved dominance generations later.

"All right," the woman said with a roll of her eyes and a slight smile curving her lips. "Run down, pick a treat—one only—and meet me at the other end."

A sweet tooth, then. The minute the mother passed the end cap, he slid into the frozen foods aisle. He sidled up to Mackenzie—such an awful name, contemporary and contrived. A classic moniker would have suited her better.

"Hmmnn. So many choices." He smiled at the girl. "What should I choose…"

Young Mackenzie looked at him and smiled. She remembered him from the produce section, or she trusted far too easily.

She didn't speak. And he was conscious of a distinct shortage of time.

"What's your favorite?" he asked.

"Today my favorite is something with chocolate chips." She nearly pressed her nose against the cold glass. "Last week my favorite was Frosty Cake ice cream."

"Frosty Cake? What's that?"

"It's got pieces of cake and frosting it!" She grinned, showing a set of tiny but perfect teeth.

"Cake and frosting and ice cream on one spoon? You must have cavities on every tooth!"

"No, I don't, see?" And she opened her mouth wide, leaned into him just enough.

His heart pounded as he leaned down. Precious girl, inviting him to enter her space. His fingers angled her jaw upward. He displayed the appropriate expression of mild curiosity, yet the ease with which he'd contrived this encounter suffused him with power and thrilled him down to his very cells.

"Bigger. I can't see," he said. In the same instant, he realized the child's mother was barreling down the aisle with her cart.

"No cavities!" he exclaimed as loud as he dared. "I can't believe it! You must really do a fine job brushing."

He turned from the child, pretended to check the case. He yanked open one of the doors, grabbed something small, and shoved it in his basket. The woman reached them and placed her hand protectively across Mackenzie's chest, pulling her back against her body into what she must imagine was a circle of safety.

He nodded at the case, as if reaching a decision. "Well if you want chocolate chips, you should get Cookie Chip Ice Cream. It's got chocolate chips *and* cookie dough."

He gave the child a conspiratorial wink, then shot the woman a small, quick smile and turned to go, as if he was embarrassed about discussing ice cream flavors with a child.

In reality, he required a quick exit, before she memorized his face. Before any hint of the giddiness that bubbled within him showed. Like a chemical reaction in the lab, spontaneous effervescence could not be contained for long, he thought, as a laugh erupted from him moments later in the cereal aisle. There was simply nothing like the discovery of someone new.

CHAPTER 2

STANDING BESIDE a borrowed police cruiser, Detective Sergeant Mitch Saunders scanned the ugly orange and tan exterior of East County High in Blakes Ridge, Pennsylvania. He blew out a shaky breath. Ever since last night, when he'd found out his younger sister had run away—over two weeks ago—he'd been trying to dislodge an awful sense of foreboding.

Mitch hit speed dial for his mom.

"All right, Mom, I'm here. Who am I looking for?"

"Tiffany's best friend is Carrie Holland. Last time I saw her, her hair was dyed an awful shade of red—bright and unnatural looking. It always looks sloppy, teased up into a ponytail. Lots of heavy makeup. Clothes too tight..." Deirdre Scott heaved a sob. "She used to be a nice girl. But, you know, they are way past the age of tea parties and teddy bears, so I just don't know anymore."

"It's okay, Mom, I'll sort it out."

"I know, I know you will, I'm just—I was so sure she'd come back. I thought to give her some time, just enough to realize how much better it is to be at home...with people who love her. And now, I'm so scared." Her voice dropped to a whisper. "Maybe something horrible happened."

"Don't borrow trouble," he said, knowing the advice was worthless. She'd buried a son and a husband. Deirdre would always fear the worst. "I'll find her, and then, after I skin her hide for you, you can play the good guy at home, okay?"

He heard sniffling, and frustration welled. Nothing he could say would ease his mother's heartache and worry. Nothing would help until he'd found Tiffany. Again, he wished his mother had gotten word to him right away. But he'd been undercover and just about to bust a fledgling narcotics ring when Tiffany had split. Unfortunately, that career move had rendered him unavailable to his family for much of the last few years.

The bell rang—a far-reaching metal reverberation signaling the most important part of the school day: escape.

"Mom, they're coming out. I'll call you later."

He rounded the hood and went to lean against the passenger-side door. Eager to be released, especially on a Monday, kids poured from the doors and fanned out, though most of them had to flow in his general direction. He'd parked between the main doors and the seniors' parking lot. Anybody tight with his sister wouldn't be caught dead heading for the buses lined up like neon sausage links off to the left.

They paid him no mind, just streamed past him. Cops came to the school often enough. Given that most of Mitch's years in law enforcement had been spent right here in Blakes Ridge, he'd been back to the school numerous times himself since his own graduation seventeen years ago. LEOs, or law enforcement officers, often checked kids out, followed up on reports of vandalism, and searched lockers for drugs. Today, he'd purposely worn his uniform, marking him clearly. Otherwise, a thirty-six-year-old man sporting torn jeans and a day's growth of beard loitering on the premises might creep the kids out—something he hoped to avoid.

He fixated on a girl who'd paused to light a cigarette

before stepping off the sidewalk. The hair, makeup, and retro Madonna-era clothes made her look like a ten-dollar hooker. Mom had nailed the description.

Mitch crossed to her and her friend—nearly a twin, except this one remained a brunette.

"Girls." He crossed his arms, but remained in the street. Although they still had to look up at him, he wasn't aiming to intimidate them right off the bat by towering over them.

They didn't return the greeting. The redhead—if you could actually call that screaming mop red—squinted and blew out a stream of smoke, testing him. The friend shifted her hips, attempting to look cool and undisturbed.

"I'm Detective Saunders. Are you Carrie Holland?" He nodded at her.

"Depends."

He rolled his eyes. "Listen, this isn't the movies. You aren't in trouble. I just need to ask you a few questions—about my sister. So, are you or aren't you Carrie Holland?"

"I am." She sighed, like admitting that took some great effort.

"Tiff's your sister, then?" Carrie scrutinized him. "You're older than I expected."

Kids these days had no respect for adults or, for that matter, the law. Yes, compared to Tiffany, he was old. He'd been seventeen himself, when—surprise—his mom and new (but temporary, as it turned out) stepdad had announced a baby sis was on the way.

"Uh," the other one interrupted, "can I go?"

"Depends," Mitch said. "Do you hang with Tiffany at all?"

"Yeah, for a while."

"Then stay. What's your name?"

"Jennifer Mayberry, but everybody calls me JayMay."

Well, that should be easy to remember. "So, let's start with the main thing—either of you know where Tiffany's hiding out?"

Shakes of the head. Jesus, teenagers. They never wanted to tell you a thing.

"Come on," he said.

"We're not that good of friends anymore," Carrie said, looking sideways.

"Nothing you tell me is going to land you in trouble. Seriously, my mom's worried sick, and frankly, so am I. I know you know she's…not well." Hardly a secret, given that Tiffany had missed a couple of months of school first semester. He'd pressed his mother to stage an intervention and force her into rehab. For a while, they'd thought, she'd stayed clean.

He felt almost physically sick every time he thought of his sister like so many of the kids he'd seen in the system and on the streets, and he had to look away for a second. "I'm trying to help her, keep her from hurting herself." He held his breath, waiting.

The girls exchanged a glance, and Carrie shrugged. The leader of this duo, for sure.

"We don't know where she is. None of us do. She won't even text us back. Everybody was talking about it last week. She skips all the time." She gestured to the school. "That's not a big deal, but then she missed a big party last Saturday night. One she wouldn't have wanted to miss."

"One that promised lots of drugs and booze?"

The ratty red knot on Carrie's head bobbed up and down as she nodded.

But it was JayMay who piped up. "She was always up for that stuff. Everybody does some things, but she was getting kinda scary, you know?"

Carrie looked up, the brown eyes behind the black eyeliner holding his. "You're not the only one who is worried. Tiff used to be cool. She was my best friend. She was a good person, too—helped all those old folks even though I couldn't see how she could stand it. But she doesn't care about anything anymore, not me, not anyone—only the next fix."

"Where'd she get her stuff?" He wanted to fire questions at them like bullets. Instead, his tone remained cool, his pace slow. "Who'd she hang with?"

"Some old dude, her boyfriend."

JayMay snorted. "Her dealer, more like."

"Yeah," Carrie said. "She calls him her boyfriend, but he doesn't hang. She would just go over there, so I've never even met him."

"You know his name?"

JayMay shook her head, but Carrie spoke: "Tommy, I think. But she didn't say much about him."

"How old is he, d'ya think? What's he look like?"

"I only saw him once, from a distance," Carrie said. "Definitely older than you, but not ancient. Blond hair. Looked like a classy guy—not like some scumbag dealer."

"Any idea where can I find this guy?"

Carrie nodded. "I dropped Tiff off a couple of times when her mom took her car keys away. Lives over on Dale Drive. Way out of town, off the access road that runs along the highway."

Mitch's heart pumped harder, and he felt a crack of hope. Not only something concrete he could use, but also an address that rang warning bells for him.

"I don't think she's there, though," JayMay said. "A few weeks ago, she told me"—her fingers hooked the air like quote marks—"'Everyone's so stingy out here with their goods, but

I hear it's easy out in Cali'—California," she added, making sure he understood.

"You've been a big help." He handed them each one of his cards, anxious now to follow up on what he'd learned. "Call me if you hear from her, or think of anything, and tell the other kids, too, okay?"

They nodded.

"And hey, you better get off school property with that cigarette or someone's going to accuse me of not doing my job." He winked, and Carrie jumped. She'd forgotten about her smoke.

Mitch called his mother to let her know he'd connected with Tiffany's girlfriends, then headed back to the station just long enough to return the cruiser and change clothes— investigative work, especially unearthing a person who didn't want to be found, was best done undercover. The rest of the day—the rest of his life, if necessary—would be devoted to tracking down Tiff. First stop, Dale Drive.

As far as Mitch was concerned, that particular street could be considered the scene of a double crime. His own personal disaster: his career path halting in its tracks. And a true tragedy: a teenage runaway named Laura Macnamara who'd abandoned her nearly comatose mother—a case he'd been unable to solve. Although there had been no good leads, no real motive from any angle, no body ever found, the media had a field day making him look incompetent. Eventually, he'd been forced by the chief to give up and move on to cases more pressing.

As for a promotion, the higher-ups had been forced by public opinion, courtesy of those piranhas called the press, to pass him over—and over. Until he'd finally thrown his hands up and switched to narcotics. Scranton had needed faces the drug runners didn't know. It was no more than forty minutes north by car, so he'd kept his apartment in Blakes Ridge in order to have a home base near his mom and sister. Truth be told, though, he'd been relieved to ditch this town for a while, and therefore, he rarely spent time at home.

In terms of the Macnamara case, he'd always believed that someday the clues would fall into place, and he'd finally solve the runaway mystery, regardless of the departmental shift. He'd never really let go of it, and didn't intend to.

Dale Drive came up quick if you weren't prepared, so Mitch slowed his truck. The street curved in a wide but shallow arc, where only four houses stood, unless somebody had subdivided their lots in the last couple of years. Room to do that, as each house claimed a couple of acres. All of them sat to the right of the road, with deep wooded areas behind. The lots to the left had been leveled and mostly cleared but never built on, and he'd never seen them look anything but overgrown. He made the right onto Dale Drive, and slid to a stop without pulling over.

The runaway's house looked well cared for—otherwise, very little had changed. Still a ton of kitschy yard art in front of the third house—this time heralding Memorial Day, all red, white, and blue. When he'd first landed that case, the yard had screamed St. Patty's day. The fourth house still looked a little sad, forlorn, with an old Caddy in the drive. That couple had seemed ancient then, and Mitch wondered if they were both still living.

If Carrie and JayMay's info was solid, the first house, the one sitting just ahead on his passenger side, had to be the one. Tiffany's "Tommy" could very well be that self-righteous, smug neighbor he'd met in the first case, Thomas Hadfield Weihle.

Mitch parked in front, walked the gravel drive, and took a

deep breath before ringing the bell. He waited, adrenaline and tension sparring for the top spot in his chest.

He pushed the bell over and over—obnoxious, yes, but no way a person could ignore it. Three forty-five. If Weihle was still a nine-to-fiver then it'd be a couple of hours at least before he arrived home.

Mitch trudged back down the stoop steps and headed for the car, more disappointed than he'd expected.

Somehow, he'd hoped against hope that Tiff would stumble to the door. That she hadn't gone to California as her friends suspected. That she'd been holed up in Weihle's house. That he'd be able to save her from Weihle and from herself.

He moved the truck opposite the Macnamaras' old house and let all the details of that case ricochet through his mind. Was it possible the two cases were linked via Thomas Weihle? When he could stand it no longer, he crossed the yard in long strides and skirted the left side of the Macnamara property. No one seemed to be home, so there was no one to mind.

A play set—the wooden kind boasting swings, slides, a climbing wall, a fire pole, and even a roof—pushed the borders of the mowed lawn. The wood, apparently just as much fun for squirrels, was gnawed in multiple spots along the top. To the right sat a plastic log cabin, its bright red shutters now a mottled pink—color leeched out from the sun. This new family had been here a while, likely moved in soon after the property was foreclosed.

He looked at the back of the two-story, reacquainting himself mentally with the interior layout. Typical second floor. Three average bedrooms, one hall bath. Before the time of master baths and walk-in closets, and fancy built-ins for kids who had more toys than he had furniture. Downstairs had been rather average, too. Linoleum and Formica. A La-Z-Boy recliner and matted wall-to-wall carpeting.

There'd been a dish rag with blood on it tossed haphazardly on the kitchen counter—otherwise, nothing. At first glance, nothing out of the ordinary, anyway.

Laura Macnamara's school backpack had sat on the bed, unzipped, yet intact. Clothes spilled out of her hamper. A lone suitcase showcasing Hello Kitty seemed more appropriate to sleepovers than travel. And, in fact, there were no empty spots, either in her mother's room or her own, where a suitcase or duffel might have been yanked out of storage.

The mother, Ellen Macnamara, she was the catch. At the time of Laura's disappearance, Ellen had recently entered a long-term care facility—the same one where Tiffany had done community service. Another coincidence?

Ellen's stay had been paid for in cash, although she herself was near comatose. Oh, she functioned physically, if you called sitting and staring out the window functioning. She slept, she woke, she ate, she shit. But beyond responding to the most basic physical needs, there was no desire, no initiative, no forethought, no speech. She didn't shower, unless she was made to. She would eat if spoon-fed, but likely hadn't seen the inside of her own refrigerator in, well, who knew how long. The neighbor—Thomas Weihle, of course—had said she'd been "unwell for ages."

Mitch could just hear his well-to-do tone. A concerned neighbor, supposedly, though clearly a man who felt himself above petty matters like illness or heartbreak.

"Ellen was always prone to depression," Thomas Weihle had said in that cultured voice of his. "Medication worked nicely for some years, but when her husband died, well…I saw her rarely after that."

Mitch had disliked the man on instinct. Being a cop, you learned to trust your gut, to read a person's eyes. Mr. Weihle's eyes had been off—too hot. Deceiving, like a skillet on a gas range. Just because the flame underneath had been snuffed, didn't mean it wouldn't give you a third-degree burn. Mitch could have attributed some of that heat to the cop cars lining the curb, their flashers bouncing like strobe lights, disturbing an otherwise quiet evening. In those situations, most folks showed pity or concern and usually even a degree of morbid curiosity. Yes, sometimes the selfish ones radiated annoyance at the intrusion. But Weihle's wasn't garden-variety frustration, the kind born from disturbed sleep or trampled flowers. His was something deeper, something angry simmering furiously below a tightly clamped lid. Worse yet, Mitch had sensed excitement lurking behind the smooth exterior, too.

Of course, he'd checked out Weihle as a possible suspect in Laura Macnamara's disappearance. He was an R&D—research and development—scientist at a local pharmaceutical company called Novatru. Well thought of by his superiors. Owned his own home, and, given the way it was decorated, appreciated the finer things. A bachelor, but the serious, conservative type. No dating, no partying, no Sunday tailgates. Weihle went to work, he came home, he did some errands, nothing out of the ordinary. In fact, the complete lack of a social life seemed odd to Mitch, and yet there'd been no red flags, nothing to follow up on, nada to investigate further without crossing the line.

And yet here I am again. Mitch smirked, then immediately sobered. He hoped with every fiber of his being that his gut telegraphed wrong. That Weihle wasn't involved. That Tiffany was just a temporary teenage runaway who'd left of her own volition. *Please,* don't let her end up like Laura Macnamara—a missing person, murky clues, dead ends, and an eventual cold case to everyone on the force but him.

He turned again to the woods pressing in behind the jungle gym and walked it as he had so many times before. He squished through earth dewy from a recent spring rain, stepped high to tamp down young pricker bushes, and ducked under low branches. Two hundred yards, give or take, and you popped out on PA Route 80 Westbound.

Just that easy.

Mitch's boots slid on cinders that had been pushed to the wide shoulder of the highway. A few cars whizzed past, and the hood of his thick sweatshirt blew wildly against his neck. He yanked it up, turned to avoid a face full of road dust, and scanned the woods. At this time of year, the bushes were thick, the tree cover dense; everything was lush and green.

When Laura took off from this very spot, the branches would have been bare, the color gone. Lights would have been visible in the backs of the houses, winking on and off as drivers sped by the staggered silhouettes of tree trunks. And at night, the woods would have looked black. Wide and stark. Empty and menacing.

What was it the semi driver had said? Oh yeah, he'd likened the dark that night to an eerie thing right out of a horror movie, like something living that could suck you up.

The burly driver's words came back like it'd been just yesterday. "I could just see a figure, standing near the guardrail. Wouldn't have seen her so early, except her coat was white. I downshifted, but overshot her, o' course. No way not to with a semi and a full load, so when I passed I could see she was a female. That was about it, 'til she climbed in my cab."

The driver had shaken his head, scuffed his boot in the cinders, right here at mile marker 291.1. "The lights in my cab come on automatically, o' course, so before she shut the door, I got a look. All beat up. Black eye, split lip. Had a down parka on—one o' those teenage things. Ain't for warmth, but for looks. Barely covers their middles." He'd gestured to his own stomach, well hidden under thick black and red flannel.

He'd nudged up his cap. "Fur all around the hood. She kept that hood up the whole ride."

Mitch had waited. Sometimes, if you just let people talk, they'd let loose just what you needed.

The trucker had looked at him sideways. "This girl, she ain't no stupid teenager. This one, she was serious, probably smart. Well, I don't know, maybe not smart, but she ain't no child. I'd wager she'd already seen too much o' this world."

Mitch hadn't expected an answer, but had asked anyway: "Did she mention a destination—a town, an area of the country?"

"Nope," the trucker had said, sighing. "I asked how far she was headed. She said, 'As far as I can get.' She didn't go no further than Ohio with me, but every time I drive this stretch I wonder if she got as far as she needed to."

CHAPTER 3

A VOLUNTEER SHUT the heavy double doors of the church behind the last man in line, blocking out the early evening sunshine that blessed San Francisco today. Charlie Hart sighed as her concern ratcheted up several notches—Tiffany Scott had missed another meal at Glide.

She looked over her shoulder at the blue and orange trays lined up on the metal runners, five here, about ten across the glass in the works, being filled with pot roast, fruit cocktail, rolls, various condiments, and the necessary utensils. Nineteen meals between her and the last guest.

"Only four more, Henrietta," she said to her friend who was stationed at the start of the trays.

"Hallelujah," Henrietta Plummer said with a weary smile. Plenty of girth and an advanced age always made Henrietta tire long before the end of a shift. And yet she showed up—nearly every day now that she was retired and her grandchildren were in school—to give back to the organization that had helped her feed her family so many years ago.

"Uh-huh," Charlie said, though she could have served forever, hoping that Tiff would walk through the door. She was really getting worried about the teen.

"*Hola*, Juan," Charlie said with a smile, handing him one of the oversized plastic trays laden with warm, filling food.

"*Gracias*, Charlie." Juan, an older man, was still embarrassed to be there and ducked his head, but Charlie always greeted everybody by name if possible. She knew firsthand that this soup kitchen and its affiliated church might be the only place these folks felt welcome today, or all week.

Charlie bent down and greeted a young black boy who had wrapped himself around his mother's leg.

"Hey, Chief." She smiled. "I gotta a little something extra here for my favorite guests," she said, and slipped a Hershey's Kiss from her oversized cargo pants pocket to his. She made sure he got a good look at the silver foil in the palm of her hand, and was rewarded when his eyes turned into saucers and a smile tugged at one corner of his mouth.

"Save it for later, when you really need a treat, 'cause I don't have enough for everybody, 'kay?" She winked at the boy, and the young mother thanked her with a smile.

Always, the single mothers and their young kids got to her. The runaways, too, of course. *There but for the grace of God, go I...* She always recalled the phrase, though she'd no clear idea where she'd heard it first.

Charlie loved coming here. Loved giving back. Loved the success stories. Some days she felt the heaviness of it all—such a cruel world, so many needy, some who never seemed to make any progress. But mostly she felt some peace for having done what she could, and always a bone-deep sense of gratitude for having gotten out herself, after spending years on the run. Homeless, scared, and alone was never far behind her.

Although she could relate, she tried to remain unattached to the people who came through Glide, giving kinds words of advice and hope without getting too involved. But Tiffany Scott was a special case.

A couple of weeks ago, Henrietta had mentioned that

a girl came through Glide whom she believed hailed from Charlie's hometown. Henry only suspected Charlie was from Blakes Ridge, Pennsylvania, as she'd noticed Charlie's white knuckles during a newscast about a gruesome fire at a nursing facility there last year. Somehow—probably because Charlie had been cagey about confirming or denying the fact—the town's name had stuck in the stubborn woman's mind. The idea of talking with Tiffany had stuck in Charlie's.

Against her better judgment, Charlie had tracked the girl down in line for another shelter. Dirty and hollow-eyed, at turns twitchy or zoned out—it'd been clear from the first that she'd been pretty well gone.

Right off, Tiffany had asked her where she could find a safe place to sleep. And then asked about a clinic. Charlie's shell had cracked, as it always did when she felt a young addict truly wanted help. Charlie invited Tiffany to take meals and shelter at Glide. As they'd walked, she'd asked where the teenager was from, biting her lip as she waited…hoping she was and hoping she wasn't from the same area.

"Nowheresville, PA," came Tiffany's answer with a roll of her eyes under her knit cap and stringy blond hair.

"Hmmn," Charlie had replied, with a knowing look. "Sounds just like where I came from in Pennsylvania."

"No shit, you're from Pennsylvania, too?" Tiffany'd said.

"Yeah, but I bet your town wasn't as backward as mine."

"Blakes Ridge'll win hands down."

"Wow." Charlie gulped.

The Poconos to the east, some minor college towns to the west, her and Tiffany's hometown sat somewhere, nowhere, in between.

She'd hoped never to meet another person from home again. Tried hard never to think of the place or the people she'd left behind. And that got easier, mostly, as the years went on. But here was Tiffany Scott, inadvertently chiming a giant gong that rang on in Charlie's soul for days. Making her yearn for things better left behind. Making her desire for answers grow more demanding, almost heedless of consequences.

She'd had to refrain from blurting out the questions that plagued her, from giving too much away. Even though Tiffany was in bad shape and probably not paying enough attention to become suspicious, clearly she also couldn't be trusted to keep secrets. And Charlie had been so careful, for so long.

They'd talked, little by little, day after day, though Charlie gleaned precious little information. Tiffany's accent was so familiar—not glaring like a Southern or foreign one would have been, but with an earthy, no-nonsense quality that spoke of generations of Northeastern Pennsylvanians, proud of their small-town, blue-collar history. Overall, however, Tiffany hadn't wanted to talk about home, had trouble focusing, and was rather unreliable. In fact, she hadn't shown up at all the last few days.

And yet because of their shared roots, because Charlie had come to care, because also—yes, she'd admit it—she still hoped she'd stumble onto a bit of information that might provide her a measure of comfort, she'd continued to look out for the girl.

Charlie sent the last man in line off with his tray and a smile.

"Henrietta, I'm going to visit. Be back in a few." She tugged off the plastic cap she'd worn, ran a hand through her choppy, bleached hair, and headed for the cafeteria-style tables.

Charlie looked over first one dining room and then the other. About one hundred guests today, she'd estimate. A small crowd. Glide Memorial Church could fit two hundred when full, and usually did, being located in a real hot spot for the homeless, the addicts, and the poor—the Tenderloin district, arguably the roughest section of San Francisco. Glide and St. Anthony's, a group of Franciscans, worked together, making a serious dent in hunger and providing shelter to as many as they could. Their numbers always increased when folks needed a respite from the rain, fog, and cold that so often invaded the Bay Area. Today, though, the weather spun California perfection. Spring bloomed, but the warm wind and toasty sunshine felt almost like summer.

She made a beeline for one teen after another. So often they knew each other from the shelters and the rehab clinics, even if they kept to themselves here.

"Hey," Charlie asked one after another, "you seen that girl Tiffany lately?" Nobody had, until she spotted Ian Cross.

"How you doing, Ian?"

"Fantastic, Charlie. Love the pot roast, and it's a beautiful day." Ian grinned at her with a knowing look. Once, she'd remarked on how positive he always was, so now he played it up just for her. Still a growing young man, he never missed a meal. Charlie also suspected that if his table companions left anything untouched, Ian pocketed whatever traveled well.

She couldn't help but grin back at him, but quickly brought the conversation around to where she needed it.

"Have you seen Tiff lately?"

"No show, huh?"

"Yeah, I'm more than a little concerned."

Ian shook his head, inky black hair sticking straight up from a recent cut. In fact, he'd shaved it off himself as a symbol of his commitment to stay clean. But judging from his thick eyebrows, he'd have a full head of hair again in no time.

"You might want to lower your expectations," Ian mumbled to his tray.

Charlie bit down a nasty retort and opted for the truth instead: "I know it, but I just can't."

Ian frowned. "She hasn't been at the shelter for a few nights, so unless she's at one of the others…" He shrugged.

"Damn." She sighed and smoothed out the white plastic apron over her thighs. "Will you let me know if you hear anything?"

"Yeah."

"Thanks, Ian."

"Uh, Charlie?" Ian fidgeted with his spoon. "I really have a bad feeling about her."

"Why? What makes her any less likely to succeed than any of these other people sitting here?" She swept her hand out to encompass the room.

Charlie had been eating at or working in this soup kitchen for years, and had seen other teens kick it—whichever addiction they'd had. Unlike her, most teenagers had families somewhere, who could forgive and could help them get the care they needed. Teens also had physical strength in their youthful bodies made for recovery, a long future ahead to face and fill, and most important, if they'd been living on the streets, usually a hard-won maturity to fight through the tough weeks.

Ian shrugged, yet his lips pressed in a flat line and he refused to look at her. Charlie figured he'd bend the cheap metal spoon if he clasped it any harder. Her heart sank watching him; however, she herself wasn't giving up on the girl.

"Okay, Ian." She squeezed his shoulder as she stood.

"Thanks for the warning." She blew out a breath and clenched her fists.

Little did Ian know that when it came to Tiffany Scott, far more than Charlie's emotions were at stake. For her, anybody hailing from Blakes Ridge presented a minefield of danger. Yet her craving for information from that very spot was so intense, she—inconceivable as it was—ignored the risk.

CHAPTER 4

MITCH HAD KNOWN about his sister's various arrests for possession—knew more than any big brother should have, being that he had access to the system. He'd also called in some favors to get her a decent assignment for her community service—he'd desperately wanted her somewhere insulated, somewhere safe. As it turned out, she'd enjoyed helping out at Rolling Meadows, a seniors' nursing facility, and she'd continued to volunteer even after the obligation to the state had been met.

The last time she'd been busted, she lost her license and the rest of her freedom. He now knew that was when she started disappearing. A day here, a night there. A couple of days sometimes, but always she'd turn up. Until a night turned into two nights, turned into a week and then another, at which point Mitch answered the bell last night—he'd only been home a day—to find his mother sobbing on his doorstep, railing against tough love and begging him to bring her baby home safe.

According to Mom, Tiff hadn't been to the seniors' complex in a couple of weeks. But Mitch had time to kill before returning to Dale Drive to intercept Thomas Weihle after work, and here, at the center, he could kill two birds with one stone.

Rolling Meadows Assisted Living Facility had established

a good reputation catering to those who thought ahead and realized they'd prefer to make their own choices in conjunction with their spouses and families before they became unable to do so. Rolling Meadows offered a graduated system of care, so that one might live in a small apartment, then move to an assisted living suite, then to a skilled nursing room, as one's health demanded. All the while, the members enjoyed access to the restaurant, the community's social calendar, and, of course, the doctors and nurses.

Carrie had been right in her estimate of the age of people Tiffany had helped, he thought as the doors slid shut with a soft whoosh behind him. Every person here had gray or white hair and could certainly be classified as "old folk," as she'd put it.

That's why it was unusual that his runaway's mother, Ellen Macnamara, resided here. Last he'd seen her she'd had some streaks of gray in her brown hair—the same rich color her missing daughter had, according to her pictures—but she was a good twenty years younger than most of the other patients.

Mitch veered away from the crowd heading toward the restaurant for dinner and aimed straight for the reception desk to his right. He inquired about seeing the director of the complex, then sat down to wait in a cozy seating area that faced a stone fireplace. Apparently the woman, Rowena Leonard, who'd headed up the place when he was searching for Laura Macnamara was no longer here. That should be a good thing. She'd been too by the book on the client privacy thing. In fact, she'd been no help to him at all, saying only that Ellen's care was paid in full by an anonymous donor. His warrant yielded no further information. Whether she'd destroyed the paper trail or truly didn't know where that money came from, he'd never been able to figure out.

Mitch didn't bother grabbing a magazine from the end table, just leaned his head back and drummed his fingers surreptitiously on the side of his right thigh. The questions to ask about Tiffany were fairly straightforward, and, frankly, he'd be surprised as hell if the new director could help him in that regard. You never knew, though. But could he push and fish for new information on Mrs. Macnamara?

Given that he hadn't yet spoken to Thomas Weihle, his tip from Carrie and JayMay was the only thing that even remotely connected the two cases. Except he already had that feeling, the one that said he was onto something.

"Officer Saunders, sorry to keep you waiting. Mondays are always busy," said a middle-aged guy with striking blue eyes and a full head of blown back salt-and-pepper hair. "I'm Gus Standall." He extended his hand with an enthusiastic shake and hearty smile.

"Come." Gus motioned and turned, already on his way, "Let's head to my office where we can talk privately." Mitch wouldn't have been surprised if the guy had winked. Big in the belly, overly energetic, and a snazzy suit—should have been a car salesman. Wait, he *was* a salesman, just for living space instead of wheels.

"So, sit." The director motioned to a tan leather chair with wooden arms as he slid behind his desk. The whole place had a rustic lodge feel—nice, but sorta fake. "What can I do for you today?"

"Well, Mr. Standall—"

"Please, call me Gus."

"Gus it is. I'd like to ask you some questions about my sister, Tiffany Scott."

"Of course. A lovely girl, Tiffany."

"Well, she is that. I'm sure you approved her community

service work here, so you know she'd been working off a drug violation." Why not clear the decks and get it out of the way, thought Mitch.

"Of course, but I assure you, we had no trouble with her, until just the last few weeks when she stopped showing up. The staff found her very helpful, and our residents think she's an angel. I hope she hasn't…slipped back into bad habits?"

"I'm afraid so. And to make matters worse"—Mitch looked at his own hands rather than at Standall—"she's run away from home." His chest felt tight. He'd failed Tiff and his mom.

Gus shook his head and shut his eyes for a few seconds. "I'm so sorry to hear that. I'd hoped she'd just been acting like an unreliable teen. Your poor mother. What do you need from us?"

"I'd just like to ask some questions of the people Tiffany spent the most time with. The head nurse, or other staff that would have overlapped with her. Perhaps a few patients she was friendly with?"

"Of course. Normally, she would have helped out in assisted living. I'll take you over there myself." He rose.

"Gus…" Mitch stood as well, and leaned in as if imparting a bit of privileged information. "There's actually one more thing."

Gus raised his eyebrows and nodded, both willing and curious.

"I haven't connected all the dots yet, and I'm not able to divulge the details, but I'm thinking there's some sort of connection between my sister's situation and an old case I had."

"Really?" Gus said.

"Yes. Do you still have a patient here named Ellen Macnamara?"

"I was about to say, we don't call them patients, we call

them residents, but in Ellen's case, sadly, you're right, she's more of a patient." Gus sighed. "I wasn't here when she arrived, though I certainly remember the news reports." At that, his eyes slid away from Mitch's. If the press hadn't gone and sabotaged him but good, Mitch thought.

Gus continued, "The nurses assure me that her situation hasn't changed one iota."

"I'm sorry to hear that," Mitch said, and he genuinely was. "I'm wondering if she's had any visitors, and, though I'm sure you can't give me details without us going through the proper channels, I'm wondering how it is she's still affording this quality of care."

Gus nodded thoughtfully. "Let me see what I can find out and get back to you."

"I'd appreciate it, more than you could know," Mitch said.

Gus led Mitch to the assisted living wing—just as inviting as the lobby, but set up somewhat like one floor of a hotel—and introduced him to Yvonne, a short, curvy black woman—probably mid-to-late forties—with a friendly face, close-cropped hair, and oversized silver hoop earrings. As soon as she learned that he had questions about Tiffany, her beaming smile turned to a pressed line of generous lipstick.

"Hmmph. That poor girl. Such a way with our folks here. But I know she had her troubles. I do believe she was a good egg inside, though, that sister of yours."

Gus excused himself to look into that *other* matter, and Yvonne suggested that Mitch follow her and ask whatever he needed while she made the rounds.

"Your boss seems like a decent guy," Mitch said.

"He really is," Yvonne said as she bustled down the hallway in her nurse's uniform, a printed top and light purple pants, and, of course, the requisite white shoes. "We were worried about who we'd get next when Mrs. Leonard died, but Mr. Standall's nice to work for."

"I met Mrs. Leonard here a few years ago. I didn't know—assumed she'd changed jobs."

"Nope. That wonderful woman dropped dead right there in her office of a heart attack. Horrifying, you know, with all of us medical staff right here. But it must have happened just like that"—she snapped her fingers—"because she didn't even pick up the phone."

"Terrible," Mitch said. "How long ago was this?"

"Well over two years now." Yvonne shook her head. "And it was terrible. She hadn't been sick, had no history of heart trouble. Such a shock."

Yvonne checked a chart, spoke briefly to a young nurse, sent her off on a task, and then walked over to another door and knocked.

"Mr. Donovan?"

"Come in, come in," said an old voice.

Yvonne swung the door wide and entered a two-part room. On the left was a standard hospital bed with a duvet cover, an antique dresser, and one of those fancy stained glass lamps, and on the right Mitch found a small sitting area with two comfy chairs, a TV, and a radio. An elderly man, bald with bits of white, frosty stubble, and thick glasses, sat in the recliner with the crossword page of the newspaper folded neatly on a rolling tray in front of him.

"Mr. Donovan, I brought you a visitor. This is our young friend Tiffany's brother."

Mr. Donovan peered over his glasses. "Yvonne, you better have the doc check my prescription again. He looks like her father to me," he said, cackling a bit.

"Officer Saunders—"

"Not an officer, too! I really do need my eyes checked. I don't see any uniform!" he said.

Yvonne rolled her eyes in a good-natured way. "As I was trying to say, this one here is our resident jokester."

"Hello, sir. Nice to meet you," Mitch said, and extended his hand, which the old man gripped in a firm shake.

"Yvonne's right. I've got to get my kicks somehow. Now sit down and keep me company for a bit."

"I'd be glad to, sir."

"But stop calling me sir. Just makes me feel my age."

"Sorry, it's part of my training, not to mention my upbringing," Mitch said with a wry smile.

"About that. Your parents did a fine job with your sister. Tiffany's a real doll. Always takes time to listen to my tired stories and jokes, though I know full well I've told them to her before."

"I'll be sure to tell my mom." Mitch smiled, glad for anything positive to pass on.

"I've been wondering where she's been, and now you're here. Out with it."

"She's either run away, or she's missing."

Mr. Donovan raised his eyebrows.

"Tiffany's an addict," Mitch choked out. Memories of a cherubic toddler with blond pigtails flying were still lodged firmly in his brain. "Drugs. She's in bad shape." He shook his head. "I've promised my mother I'll find her, but frankly, I'm worried."

Mr. Donovan nodded. Crossed his arms over his thin middle and leaned his head back.

"Her friends haven't seen her," Mitch said. "Most of her sober time was spent here, so here I am, looking for information—for anything that might lead me to her."

"California," came the whispered word.

"You know, a friend of hers mentioned that, too. But it's a big state."

"She said she really wanted to move there. I joked that I hoped she'd wait until she graduated, or at least until I died." Mr. Donovan looked Mitch square in the eye. "I told her all about San Francisco. I used to live there. She asked me question after question."

The old man shook his head. "All teenagers dream about the world, think their hometowns are so stifling. My God, I never thought…"

"Mr. Donovan, do not put any blame on yourself. Tiff is not well—the decisions she's made aren't rational ones. I work narcotics. I've seen…" Mitch couldn't go down that road. "I pushed my mom to use the tough love approach. We forced Tiff into rehab. But I wasn't around enough on the other side. If I'd been there, I would have seen what was happening. I could have…" He gripped his knees hard and tried to get a hold of himself, lest he end up sobbing like a baby.

Mr. Donovan reached, shaking slightly, and gave Mitch's hand a squeeze. Mitch looked up from the gnarly knuckles, past the thick lenses, and into watery, pale eyes, and turned his hand over to grip him right back.

After a few moments, he said, "Thank you, Mr. Donovan. You've given me somewhere to start."

Mitch found Yvonne in the hall. He inquired about Ellen Macnamara, mentioning only that he'd been the one to work her daughter's case.

"Such a sad thing, isn't it?" Yvonne said. "Some days I wonder if it isn't best, because if Ellen understood about her daughter's disappearance all those years ago, the heartbreak would be crushing." She tsked then added, "That poor girl's got to be dead. Otherwise, what could keep a daughter from a mother in this state?"

"I've wondered the same thing," Mitch said. *At least a million times.*

"I know she didn't have any family other than her daughter. Does she get any visitors at all?"

"Only her neighbor. But he's here every few days, like clockwork."

Mitch froze. He cleared his throat to jump-start his voice. "Which neighbor is that?"

"Thomas Weihle."

Mitch's mind raced. "The blond man who lived next door to them."

"That's right, the good-looking one. All our single girls here have a crush on him." She rolled her eyes at him, this time with something that looked like disgust. "You know him?"

"His name came up in the investigation pertaining to her daughter." *And now the one involving my sister.*

After a few more questions, Mitch learned from Yvonne that Weihle always visited on Mondays—as well as Wednesdays and Fridays—normally around the dinner hour or early evening, so he chose to hang around.

First, he peeked in on Ellen Macnamara. Except for hair that showed more gray than brown now, she seemed just the same. Indeed, what kind of daughter would abandon a mother this bad off? He'd imagined a million scenarios, but in his mind, very few would justify willingly taking off. If Laura Macnamara turned up alive, she'd crush his belief in humanity to rubble.

As Mitch headed back toward the common area, Gus Standall found him. Apparently, there was no paperwork to be found on Ellen's intake and anonymous donor; however, their in-house accountant—who previously, Mitch guessed, had been under orders from Mrs. Leonard to keep quiet—now recalled that there'd been three lump sums in the first year, and nothing since. She believed they had been cash deposits.

Mitch parked himself in the lobby, squarely facing the sliding doors. He settled into a comfortable upholstered chair and noted the warmth from the gas fireplace heating his left side, but he wasn't about to relax—not when the one link between his runaway and his sister could slither right through that door.

CHAPTER 5

AFTER CLEANUP, CHARLIE stepped out of Glide with a grocery-sized brown bag of sandwiches made from Glide's leftover rolls under one arm, and her satchel slung crosswise over her chest.

She headed for the playground on the block between Leavenworth and Hyde, unsnapped her triangular knife out of its leather sheath, and snugged its curved, T-shaped base into her palm. The knife itself was tiny, barely over an inch long, and stuck out between two knuckles, but it gave her a measure of comfort now, hiding in the hand under the bread.

The Tenderloin had become home to her and was safe enough most times—especially in the bright sun of midafternoon. There were always some rough characters who roamed the streets, but she'd come to find that they, like any other neighbors, looked out for their own—the regulars, the faces they knew.

Trouble was, today she'd be venturing out of that safety zone, looking for Tiffany Scott in all the wrong places. Chances were things would be fine, but Charlie believed better safe than sorry. Luck hadn't exactly prevailed in her life.

The homeless and anybody who lived on the wrong side of the law were wary types, not that she blamed them. Besides sustenance, the sandwiches she carried provided an excuse to strike up conversation.

For a good weather day, the playground was nearly deserted. A homeless woman, surrounded on her bench by a fortress of plastic bags, talked an endless stream of nonsense.

"Ma'am, have you seen a pretty blond girl here lately?" Charlie asked as she held out a wrapped sandwich. The woman took it and shook her gray head, but the blather didn't cease for a second.

Two kids, both Hispanic, stood in a corner, trying to look old, cool, and tough dragging on their smokes. They wore jeans that hung low, hoodies pulled up, and shades to hide their eyes. They were either dealing or looking to buy, and Charlie felt a smidge of hope that this pair might have seen Tiff. But they claimed not to. And they refused the food. She sighed. Likely they were older than their years, tired of taking handouts, ready to make their own way, no matter what it took. She could relate.

"If you do see her, tell her…that her friend from Glide was asking. Thanks."

She veered out of the park and headed for the next stop in her mental catalogue of places the kids went to get high—for surely Tiffany would have hit those spots herself. Maybe the abandoned lot three blocks over that hid between two buildings and behind a tall, spray-painted fence. Back when she spent time on the streets, she'd seen slouched figures slip in and out of there with amazing frequency.

But today—broad daylight and nobody around. If she was braver, and stupid, she'd do this tour in the middle of the night.

There was a rehab clinic next. The one she'd mentioned to Tiffany. Maybe she'd get lucky and just spot the girl.

On the way, she passed a black man with a short gray afro, enormous tennis shoes with missing laces, and layers and layers of clothes. He had street dust from head to toe, and she could smell him ten feet away. The sharp stench of the unwashed, like still air in a corner that had been peed in repeatedly, always made her stomach pitch. Too many bad memories.

His hand-lettered cardboard sign read, "Help, I'm hungry," but he waved off the food. "How 'bout some money, sweetheart?" He grinned. A few yellow teeth stuck up out of his gums like weathered gravestones ready to topple. He stretched out a paper coffee cup, its few coins rattling. He wanted money for drink. Charlie shook her head and moved on.

She'd get the same reaction near the rehab clinic, but with more desperation. Drugs cost a lot more nickels than cheap alcohol, and not everybody visited the clinic for help. Some went because dealers hovered in the shadows nearby.

She'd check the bright clinics and the dark shadows.

And if she managed to find Tiff, what then?

Sure, Charlie could feed her, force her to shower, clothe her in something of her own, let her bunk on her couch a night or two…but honestly, she knew enough to realize that nothing she did would truly help, nothing would stick, unless Tiff chose to make it so. Some people could swim to the surface at any point, others simply had to crawl around on rock bottom for a while before they'd find the strength to stand up and kick for the sun.

Even so, where would she herself be if it hadn't been for people who'd extended their hand when she was down? Broke and terrified, hungry and dirty, heartsick and guilt-ridden? Granted, she was less of a risk having never been an addict, but most people never knew what another soul contended with when they offered to help.

After a few hours, she'd run out of places to look for Tiffany, and too many sandwiches remained in her bag. She simply couldn't stuff them in a garbage can. She'd spent too much time hungry herself, so she'd take them back to Glide's kitchen. There, they'd get eaten. If not by patrons, maybe by staff or volunteers.

As she exited Glide for the second time that day via the carved wooden double doors in front, she walked three steps toward the intersection and halted. She'd planned to head home to her apartment to chill for few minutes before she changed into the requisite all black for her shift at Cleo's Bistro. But she was too wound up—determination and impotence, defeat and stubborn hope all vied for top spot in her chest. If she went home she'd only end up brooding about Tiffany. So where to now?

"Hey, girl," said a rich, but breathless voice behind her. "What you doin'? Counting cars?"

Charlie turned and smiled at Henrietta, used to the slow progress the heavyset woman made. "Honestly, I have no idea what I'm doing."

"Ain't like you. You always have a plan."

"Hardly," Charlie scoffed.

Henrietta narrowed her eyes and tilted her head at Charlie, as if changing her perspective would provide an answer. "Everything okay?"

Charlie sighed for what felt like the hundredth time that day. "I'm really worried over that girl I've been talking to—the blond one. She first came in about two weeks ago."

"Honey, don't waste your energy on her—"

"But—"

"No, Charlie, you listen to me." Henrietta held up a hand. "That one's a heartbreaker. She was meant to be breaking boys' hearts with those eyes, that blond hair, and those long legs, but it ain't never gonna happen that way. I'll wager she's already broken her momma and daddy's hearts back home, and if you let her, she'll break yours as well."

"How do you keep them from getting to you, Henrietta?"

"Oh, some of 'em get to me but good, darlin'. But there's some you just have to refuse to let in." Henrietta reached her arms out wide, and Charlie went easily into her embrace.

Charlie sighed. "I hope you're wrong about Tiffany."

"Well, so do I." Henrietta squeezed harder. "Time will tell, I guess."

———

In the end, Charlie decided to stop at the PO box she'd rented for herself a few years ago, once she'd decided it was safe to stay in San Francisco.

She crossed the drab lobby and headed to the back where her slot hovered, close to the bottom, one among many. As always, she stared for a moment at the rows and rows of little silver doors and wondered which hid secrets, which kept away demons, which allowed a sense of security.

Hers managed all three.

She glanced down at her key ring and fingered the one she needed.

Charlie hated to open the box when it was empty, which happened more often than not. Birthday pictures were the only ones she could count on, except her girl didn't turn six until September. Once in a while they'd do better than the promised annual milestone and send photos of a new dress or a special outing. Who knew? Maybe there'd been a spring vacation to somewhere warm and notable, somewhere far from the lingering snow that plagued the mountains of Pennsylvania.

She'd never know if she didn't open the damn box and find out.

Charlie took a deep breath, squatted down, and inserted the key. She turned and pulled—

Empty.

She slammed the door shut, yanked out the key, and bolted.

She hated that dark, deep, gaping hole—it was too close. Too close to the feeling that still sometimes rose up inside her. The one she'd felt when she handed her mother over. The same one she'd felt when she'd handed her baby daughter over.

Charlie stifled a sob and pushed out into the sunshine on the streets of the city.

CHAPTER 6

HE HURRIED UP THE RAMP toward the doors of Rolling Meadows. He hated to be off schedule, but there was no help for it today.

He'd checked out of the supermarket well ahead of the little girl and the woman. He'd had only a basket, to their full cart, and had ignored the rest of the items on his mental list in his haste. Waiting in his car for them to leave had been torturous. Their subsequent stop at a toy store had nearly made him climb out of his skin. He had run out of time to stop home—he preferred not to make Ellen wait—so his own groceries remained in his trunk, the ice cream certainly melting into a mess.

A few ruined groceries? He smiled. Well worth it. For he now knew where this gorgeous child lived—where to watch, where to wait: in a cookie-cutter subdivision only a half an hour away. Surely his neighborhood supermarket couldn't have been their usual haunt. Given the distance, he'd need to consider carefully how best to become part of Mackenzie's life. She was too young now, but if he planned well and came upon a diversion or two along the way, his patience would pay off.

"Thomas Weihle."

Thomas stopped short, nearly colliding with a man—one

he would have recognized, if he hadn't been so firmly rooted in thoughts of Mackenzie.

"I'm a detective with the Blakes Ridge PD. I have some questions for you."

Ah, Thomas thought—his mind focused again on what was, instead of what would be—the officer who had no more luck than he himself had had in chasing down lovely Laura.

"Saunders, isn't it? Excuse me. Such a shock, seeing you after all this time." Interesting, Thomas mused, this detective's persistence when he had suffered such public humiliation in his failure.

"A shock, huh?" The officer crossed his arms over his chest and planted his feet.

Did the crass man intend to talk right here near the sliding doors?

"Well yes, of course, it's been, well, how many years exactly since my young neighbor vanished?"

"Six."

"Has there been a new development in the case, then?" Thomas had always believed she had run—the little bitch— but forced his face to show concern and whispered, "Has—has Laura's body been found after all this time?"

———

Before Mitch could stop himself, he'd moved a full stride closer to Weihle. He looked past the man's worried façade and perfectly presented exterior to the snaky eyes beneath. The thought of this creep anywhere near his sister was so disturbing that his arms nearly rose to grab the poser's throat and throttle him. But with no warrant, no proof, nothing but hearsay in either case, he'd have to rein in the need for aggression and play the game.

"I'm here on another matter." Mitch paused. "I'm looking into the disappearance of Tiffany Scott."

Weihle's eyes widened, just a fraction, before he recovered himself, and Mitch felt a great satisfaction. If the pompous jackass hadn't expected his connection to Tiffany to surface, then he sure wasn't as smart as he'd thought himself to be. Or perhaps he was just getting sloppy.

"Who?" the man had the gall to ask.

"The teenager who helped out here at Rolling Meadows."

"Hmmn. There're a number of girls who assist the nurses here."

"Right. Maybe you'll remember the beautiful blond one who calls you Tommy and has spent time at your house?"

Weihle's face blanched for a second, then his light blue eyes hardened like ice chips. He smoothed his blond hair, even though not a strand was out of place, all of it flowing straight back from his face, like it'd been blow-dried or gelled or something. Mitch noticed grays mixed with the pale strands, and put him in his mid-to-late forties.

"Ah, yes, of course, Tiffany. I attempted to tutor her when I found out her grades were slipping. I'm quite proficient in science and math; however, even I couldn't help that girl. She was only at my house perhaps twice, probably two hours altogether." He smiled and shook his head. Such an act, Mitch knew.

"It became clear very quickly"—Weihle leaned in, as if to keep a dirty secret hush hush—"that she was high as a kite. There was no help for her grades, unless she got help for herself first. I told her that in no uncertain terms."

"And did you help her with anything else, Mr. Weihle?"

"I'm sorry. I don't follow your meaning."

"Perhaps keeping her 'high as a kite.'"

"Certainly not. I do not do drugs, Officer."

"Detective."

"Detective, then." Weihle sighed. "I'm not sure I appreciate the direction these questions are heading."

"I'm sure you don't. One last question." Mitch was dying to haul this asshole in for a true interrogation. "Do you know where Tiffany Scott is?"

"I haven't the faintest idea." Weihle smirked. "And since you aren't—apparently—very good at finding people, we may never know."

"Oh, but Mr. Weihle, now that we've renewed our acquaintance, I find myself incredibly motivated to rethink the Macnamara files." Mitch smiled, feeling feral as a wolf. "Besides, I have a personal stake in this new case. Tiffany is my sister."

———

Mitch rapped on the window of Chief Dominic Marcone's door and waited with his hand on the knob for his mentor to look up. The man had aged considerably since Mitch first met him fifteen years ago. Still beefy and imposing, he now sported deep grooves in his face. His thick shock of hair had, somewhere along the way, gone completely gray. Looks were deceiving, though, because the chief's energy level put the younger men on the force to shame.

Marcone motioned him in, and Mitch slumped into the wooden chair facing his desk.

The chief narrowed his eyes. "So?"

"So, it's worse than I'd hoped. I have to go after her."

"Take as much time as you need—you've got years worth

of vacation time racked up on this end, and I hear you're due a break after the last undercover assignment. Congrats on the collar, by the way."

Mitch nodded in acknowledgment.

Marcone braced his arms on the desk and asked, "Where do you think your sister is?"

"Looks like Tiff took off for California to get wasted in peace. I have a visual ID from the ticket guy at the Martz Trailways station in Wilkes Barre." Mitch grimaced and said, "He remembers because she was so stoned he bet that she couldn't count out the cash, but she handed over the exact amount—$243 one way through to San Diego—already prepared in an envelope. Apparently she kept saying 'San Francisco' even though the route was to San Diego. He did check her ID for proof of age. Unfortunately, he couldn't show me the records because Martz doesn't have them. The bus was a Greyhound, so I'll need to confirm with them."

Marcone leaned back in his chair with his hands steepled—his classic thinking pose. "Where'd she get that much cash?"

"Damn good question, isn't it?" Mitch shook his head, although he had an idea or two on that score.

"You're going out there?"

"Yeah." Mitch nodded and then rubbed his hand over his face. "But it's not that simple."

The chief crossed one leg over the other, got comfortable. "Enlighten me."

"Tiff's friends pointed me to this guy she's been hanging out with, Thomas Weihle."

"Sounds familiar. Why?"

"Because he's the good neighbor from the Macnamara case on Dale Drive."

"The one you had a feeling about?"

Mitch shot him a wry smile. "That's the one. Turns out he still visits Ellen Macnamara, three times a week, every week. Guess where Tiffany did her community service?"

"The very same facility."

"Yep. Rolling Meadows." Mitch got up, moved around the small space. "Tiffany has spent time at his house. He claims he tutored her. I had a little run-in with him at the center."

"Mitch." Marcone's voice held a warning note. "Your sister is not one of your cases, you don't work in this department any longer, and we can't just open an old case because this guy happens to—"

"I know it, Chief, I fucking know it." Again, Mitch rubbed his fingers over his eyes. "But you gotta admit, the coincidences are stacking up."

Mitch turned and faced his boss. "You know I can't let someone else handle this thing with Tiff, and now the stakes might be even higher. I'm between assignments in narc, anyway. I've already worked it out. Taking leave until I can bring her home." He lifted a softball trophy from the chief's bookcase and spun it around in his hand. "I need to open an official investigation, though—Mom should be in anytime. Do me a favor and put O'Dell on it. I don't trust the rest of these imbeciles to take it seriously. Some of them watch way too much TV. They could be sick enough to think I deserve this thing with Tiff."

Marcone raised his bushy eyebrows, but nodded. "All right. O'Dell's your man."

"I'll brief him, then I'm gone."

Mitch moved to leave, but turned back to face the chief before reaching for the door.

"Chief, you gotta know. My priority is bringing Tiff

home safe and sound. But if I find out that Weihle is in fact involved..."

"Understood." Marcone pushed out of his chair. "Good luck, son."

———

Mitch's initial relief evaporated as he hung up the phone. The bus company had confirmed that one Tiffany Blanche Scott had transferred through Harrisburg, St. Louis, and Los Angeles, and had actually arrived in San Diego, CA. The question was, did she remain there or find a way to San Francisco?

A rap of knuckles on his desk made his head snap up. Carson O'Dell. About time. Mitch itched to go tearing off after Tiffany.

"Chief says you've got a case for me," O'Dell said.

"Yeah." He looked over Carson, always surprised at how young he appeared. But Mitch knew the kid had far more experience—in life and on the job—than his baby face would let on. He also happened to be smart and hardworking, but most important, he had a baby sister of his own. "You got a notebook?"

Carson pulled it from the pocket of his army-style jacket and held it up.

Mitch shot a look at the officers hanging about the bullpen. Already they were all ears because of his closed-door meeting with Marcone, the phone calls he'd had to make, and the impending arrival of his mother. Although Blakes Ridge PD was a decent-sized department, having long ago absorbed others to cover the bulk of Carbon and Lackawanna counties as well as part of the Poconos, Northeastern Pennsylvania was a revenue-poor area. There was only so much manpower they could afford. That meant, in terms of mentality, the place had a memory like a small town and gossip was nearly a job requirement.

Mitch required privacy to brief O'Dell. He planned to voice every last suspicion he had regarding Thomas Hadfield Weihle. And if the other officers heard the name "Dale Drive," there'd be a shitstorm of conjecture.

"I need to get to the airport. What do you think about riding with me and taking a cab back?"

"Expensive taxi. I could drive your truck back," Carson said.

His shiny black Ford F-150? His one major splurge? Mitch's crummy apartment looked as if he hadn't spent a dime on it, which he hadn't, but his truck sported all the bells and whistles. He figured it made sense. Both were like flushing money down the can, but he spent far more of his waking hours in his vehicle than in his empty apartment. He might as well enjoy. That vehicle was his only item of value, and therefore a source of pride as well.

The kid caught the look on his face and tried again. "Cab fare's on you, man."

"I might make you take the bus for that, O'Dell. Let's go. I need to get out of here."

CHAPTER 7

THE CLANK AND BANG of trays, ladles, cups, and utensils soothed Charlie the instant she slid in the back door of the kitchens. Somehow all that noise had come to symbolize a home away from home for her. Maybe, just maybe, that same sense of comfort that she always felt at Glide and St. Anthony's would have drawn Tiffany back tonight as well.

Charlie greeted everybody on staff as she weaved through the chaos, but didn't stop to talk. She had only a few minutes before she had to hustle over to Cleo's and make some money.

She stepped through the line of guests, already scanning the tables. Then she headed down a middle aisle, checking every table, but her attention was yanked to a man who'd just come in the main door. He wasn't facing her, engaged as he was in conversation with the aide posted there, but her breath caught anyway—because he didn't belong here.

He stood tall and straight and was fit and clean. One glance told her he was both confident and determined. He hadn't shaved recently, but usually did, she guessed. Good-looking, too, but in a rugged way. *In another life*, she thought as an aside, *you'd have been my type.*

Sandy brown hair—too long, for a gust of wind blew through the door and pushed it into his face. He swiped it back with a large hand. In the other, he flashed a photograph.

The aide, Aaron, a good guy who helped out when he was able, shook his head.

A cop, then. Looking for someone.

Out of long habit, she tensed, ready to flee—but Aaron was pointing at her already, and the intruder's eyes locked with her own.

Charlie felt her stomach drop out and her whole world tilt precariously. Cops were to be avoided; they asked too many questions and might look too close. She willed her legs to move, to turn, to run, but she was frozen in place. There were too many people watching. And she wasn't ready this time. She'd been caught off guard.

Don't panic. Think, think! She ran a hand over her hair—short, tousled, blond. Had she remembered her contacts? Yes, her eyes were blue.

No choice, she'd have to play it cool. She was Charlie Hart. She was Charlie Hart...

———

Mitch covered the distance in seconds and approached the blond—could you call it blond, he wondered, when it was nearly white? Her look was kinda funky: black cargo pants, a tight black top—high-necked but sleeveless—big silver earrings that hung down and swayed, and, now that he was up close, black tennis shoes, too. Her chest and perfect breasts—he'd somehow, inappropriately, zeroed in on those—rose with a deep breath, and then she tilted her head up to accommodate his height.

Large blue eyes—a deeper hue than normal—blinked once at him, and he felt a low thrum start in his core. A heart-shaped face, a few freckles, minimal makeup over smooth skin and full, lush lips—lips that were *not* smiling at him.

"You're Charlie?"

"Welcome to Glide. Line's over there," she said, and tilted her head to her right. "Fried chicken and dumplings tonight." She was terse and tense—and hot as hell. A point he'd do well to ignore.

Mitch cleared his throat. "Thanks, but I'm not here to eat." He looked around a little. No Tiffany, at least not right here in the immediate vicinity. "That guy"—he gestured to the man at the door—"says you're definitely the one I want."

Her face seemed to drain of color, so he smiled to put her at ease. "I'm looking for someone. She's—"

"Do you have a warrant?" Her hands fisted on her hips and she got in his face.

He nearly took a step back at the abrupt change in demeanor. "I—"

"Because this is a place of sanctuary. We help people in need—and that doesn't include cops." Her eyes flashed, and while her attitude ticked him off, he also found himself intrigued by all that fire.

Mitch raised his eyebrows. "Listen, lady, I'm not here as a cop."

"But you are one—that's plain as day."

He said, trying hard not to growl, "I'm off duty." She scowled, and took a breath to speak, but he jumped in. "I'm here as a brother."

Her bare shoulders drooped a full inch.

"I'm trying to locate my sister, Tiffany Scott." The shoulders shot back up. Mixed signals for sure, but she definitely reacted to the name. "She ran away a couple of weeks ago—"

"I'm not answering your questions—"

"Christ! Do you ever let a person finish a sentence?"

"Not when that person isn't listening to what I'm saying: no warrant, no answers. Get out."

"You've got some nerve!" he shot, but she'd turned her back and was stalking away. "And zero compassion," he muttered, noticing that all the men and women sitting around them had nearly disappeared into their plates.

Mitch strode back the way he came, fists clenched. He jerked a terse nod to the long-haired dude still at the door and went out for some fresh air. She'd thrown up a blockade. For the moment, at least, nobody within earshot of that argument was going to fess up to seeing Tiffany now.

In the meanwhile, he'd question any folks just arriving for dinner, *before* they had a chance to talk to their fearless leader.

––––––––

Charlie glared daggers at the man's back as he stormed out of Glide. When he stepped over the threshold, she pivoted and marched to the kitchen without a glance to the left or right.

Henrietta held open the swinging door for her by casually leaning against it, while she fanned herself with a plate. "Quite a show," she murmured.

"I suppose you had a front-row seat," Charlie muttered as she slid past. She didn't want to talk about it, so she attempted to adjust her tone to sweet. "Another hot flash, Henry?"

"Woo, yes. Brought on by all the excitement." She ambled in, the swoosh of the door just missing her as it returned.

Charlie headed for the far counter and slammed empty tins into the industrial-sized washbasin. She yanked down the oven door, and reached in—

"Ow!" She jumped back and lunged for the sink, pulled

the cold faucet handle, and shoved her hand under the rush of water.

Henrietta grabbed two mitts and slid out the tray of chicken. "A little rattled, are ya?"

"Just not paying enough attention, that's all," Charlie grumbled.

The older woman set the food under the warming lights without looking at Charlie. "My mind's lingering on that hunk of a man, too."

"Henrietta!"

"Well, he is a looker." She returned to the oven for some warm dumplings. Charlie rolled her eyes and caught Henrietta's smirk. "What'd he say to make you so angry?"

"Nothing really." Charlie eyeballed the pad of her index finger, found it slightly red, and stuck it back under the stream of cold water. "He just rubbed me the wrong way."

"What's he want?"

Charlie huffed out a breath, turned off the faucet, and grabbed a towel. "He's a cop. He's looking for his sister." She faced Henrietta. "Tiffany Scott."

Henrietta stared. "Then what was all the yelling about?"

"I wasn't willing to give him any information without a warrant."

Henrietta put her hands on her hips. "Why ever not, child?"

"Because how do I know she wants to be found? That he's who he says he is? That he's not the cause of her trouble, or that he's doing what's right for her?"

Henrietta cocked her head. "Isn't this the very girl you been worrying over?"

Charlie nodded, sheepish.

Henrietta shook her head. "You are somethin' else, if you

withheld information that could help that girl. From an officer of the law, no less!"

"A job or a title doesn't make a person automatically trustworthy, Henry." Appearances could be deceiving—a truth she'd do well to remember. "Besides, if I knew where she was, I would have helped her myself."

"Mmm-hmmn. Just by looking at that fine man, I can tell he's on the up and up, and I bet you know it, too."

Charlie frowned. Maybe—except if he was Tiffany's brother, then he was also from Pennsylvania. Add that to the fact that he was in law enforcement, and the chances of him recognizing her skyrocketed.

She threw the drying towel on the metal counter. "What I know," she said, "is that the good-looking ones can be the worst kind."

Henrietta clucked her tongue. "What I know is that a good man could be just what you need to force you out of that box you live in."

"You rent me that box!" Charlie stamped her foot, then immediately regretted the petulant action. A landlady who acted more like a mother naturally brought out her inner child.

"That's not what I meant and you know it." Henrietta raised her chin in challenge.

Charlie blew out another breath hard—this one forceful enough to make her short bangs move. "Stop pushing. I have everything I need."

"You most certainly do not! You serve at this mission and you waitress at night. Otherwise, you hide out in your apartment. No friends to speak of—"

"I have you and Cleo—"

"No friends your own age—real girlfriends! Never a date,

no hobbies, and not a lick of fun as far as I can tell." Henrietta had started fanning herself again in the middle of this tirade with a work-worn hand.

"You should talk," Charlie said.

"I'm old! I've lived life, child!" She flapped both hands in exasperation and her generous bosom heaved. "You deserve more."

Charlie shook her head. "Please, Henry. This is the only way for me." Tears threatened, so she clenched her jaw. "I promise you, I'm content. It might not seem like much from the outside looking in, but this life is a *blessing*."

CHAPTER 8

MITCH ROUNDED THE CORNER and leaned against the wall. He needed a second to regroup—a deep breath and an order to his body to relax. As soon as the tension left his fingers, he realized he'd crushed the picture of Tiffany. *Damn.* He smoothed it against the thigh of his jeans, then held it up.

Just then, he caught a movement down the street in his peripheral vision. Someone in all black scooted out the back door of the church and darted across the street.

Where are you off to, Charlie? Tiffany's place, maybe?

He stuffed the picture in his back pocket and followed. Around the corner, up the block, a right turn, straight uphill for two blocks—man, the hills in this town were brutal. Pennsylvania's hills rolled, but these shot up at what felt like right angles. Charlie had no trouble, though. Her strides got longer, her messenger-type army bag swung instead of bumped, but her pace didn't slow.

Finally, she halted at a happening corner—meaning there were a few shops actually open, a couple of restaurants with updated, freshly painted signs. Near Glide, in the heart of the Tenderloin, he'd noticed that metal barriers padlocked nearly every business.

Charlie looked into a window, pushed at her hair, wiped a hand across her forehead. She rolled her shoulders back and then dipped her head to swing like a pendulum over her collarbones, as if she needed to release tension. Even though she didn't seem to have any idea that he was there, Mitch stepped into the alcove of a doorway as a precaution. She dug in her bag, puckered up to the glass for a quick swipe of lipstick, then whipped out a black—of course—apron, tied it on, and slipped into the nearest restaurant's entryway.

Mitch clunked his head repeatedly against the wall behind him. She was only going to work. As a waitress. At a place called Cleo's Bistro. *Shit.* So much for her leading him straight to Tiffany.

The front of Cleo's was all glass, and the light was currently in his favor, so he found a spot to watch the restaurant. Surely Tiffany hadn't cleaned up and gotten a job in such a short time period? Nor would she be a patron.

Nonetheless, something niggled at him, something didn't feel right. The woman had shut him down quick as a shot. Was she protecting Tiffany, or someone else? It wouldn't hurt to stand quietly for a while, keep an eye on this Charlie, and let his mind wander over the possibilities...

He admitted to a rampant hard on where Charlie was concerned. She was smoking hot, and he always preferred strong women. She'd be a challenge, though, given her obvious and deep-rooted distrust of the law. There'd be a good reason for that, at least in her mind, and he wondered about it. If the situation were different, he'd like to get to know her better, figure out all those question marks—not to mention getting his hands on her. Fat chance, though.

He had zero time for distraction. Hell, he didn't even plan to get horizontal to log sleep, let alone get into trouble with a woman. He was here to find Tiffany. Period. He'd stay in San

Francisco only as long as it took to track her down, and then he'd have his hands full dragging his unwilling sister home.

Mitch shifted. He'd reached his limit for standing still, when he could be making forward progress. But the few minutes lost had been worth it. Charlie proved to be a capable waitress, owning her space, moving fast and sure, catering to the needs of each client. She seemed professional and friendly with one table, at ease and laughing with another. Her smile lit up her face, making her look like an entirely different person than the front she'd put on with him. Now that he'd seen her smile, she reminded him of someone, he just couldn't put his finger on who...

Didn't matter, though—his time was up. Gazing like a fool at some woman who had taken an instant dislike to him would not bring Tiffany home. Furthermore, he intended to make good use of his time while Glide's lovely watchdog fulfilled other obligations.

Mitch retraced the blocks downhill toward Glide. As he crossed the street in front of the soup kitchen, he got out his wallet for the picture of Tiffany. Where'd it go? He checked another flap—here it—

No, that was the picture of Laura Macnamara. He shoved it back in and stopped cold, replaying a slideshow full of pictures in his mind.

Holy mother of—

BWWAAAAAHHHH! A horn blared.

Mitch jumped out of the crosswalk just in time. He pressed his shoulder blades into the cool stone wall of Glide and slid heavily to the ground. His hands shook as he reopened the wallet and slid out Laura's old school photo, worn from carrying it with him for so many years.

He curled his index fingers to blot out the brown hair, picturing a crop of white blond instead—and nearly blew his own mind.

His brain spun out of control for a few minutes as he tried to grab hold of the probability of accidentally finding Laura. He knew he'd find her—or her body—someday, but this was…insane? Unbelievable? Wrong? Because, apparently, he'd just morphed into one of the luckiest shitheads on the planet.

But was it really just dumb luck, or was there a reason he'd found Laura where Tiff should also be? A connection between her and Tiffany? Her, Tiffany, and Thomas Weihle.

Mitch fished his cell phone out of his jacket pocket to call Marcone. He'd need permission to bring her in. Hell, he'd need proof, too. A DNA sample to send in. Or perhaps he'd force her to admit her true identity. He rubbed his thumb up and down over the cell's buttons, thinking. He'd have to watch her like a hawk. She ran once, she'd take off again. Definite flight risk.

He shook his head. *Fuck.* He couldn't risk it. His first priority had to remain Tiffany. After a tip at the San Diego bus depot, he'd driven straight here. He'd covered some ground checking shelters and soup kitchens in San Fran already. However, if Glide didn't pan out, there were plenty more to canvass. He couldn't afford to get off track. For a girl like Tiffany—young, attractive, alone in an unknown city, and constantly desperate for a fix… Jesus, trouble would be jumping out at her around every corner.

He had to keep mum, hiding the fact that he knew that Charlie was Laura Macnamara—Christ, he still could barely believe it—just until his sister surfaced, then he'd call the chief. Call the press, too, to vindicate his own ass. Even call

Gus Standall at Rolling Meadows to let Ellen Macnamara know—her daughter lived.

Mitch shoved the phone in his pocket, ran his hands over his face, then raked them through his hair. Enough. He had to get moving—the quicker he found Tiff, the quicker he could expose Laura and put both nightmares behind him.

CHAPTER 9

THOMAS GRINNED as he slid open the kitchen window of the modest two-story home in Grove Point. It felt as if this sash had been unlocked and lubricated just for him. He swung a leg over the low sill, stepped in onto hardwood floors shined so well they reflected the moonlight, and quietly shut the window.

He'd called in sick the last two days, to watch the house and map out both its layout and the inhabitants' routines. The glimpses he caught of young Mackenzie kept the task from being a chore—indeed, he'd felt invigorated. He thrived on careful crafting of a foolproof plan. Setting in motion things to come. The only thing better was the surge of exhilaration when all his hard work paid off.

Now, at nearly three o'clock in the morning, he paused at the kitchen counter, to sift through the mail for names. The Hudsons. Pamela…and ah, here it was, Raymond.

Pleased, Thomas moved quietly toward his goal: to gaze upon a sleeping Mackenzie—the first step in getting to know her. During daylight hours, he couldn't get close—not yet, anyway. Unless she was at school or after-care, her parents were always hovering, and the mother would remember him from the grocery. Even if he could get near, he'd be rushed; the child was nearly always in motion, delightfully animated. He needed to peruse her still features at leisure, to figure out just why she reminded him so much of Laura. The glossy brunette locks of hair, the rosy cheeks, the full pink lips, so large in a tiny face... He longed to be up close and personal, where he could inhale her scent and embed it in his memory to get him through.

He'd waited years—and been willing to wait longer—for Laura. Interim catches, like Tiffany, were invariably rushed, and therefore nowhere near as satisfying. This child was young at discovery, just like Laura. He'd require just as long to groom Mackenzie: first, to twist the situation to allow him entry into her world, then to learn how best to control her. By the time she was old enough, she'd be so thoroughly snared that there'd be no risk of exposure for him. The years ahead would require torturous restraint, yet they'd be a delicious torment—well worth his time and effort.

The stairs creaked with nearly every footfall. He held his breath—as if that would help—and attempted to tread lightly. Finally, he reached the second floor, which was carpeted wall to wall and therefore much better suited to sneaking around. Four doors were visible from here. The master to his left and three down the hall a ways. The bathroom glowed with a nightlight that illuminated the hall just enough. As he approached the doors, he spotted a wooden fairy hanging on one. She brandished a sparkly wand that spelled out MACKENZIE.

He sucked in a breath and slid into the room. She faced the closet doors, making it necessary for him to tiptoe around the bed. Then, as his eyes lit on the child's face, another nightlight making it possible to see her clearly, he dropped to his knees as his heart beat hard and fast.

He'd been right. She was divine—slumbering peacefully, her lashes long and dark on her round cheeks, her arm hooked over something furry, her hair tangled around her head. Her features did remind him of Laura at that age. What luck to have found a child who so resembled Laura—and yet he'd need to be careful to remember that she was not Laura. She'd have her own personality, a set of unique needs, for him to play with.

Thomas desired desperately to stroke her forehead or hold her hand, but he settled for smoothing her hair and leaning close. Hovering just in front of her face, he drew in her scent, shutting his eyes to concentrate.

The bedclothes rustled. His eyes flew open to see a small hand flop up above her head. She frowned in her sleep and shifted, her chest facing the ceiling. She murmured, stretching further, and her sweet face turned away from him. Her hair splayed over the pillow, exposing the delicate tendrils behind her ear, the soft skin of her neck—

Thomas stilled, forgetting even to breathe. She had a birthmark. Just there on her neck. Even in the dim glow of the nightlight he could make out its shape. A scythe.

A mark to match his own.

Impossible.

Thomas lurched to his feet, stumbling. Horror rose within him as possibilities presented themselves as fast as the dizzying spin of a rotary evaporator flask.

He pressed a gloved hand against the wall to steady himself.

After a moment, one thought had risen to the top, just like vapor being drawn off a sample by vacuum. In his mind, however, it surged up and exploded with force.

The child named Mackenzie was his. His and Laura's. His stomach turned—he'd targeted his own offspring, even lusted after her. *Laura, you bitch, putting me in this position.* He pressed the back of his forearm against his mouth, just barely staving off vomit.

Disgust and fury swirled through his mind like a tornado, blocking out rational thought for a time.

Then, clarity. Laura had given away his child. He'd thought her abandonment the worst sin, but this deceit—the sloughing off of his own flesh and blood to strangers. Subjecting her—however unwittingly—to his desire. Ultimate betrayal.

Rage, hot and fierce—like he hadn't felt since Laura had run—boiled from within. Sweat beaded on his upper lip, and he reached for the handkerchief he kept in his jacket pocket—except he'd forgotten. He wasn't dressed as usual, but in form-fitting black clothing for this nighttime excursion. Thomas fought to control himself, pulling off the knit cap to let some heat escape, counting his breaths, consciously releasing his clenched jaw.

He must keep his wits about him, for this could explain so much.

Thomas stared hard at the child. Was he sure?

Instinct told him unequivocally yes—he gazed on a daughter that should rightfully have been his all this time. Except he was a scientist, after all. To erase any doubt, he would need a plan and proof—logical, irrefutable proof. He pulled his penlight from his back pocket and knelt again, careful to shield Mackenzie's face with his hand, blocking the light from her eyes.

Exactly where it should be. The Weihle birthmark. An overwhelming sense of virile pride suffused him.

His mother would have been pleased, too.

The scythe was the mark of good breeding, she'd always said. Just before she'd abandoned him, at age twelve, on the steps of a home for orphaned boys, she'd reminded him, *You are marked for better, my boy; remember that always, and rise above.* She'd bent, kissing him perfunctorily on his cheek. His eyes latched on to the gap in her blouse, showing the frayed lace of her only bra. Every cell in his body longed to bury his face in the softness that swelled there, yet he'd stood stoic and tall, his arms at his sides like a soldier, just as he knew she preferred.

He pushed away thoughts of his mother, again seeing in front of him Mackenzie's young skin bearing his mark. He rose, dissecting her features, fingering her hair. Indeed, blood and bone sprung from Laura.

Laura, he thought, *you will pay dearly for keeping my child from me.*

Although he did not doubt, he sought proof anyway, as thorough men were wont to do. He replaced his hat so as to free his hands. He bent to collect some loose hairs, then thought better of it. He'd have to pull hard enough to get root on multiple samples—surely she'd wake. Thomas crept out of the bedroom and into the bathroom. Quietly, quietly. Gloved hands pulled at vanity drawers, sans success. He needed just one clean Q-tip. Straightening, he saw himself in the mirror, and smiled—a loopy look. Did all men feel so strange and proud at finding out they were fathers?

Of course, he realized suddenly, the mirror was a recessed medicine cabinet. It opened with only a faint popping noise. Yes, top shelf, a small cup with white tufts peeking out above the rim. Thomas shook out a few, careful to touch only the cardboard wands between the tips.

Back in Mackenzie's room, he was pleased to find her snoring softly, mouth open. Carefully, he angled a cotton swab into the gap, and rubbed it along the inside of her cheek for buccal cells. Thomas slid the stick out just before she snuffed and snapped her lips shut. Then she swiped an arm over her face and shifted uneasily. He needed to leave.

Thomas glowed at his success. Paternity tests couldn't be done in his lab—at least not without raising eyebrows. However, sending off for a kit should prove simple.

Action had settled the frantic emotions he'd felt at discovering the mark. Now that he'd regained control, his thoughts sped along with precision and order. Patience and planning were still necessary; however, the goal was entirely new.

He'd nearly given up hope of unearthing Laura's whereabouts. Tonight, he'd been presented with a direct path to finding the little coward. His Laura was suddenly—thrillingly—within reach. Even better—he nearly laughed with the perfection of it—their child provided the elusive key that would chain Laura to him forever.

Thomas took a last look. Here lay his future, sleeping peacefully. Rightfully, this child belonged to him. The urge to scoop his daughter into his arms and simply disappear with her was powerful—all emotion, he knew, clamoring for attention. If he wanted Laura, too—and oh, how deeply he desired Laura for both pleasure and revenge—then he must wait. He must allow Mackenzie to sleep in this bed, live with imposters, continue this false life...

"When the time is right, my girl," he whispered, and touched his lips to her forehead.

Then he retreated out of her room and down the stairs. He found a sandwich baggie in the kitchen drawer, tucked the cheek swab safely within, and sealed it. He slipped it up into his sleeve then rolled the ribbing of his shirt to make the band tighter. The specimen would be safer there, along his forearm, than squashed in a pocket.

Thomas checked his watch: close to four a.m. He hadn't

counted on an additional quest this evening, but there was no denying its importance. He simply couldn't walk out of this house before discovering Laura's whereabouts, yet he'd need to hurry.

The den that sat just off the living area seemed to serve as an office, so that was where he headed. Thankful that he'd worn gloves, Thomas peeked carefully, quietly, through desk drawers and a two-drawer filing cabinet. Even though they'd have no idea he'd been here, it still wouldn't do to leave things disturbed. Thomas's frustration mounted as he reached the last file. The room had no closet or cupboards. He checked a bookshelf, then the desk. His muscles had become tense and tight, his breathing more shallow as anxiety mounted. No adoption file or lockbox. Neither a leather-bound address book, nor any envelopes with a suspicious return addresses sat among the clutter.

He paused to think, his eyes lighting on a framed photograph of Mackenzie. She wore a glittering crown and a fancy dress of gold. He picked it up to see the detail, angling it toward the penlight. He stroked his finger down the glass along her cheek. She looked as if she had eye shadow on, properly applied. Too formal for an impromptu session of dress-up. She must have been in a dance recital or, more likely, become a princess last Halloween. Laura had favored costumes that seemed to promote the holiday itself while still feeling traditional—a pumpkin, a black cat, a witch with green paint smeared unevenly on her cheeks.

But as she grew older, the costumes were picked first to scare, and then, eventually, to reveal—more skin, firm curves, and long legs. Her body had begun to bloom, and hormones had just begun to swirl into consciousness, leaving her unsettled and unsure one moment, bold and wanting another. He remembered vividly the Halloween she'd been dropped off back at home after trick-or-treating in a friend's more densely populated neighborhood. His porch light had been on, and he'd been watching. Just as he'd hoped, when her friend's parents had driven off, she'd rung his bell, her pillowcase heavy with treats.

He'd purchased her favorites, both Twix and Kit Kats, and they'd ended up sitting on his stoop, the bowl of candy between them. Munching and talking. She'd licked chocolate from her finger, innocent in the action as a thirteen-year-old should be, but her skirt had been short, her top tight, her hair sprayed and funky, her makeup too harsh. The combination had been intoxicating.

He teased her a bit, always posing as her confidant, gaining her trust for a day soon to come. "So, who is it you have your eye on now that you're in middle school and have so many more guys to choose from?"

Laura blushed, of course, and wound a candy bar wrapper around her finger. "I don't know."

"Sure you do. You can tell me—I don't know anybody at your school anyway."

She took a deep breath and looked out into the darkness toward her own house. "I kinda like Billy Butler. But I'm not sure."

"If you really liked him, you'd be sure." Thomas squeezed her knee.

"I totally like him—a lot. It's just, well, it's a little scary."

"Because you aren't sure he likes you?"

"Oh, he definitely likes me."

"Then what's the problem?"

She jiggled her legs, her skirt sliding up a little further, and clasped her hands together between her knees. "He wants me to meet him under the bleachers next Friday. That's where kids meet to, well, you know, make out and stuff." Her words rushed and tumbled around each other. "I'm afraid to go. Not afraid that he'd hurt me or anything. But he might laugh because I've never kissed anybody and what if I do it wrong?"

Thomas's chest felt tight, his head hot, his mind racing ahead. If he played this right... "There's no wrong way to kiss, you know. It might be a bit awkward at first, but it just takes a little getting used to, maybe a little practice."

"Oh," she said, and bit her lip. He'd been fighting an erection, but blood rushed to his cock at seeing her plump lower lip squeezed by her teeth.

"I can't believe I'm going to say this," he said, and shook his head. "But if you want, I could teach you."

She looked at him, big-eyed like a doe caught in the headlights. She'd leaned back as well, distancing herself from him.

"Never mind, never mind," he said, and waved a hand. Rather than dismissing the idea, however, his brain zipped wildly through options that might bring her around. "I just thought it'd make you more comfortable with Billy. I'm sure he wouldn't laugh if you were unsure of yourself, however"—Thomas cleared his throat—"you do want him to become your boyfriend, don't you?"

She nodded and tucked her head to focus on her lap.

"Mmmn, well, you need to make sure you get it right the first time, then." Thomas began to scoop up the empty candy wrappers. "We practiced on our pillows when I was growing up. I don't recommend that."

Laura slid her palms between her thighs as if to warm them. She hadn't run home, and he was nowhere near giving up for the night.

"Okay, well, listen," Thomas said, as if they were discussing homework or any other innocuous subject. "I know I must seem old compared to you." In fact, he was nearing forty at the time. "But that just means I have a lot of experience to share." He winked. "You could think of me as a tutor. If you change your mind and want your best chance with Billy, the offer stands."

She bit her lip again, and he sent up a silent plea. She turned to him, uncertainty telegraphing clearly in her expression.

"Laura," he said, "I hope I didn't scare you."

"Just kissing, right?" She was so nervous, her voice wobbled. "You wouldn't expect anything else?"

Thomas had raised his eyebrows. "Oh you think—" He shook his head. "No, Laura, you're a gorgeous girl, and I like you, but you are way too young for me. This would be a favor to you only."

She nodded, and he actually saw her chest fall with the exodus of breath from her lungs.

"All right," she said, as she wrapped her arms around her chest in a hug.

He looked at her. "Yes?"

She nodded. Thomas looked away to keep her from seeing the glee in his eyes.

"I just need one itty-bitty little thing from you." He smiled gently to ease her, when he'd really wanted to grin like the master of cunning that he was. "Because you are so young, you have to promise me that if I help you, it has to remain a secret."

She'd agreed, of course.

"Well," Thomas said, picking up the candy bowl, still brimming with chocolate he found distasteful, "let's get this over with." He stood and motioned for her to follow him through the front door for her first lesson.

And that was all it took to bring years of drawing her in ever so slowly to culmination.

He'd only kissed her that night, light licks and nibbles graduating to something only a little heated, but oh, the power of those first tentative kisses. Laura's shy eyes shimmering with uncertainty, those full lips tasting of processed sugar, hands stiff and tense at her sides, her entire demeanor so innocent—in perfect juxtaposition to the Halloween attire that screamed, *Fuck me, I want it.*

He'd strained to remain outwardly calm, while the most powerful erection he'd ever experienced surged as if possessed. Although it was an epic struggle, he refrained from pressing against her—he had waited too long to risk scaring her off.

What a rush it had been when she had capitulated to that kiss. All his careful maneuvering, the planting of seeds, tending to her like a new garden, had begun to bear fruit—seasons before he'd expected a bounty.

Thomas blinked, and set the picture of this younger lookalike back on the desk. He was breathing heavily now, and found he was damp with perspiration. He had to find Laura. He'd never stopped needing her, his desire growing by leaps and bounds as she became more and more his. Then, after her disappearance, the feverish burn to find her and make her pay.

At the time, he'd had no recourse but to wait and simmer, having exhausted the avenues with which to track her. Now that he'd discovered that not only had she left him and abandoned her poor mother, but she'd also discarded like trash his own flesh and blood? Now, upon finding out how deep her betrayal had been? He seethed and burned as if on the edge of combustion.

And yet the all-consuming rage warred with elation. Finally, he controlled the game once more. The power to root her out had landed squarely at his feet. The agony of waiting would soon come to an end.

If only he could come up with an address. A link.

There was nothing for it. The computer appeared to be on. He'd have to wake it, pray the volume was low or off, and take the time to look for an electronic address book. Or perhaps an email. Thomas closed the door to the study, careful not to let it click, then turned to lean over the desk chair.

Thirty minutes later, frustration had him seething in the small, square office. He glared at a mounted photo of the Hudsons. Was it possible this family didn't know the birth mother of their child, hadn't even looked? Surely there wasn't an adoption agency involved—not when Rolling Meadows had received such large cash payments, far in excess of what he'd given Laura for the mortgage. No, he was certain, she had dealt with the couple directly—sold his child to the highest bidders.

Quite the happy-looking family: Pamela, Raymond, and sweet Mackenzie. The man's hair was dark and receding, but thick. Not quite the same color as Mackenzie's, but she'd pass as resembling him instead of the woman. Too bad those wide smiles hid a sham. Every child needed her real mother, needed to know her father. Families should not be separated. He should know.

Although he wanted to rage—stomp, slam, and yell—Thomas trod softly and twisted the study's doorknob ever so gently. He left the door ajar—like he'd found it—and began again in the living room. He'd search until dawn, or until someone woke.

CHAPTER 10

MITCH WORKED HIS WAY steadily down the line of guests waiting to eat at Glide. They shuffled forward, and he took each one in turn. Flashing Tiffany's picture, asking questions, explaining his plight, his mother's fear, and always hoping for help. He got some head shakes, some sympathy, some shrugs, but no information.

The smell, a mixture of unwashed bodies, stale clothes, and foul breath, combined with the delicious scent of a hearty supper from the church kitchen, was making him lightheaded. He'd barely stopped since taking the red-eye flight from Philly two days ago. Hunger, exhaustion, and, more than anything, the worry that he'd hit another dead end pulled at him. But there were at least twenty-five more people queued up.

A lanky teen with short, spiky jet-black hair was next, and he spoke before Mitch could even show him the picture.

"I've seen her—your sister."

"You have? Where? When?" Mitch was jazzed instantly.

"Here, and at the other shelters." The boy shrugged. "She hasn't been around lately, though."

"Do you know where she is now?"

"No."

"Was she okay?" Mitch rolled his shoulders. "I mean, considering?"

The teen scuffed the toe of his Vans shoe repeatedly on the sidewalk. "I guess."

He'd broken eye contact—not good. "Maybe it'd be easier to talk in private. Will you step over there and give me a minute?"

"No way, man. I'll lose my place in line. They'll shut the doors soon."

"Right. What if I buy you dinner—order off the menu, all you can eat, my treat?" Mitch waited—he knew well that any kid on the street would hesitate to go off alone with a stranger. Trust wouldn't come easily. The teen held his eyes.

Either he passed muster, or the boy's stomach won out, because he smiled. "Hope you've got a fat wallet—I can really put it down."

The kid led him to a greasy spoon diner that didn't look like much, but Ian, that was his name, swore the "leftovers" were awesome.

They didn't talk much at first, chatting over neutral territory at first, like the menu. But Ian loosened up as he filled up. A smorgasbord of food covered the table of their small booth—chicken parmesan, meatball hero, chicken pot pie, lamb gyro, and Greek salad, just to name a few. The excessive ordering was Ian's test of Mitch's word, he knew, but even if he didn't get an ounce more information out of him, the ear-to-ear smile on the kid's face—between heaping forkfuls—was worth every penny.

It turned out Ian was only sixteen and had grown up near LA. He'd been on the streets for over a year, and had been an addict, too. He didn't want to go home until he'd been clean for six months.

"I want to make sure I can make it stick. Don't want to fuck it up at home again."

"Can you do it on your own, without the support of your family?" Ian's jaw set, and Mitch held up a hand. "No offense, kid. I just wondered because I've seen the long, twisted road addicts travel. Besides the fact that I work narcotics, I've been there with Tiffany, too. We staged an intervention, dragged her to rehab, rallied behind her…"

God, it'd been hard, seeing his sister cornered like that. She'd tried everything. She'd gone to each of them in turn— him, his mom, and Chief Marcone, whom his mom had become good friends with since he'd been widowed. She'd pulled at Deirdre's shirt, begging and sobbing. "Mom, I promise, I'll stop, I can do better, please don't make me go. I don't want to be alone, I need to stay with you, Mommy." To the chief: "Dom, don't let them do this, they're crazy." By the time she clawed Mitch's arms, snot had been pouring down her upper lip. "Mitchy, you can't do this. I'm your baby sis, I'm a good girl. I hit a rough patch. You know how it is with friends—bad influences. I'll stay home, I'll get new friends. I don't need to go away. How can you do this to me? My own brother?"

After she nearly plowed Deirdre over in an attempt to escape, he'd scooped her up and plunked her in his dad's old recliner. He braced himself on the arms of the chair, one knee pinning her thighs, trapping her. "It's too late, Tiff. You're going."

"You've all been brainwashed!" she screamed. "They'll kill me! You want me to die!" She'd put her hands over her ears and screamed and screamed. Finally, he'd carried her to his vehicle and shoved her in back. There was no escaping the rear seat of a police car, but oh, how Tiff had tried. Pounding on the windows, kicking the doors, pulling at the handles, throwing her body into the divider—all the while hurling obscenities like a barrage of gunfire sure to wound. He'd driven with tears blurring the road, squeezing tight to his mother's hand in the passenger seat. He'd looked at Deirdre only once. The expression of pain and horror on her face made him feel such guilt and shame that he'd kept his eyes on the road after that.

His poor mother. Jesus, his heart felt it'd break in two every time he remembered the "intervention."

"I'd thought"—Mitch shook his head—"she'd come so far, had stayed clean. But she backslid right under our noses. I was undercover. Had I pulled out, and really been there, I wonder..."

Ian swallowed hard, shook his head, and pushed the chicken parm away. "You can't do it for her. She's got to want it."

"Yeah, I know that, but in here"—he thumped his chest with a fist—"I can't accept it. I need to help somehow."

"Listen," Ian said, "I turned the corner. I was ready. I take advantage of the counselors at the shelters when I feel like I start to lose it. I avoid situations that tempt me." His eyes slid away. "Your sister..."

Mitch set his own fork on his plate and leaned in. "You don't think she has it in her?"

"Honestly, man? No. At least not yet. She's the kind will fool you if that's what you want to believe, but she doesn't really want it." Ian crushed a napkin between his hands and rolled it around and around. "There's this one lady at Glide who's really tried with her, you know? Pointed out shelters and clinics. But I've seen her walk right out the door and down the street to talk to the dealers." He shrugged.

"Any chance this lady knows where Tiffany is staying?" Mitch held his breath.

"No way. She was just asking me—and everybody else—if they'd seen her. She's worried because Tiffany hasn't been in for a while."

"What's her name and what shifts does she work? I need to talk with her."

"She's there all the time. Or at the restaurant where she works. Her name's Charlie."

"Blond hair, kind of funky, pretty? That Charlie?"

"Yeah. She's cool."

"We've met. She seems to have taken an instant dislike to me."

Ian raised a thick black eyebrow and grinned. "That's interesting. She's usually nice to everybody."

"She's protective, I think, of the Glide folks."

"Yeah."

"And maybe she's got a thing against cops."

"A lot of us around here do."

Regardless, Mitch thought, things were looking up. He'd found two people who knew Tiff. Three, if you counted that guy at the door who'd pointed him to Charlie because he'd seen them talking. He and Ian sat just looking at each other for a minute, until Mitch signaled the waiter.

"Some to-go boxes for the kid here, and a dessert menu. Thanks."

Ian grinned. "I can maybe put in a good word for you with Charlie."

"It's probably gonna take more than one."

Mitch paid the bill, and they climbed the few blocks to Cleo's Bistro, settled in to wait across the street. Now that the Thursday evening dinner crowd had dispersed, Charlie bustled around from table to table wiping up and snuffing candles. She disappeared into the kitchen for a while, at which point Mitch realized that Ian had been watching him watch Charlie.

Oh well. Surely a sixteen-year-old boy could understand the attraction to a beautiful woman?

"Here she comes."

Sure enough, she was stuffing her apron in her satchel and pushing open the door with her hip. "Cleo," she yelled over her shoulder, "I'm heading out and locking the door!"

She fished a key ring out of her purse and turned multiple deadbolts. Then stepped into the shadows of the street.

"Let's go," Mitch said. "Call out, so we don't scare her."

"Hey Charlie, it's me, Ian."

She turned. "Hey, Ian, what are you doing here?" Her eyes narrowed when she spotted Mitch. "You again."

"Yeah." He turned up his hands and shrugged.

"Unless you've miraculously produced a warrant, you're wasting your time."

Ian looked up at Mitch. "Dude, you weren't kidding." The teen turned his attention to Charlie. "He's just looking for Tiffany. He wants to help her."

"Is that all?" She'd been staring hard at Mitch, yet her expression softened when she looked at Ian. "Why aren't you at the shelter? Are you hungry? I'm sure Cleo's got extra tonight."

"Naw." He hooked his thumb at Mitch and held up his super-sized to-go bag. "We went to the diner. Had a ten-course meal."

"Oh, really? And does this jerk-off realize that although he provided dinner, he's cost you a bed tonight?"

"Oh, man, Ian. You should've said." Mitch had been so focused on his goals that it hadn't occurred to him that the queues for beds at the shelters started early. First come, first serve, and latecomers slept on the streets. "I've got double beds at the hotel. One's yours."

Ian scuffed his foot on the ground, and Charlie rolled her eyes. "Like that's a good idea. Idiot." She glared at Mitch. "Ian, you'll stay tonight on my couch."

"It's okay, Charlie."

"No, it's not, and I won't take no for an answer."

Just then the door to the bistro opened and Cleo herself called, "Charlie, everything okay out there?"

———

"Everything's fine, Cleo." Charlie waved. "We're just talking."

She had to keep the volume and her temper down. The last thing she needed was to draw attention to herself or, God forbid, rouse a cop's suspicion.

Charlie listened for the thump of the locks, and noticed out of the corner of her eye that the restaurant lights were flicking off one by one. She watched the cop. He waited patiently, but she could see he was strung tight by the clench of his angular jaw and piercing look. She blew out a breath. He was a problem, this cop. Any woman in her right mind would be trying to draw this guy in for a taste of tall, built, and hot—but she had to get rid of him, and fast.

"I can't help you with your sister."

"Maybe you can, maybe you can't. I just want a few minutes to ask you some questions."

He had a hard face, so serious, yet there was a hint of hope hiding in his caramel-colored eyes. She thought of Henrietta's admonishments and felt guilt poke a few holes in her anger.

"I have no idea where she is," she said, and watched disappointment flicker incongruously over features carved from determination.

"Do you know which shelters she stays at?" His Adam's apple dipped. "Which dealers she's hit?"

"No, to both."

"Has she mentioned a friend, anybody by name?"

"No."

"Any plans?"

Charlie rubbed her temples. "Your sister is an addict. She has only two things on her mind: avoiding drugs or scoring drugs."

He stood taller, and she sighed. She knew she was being deliberately harsh, trying to make him vanish as quickly as possible.

"Listen," Charlie said, "I have no way of knowing what Tiffany's situation was at home, whether she was loved, whether she was safe—"

"She was loved and safe. She has a home, a mother who adores her. People who care. I promise you, I want only what's best for her."

Charlie smiled, despite a sneaky tingle of approaching tears. "I'm glad, but Tiffany may not agree."

"I know my sister, as well as the effects of drug abuse. She can't even think straight right now—"

"Maybe you're right. Then again, she may not want to be found."

"Of course she doesn't want to be found!" he roared. "She knows we'll force her back into rehab to get clean, for Pete's sake!"

"I'm not denying the fact that Tiffany needs help."

"No?" He put his hands on his hips and leaned forward,

invading her space with his bulk. "You're denying me any information that might lead to that help."

"I'm telling you, I don't know anything." Charlie mimicked his posture. She refused to be intimidated.

"I've got a sure bet against the truth coming from your lips, Charlie," he sneered. He stepped in to loom directly over her.

Her heart racing, she backed up. "What's that supposed to mean?"

"All right." Ian stepped between them. "It's been fun, but it's probably time to call it a night."

"Good by me." Jeez, she'd forgotten Ian was even there. She took a few more steps backward in order to breathe. "Which hotel are you staying at, Top Cop?"

Still scowling, he raised an eyebrow. "Motel 6."

"It's that way." She pointed behind him. "We're going this way. If I even remotely suspect that you are following us, I will have the local police on your sorry ass before you can blink." A bluff, but he wouldn't know that.

"You will talk to me," he ground out.

"Not tonight I won't, because I don't have anything to tell." The man actually growled—a sound of ultimate frustration—and stomped away. He paced a tight circle, hands clapped on his head with elbows skyward. Charlie exchanged a glance with Ian. She started to retreat, reaching out her hand to the boy as she did so. The cop spun and closed the distance before she could blink.

"You have more to tell than you even know. We'll talk. Soon," he said in a calm voice, strung with utter steel.

"I—"

He held up a hand. "Stop." He shut his eyes briefly and

took a deep breath. "You should go now. I won't follow you, if you'll promise me something in return."

Charlie waited, on edge.

His eyes still bored death rays into her, but his mouth quirked. "Stop cussing me out and calling me names in front of the kid."

"That's all I know to call you."

"The name's Mitch Saunders."

"Yeah, well, I'm still hearing 'asshole' in my mind," Charlie said. She yanked on Ian's shirt and took off.

CHAPTER 11

THOMAS STOOD biding his time on the back deck of the Hudson home. This time, his visit was not a middle-of-the-night tour, but more of a social call. Tamping down the anticipation that had been building all day, he waited for Mackenzie to be put to bed and for the woman to finish tidying up the kitchen. Finally, he deemed the timing right.

The door was locked, but—how nice—they'd left his window unlocked yet again. The TV squawked now—he could hear it even outside—enabling him to enter and approach before the couple even realized they had a visitor. Certainly preferable to barging in through the front door.

Surely after this, the Hudsons would turn the house into a fortress. There'd been a set of keys hanging on the hook by the back door last time. Preoccupied, he'd neglected to borrow them. If the ring still hung there tonight, he'd take them, procure a locksmith's services, and slip back in to replace the missing set when they left for work.

He slid inside and closed the sash gently behind him, then pulled his newest purchase, a gorgeous Taurus PT 24/7 OSS semiauto, from his waistband and noted the red showing in the loaded chamber indicator. The ridged grip felt perfect in his hand. Although he had a lot to learn yet about guns, he wished that he'd discovered the heady feeling of a loaded weapon years ago.

The keys did hang in their usual spot, so he squeezed them and lifted, careful not to let them jingle, and slid them into his front pants pocket. His shoes, picked purposely for stealth, were silent as he crossed the kitchen tile and padded into the living room. And there the Hudsons sat just as they did most nights, imbeciles filling their brains with laugh tracks instead of knowledge.

Thomas rounded the couch, scooping up the cordless phone from the end table with his left hand.

The woman gasped; the man jumped up.

"Ah ah ah, Ray," Thomas said, as he raised his right arm, pointing the gun at the wife. "You wouldn't put dear Pamela at risk, would you? Sit, please."

Ray lowered himself slowly to the sofa, his expression warring between disbelief and fear.

"Now, Pamela, turn off the TV." Eyes goggled at him. "Pamela. Turn off the television. I need your undivided attention." She tore her eyes from his face, or rather, his mask, and searched for the remote. Her fingers fumbled, but the sound and light on the box went dead.

"Thank you." He smiled, for his own benefit, he supposed, since surely they couldn't gauge his expression under the thick knit fabric.

"Who are you? What do you want?" Ray babbled. "We have some jewelry, some cash—"

"I come on a much more important call. You have something of mine."

Husband and wife stared at each other, wondering what in the world he meant. Oh, but this was turning out to be fun.

"We don't even know who you are," she said, her voice shaky. "How could we have something of yours?"

"Ah, well, that's the million-dollar question, isn't it? But I'll wager you didn't pay that much, did you?" Horror began to dawn in Ray's eyes, but Pamela seemed to be slow to catch on. "You should have, though. Mackenzie is worth every penny."

"Oh my God, oh my God, Ray." Pamela sobbed, while Ray shouted, red-faced, "Mackenzie is ours!"

"In fact, no, she's not."

Ray pushed off the couch, but Thomas swung the gun toward him. Ray halted, then lowered himself in slow motion back onto the cushions.

"Your Mackenzie has a birthmark on her neck—"

"How do you know that?" Pamela screeched, and turned to Ray. "How does he know that!"

"Because she showed it to me, her father."

Pamela paled, covering her sobs with her hands, as if to hold inside the illusion of the world she'd still believed in only moments ago.

"You are not her father, you sicko! I am!" Ray hollered.

"Ray, Ray, Ray. No amount of lost time or money can change the fact that she has my blood, not yours." He pulled his mask up at the left side of his neck, careful to keep the gun trained on Ray. "Pamela, I invite you to take a closer look."

She shook her head, sobbing. "No. No. No. No."

"Yes." Thomas confirmed.

"You'd better get out of this house," Ray threatened.

"Or what?" Thomas sneered. "You'll call the cops? Hmmn, no, I don't think anybody who's bought a baby illegally will involve the police."

"There was nothing illegal about it! She was given to us!"

"She was stolen from me!" Thomas clenched his fist tight around the gun and felt the plastic of the phone crack. A minute, and he said calmly, "The state of Pennsylvania does not consider the exchange of cash for a child legal."

"You'll never have her. I'll kill you first."

"I don't believe either of us will need to resort to those measures. I've come with a proposal." Thomas tossed the phone behind him to the floor. "While I do want my child, there's something I want more—her birth mother."

"But we haven't seen her since Mackenzie's birth," Ray said.

"But you know how to find her, don't you?"

"No, we—"

"Excuses, excuses," Thomas scolded. "Laura is your only bargaining chip. I can, and will, claim the child as my own, stolen from me without my consent. A DNA test will prove true paternity, and a search of your financial records around the time of Mackenzie's birth will surely land you both in jail as criminals, along with Laura. In terms of a custodial parent, I'm a court's dream come true. Did you know that the state is legally obligated to place children with a biological parent?" Thomas paused. "No? You have a lot to learn, then." Both sets of eyes were trained on him. "Listen closely now, unfit parents. Sweet Mackenzie will remain safe, only if you give Laura Macnamara to me. If not…" He shrugged.

"We have an address only—a PO box." Pamela steadied herself. "I'll get it for you."

She pointed to the office door, and Thomas nodded, stepping back to let her rise and pass.

"Pam, we promised." Ray shut his eyes.

She looked back at him, eyes flat, but stance erect. "We have no choice."

Thomas crossed to where he could watch her through the doorway but kept the gun pointed toward Ray. Pamela reached for the photo of Mackenzie in the gold dress and came to the door. She slid out the back of the frame and handed Thomas a piece of paper.

"Thank you. Sit, please." He glanced down at the paper and noticed that his hands were trembling. "California, is it? You have no phone number?"

"No."

"How often does she check this box?"

"I have no idea." Pamela sat tall on the edge of the cushions and looked him in the eye. "You have what you want. Leave."

"A PO box won't be traceable," Thomas replied, and tucked the scrap of paper in his coat pocket. "I'll require one more favor from you. Ray, take the yellow pad and pen from the end table there."

"You've been in our house?" Pamela's hands clenched into fists on her knees.

"But of course." He waved at the side table, thinking idly that he'd prefer classier stationery.

Ray scooted forward, slid out the drawer, and fumbled around for the items.

"Pass them to your wife."

She waited.

"*Dear Laura,*" Thomas instructed, "*Mackenzie's true father has come to us, insisting that you return home where you belong. Hurry, for the child's safety depends on you.*"

He paused, and the scratch of the pen stopped.

"That'll do, I suppose," he said. "Sign your name, fold it, and hand it to me. I'll mail it."

Thomas slapped the paper against his thigh while he watched the frozen couple. "Shall I go upstairs and get a good night kiss from my little girl?"

"NO!" Both started to move.

He laughed so hard he had to wipe his arm against his eyes. "I'm enjoying your discomfort immensely."

Ray's face turned purple.

"A word to the wise." Thomas hardened his voice. "There is no escape from me. I'll be watching you, everywhere, all the time. If I see anything out of the ordinary—any deviation from your usual monotonous existence—it's Mackenzie who will suffer for your stupidity. Until Laura graces us with her presence, at which point, you and Ray will be free of me."

"What if," Pamela managed, "she doesn't come?"

"Oh, I know Laura inside and out." He grinned. "There's not a doubt in my mind. She'll come."

CHAPTER 12

CHARLIE, HUMMING ALONG to the Eagles, had just tossed the remains of her Thai takeout dinner into the fridge when someone knocked on her door. She froze. Why hadn't they rung the buzzer downstairs? Charlie spun the dial on the portable AM/FM radio, the strains of "Hotel California" disappearing with a crackling pop.

She was home early because Cleo's had been a bit slow, but still—who would be knocking at eleven o'clock on a Friday night? She kept to herself—purposely—and never invited people to her place. Henrietta, also her landlady, always accompanied her knock with a "Hey girl, it's me." Actually, now that Charlie thought of it, nobody but Henry had *ever* knocked on her door.

Knock, knock. "Charlie, it's Mitch Saunders."

Shit, she thought, that bastard.

"Let me in. I know for a fact you're in there. I saw you enter, I smell your food, I heard you moving around."

"You promised you wouldn't follow us," she called, approaching warily.

"And I kept that promise—last night. It seemed to me to be a one-time request, so I followed you today. Don't be mad," Mitch said.

"Don't be mad! Are you nuts? I've got some psycho cop

tailing me everywhere—seriously everywhere: the church, my work, my home—and I'm not supposed to freak out?" But she wasn't just angry or weirded out, she was terrified. Here was a guy—a cop, no less—from Blakes Ridge. He was focused on his sister now, but if he put two and two together...

She heard a clunk against the door—hopefully his head.

"Listen, I'm sorry, Charlie, I really am"—his voice cracked—"but I'm desperate to find my sister and you are one of the only links I've got."

"But I don't know anything!"

"You do, though."

"Goddammit, I do not!" She smacked the door with her palm.

"Fuck that! You do!" he yelled, and hit the door himself—with his fist, the way it reverberated.

"I'm calling the police!" she threatened.

"You do that, *Laura*," he spat, "and I'll invite the news teams to join the party."

She gasped and backed away from the door in horror. It was too late.

"Nothing to say to that?" he taunted.

She turned this way, then that. My God, what to do? Grab her bag and go down the fire escape? Try to reason with him? Beg him to keep quiet? Pummel him with a lamp?

"Laura?"

She halted.

"Laura? Open the door."

She stepped forward, one foot in front of the other, and watched her hand shake as she flipped the deadbolts. She curled her fingers around the knob, shut her eyes just for a moment, then pulled it open.

Mitch had one hand braced on the doorframe, shoulder muscles bunched, jaw tight, caramel eyes hard. He looked every bit like a man who could be her downfall.

"Please," she whispered as her eyes filled. "Don't call me that."

His brows lowered, then he nodded once and straightened.

She turned and went back into the apartment, leaving the door open. She rubbed her hands over her arms, hugging herself.

The door clicked shut.

"Lock it," she said.

There was a pause, then he complied. She forced herself to turn and face him. He looked even more imposing than yesterday—unshaven and haggard but still mega-sexy, even in a ratty hooded sweatshirt and jeans ripped over one knee—his tall build filling her tiny living room. Oddly, he was no longer glaring at her. Instead, he appeared puzzled.

She let out a shaky laugh. "Please don't tell me that was just a guess."

"No." He spread his legs, shoved his hands in the pockets of well-worn jeans. "I knew without a doubt it was you."

Just then, a deafening racket clanged against the door—metal striking metal—and they both jumped and cringed.

"Girl," Henrietta boomed, "I got my gun in one hand and my phone in the other! You don't open the door in the next ten seconds an' tell me everything is all right, I am calling the police and blasting that lock myself!"

"Don't call! I'm okay, Henry!" Charlie lunged for the door and started flipping locks. She could feel Mitch directly behind her, ready to protect her if need be. The "threat" was only Henry, but he wouldn't know that.

She swung the door wide and was greeted by a fierce-looking Henrietta. Her round face and full lips were set in a scowl, her cordless phone stuck out of the patch pocket on her favorite printed house apron, and both hands were wrapped around the handle of a mean-looking skillet, raised above her shoulder.

Charlie started to laugh, and kept on going, until her eyes watered.

Henrietta lowered the frying pan and her posture relaxed.

"You don't even own a gun, do you?" Charlie asked, swiping the back of her hand under her eyes.

"Do just fine without one." Henrietta sniffed. Then she put one hand to a generous hip and set to eyeballing Mitch.

"I mean Charlie no harm, ma'am," he said. "I just really need to talk with her."

"Awful loud for just talking."

"I apologize."

Henrietta raised her chin and turned to Charlie. Her expression softened as she reached out and laid her palm against Charlie's cheek. "This okay with you, child? Him in your place?"

Charlie nodded.

"I'll stay and chaperone if that'd help."

"It's really all right, Henry, but thank you." She stepped into the hall and hugged Henry hard, loving the feel of this wonderfully maternal woman. Part warrior, part tender mother. Tears of a different sort threatened, and Charlie pulled away with a wobbly smile.

"You"—Henrietta pointed her pan at Mitch—"keep it down." Then to Charlie, "And you—you know how to reach me." She rolled her eyes upward.

"That I do," Charlie said with a quick look up in confirmation. She and Henry occasionally used a broom handle to clunk the ceiling or floor between them.

Henrietta lumbered toward the stairs, once again looking her age.

"After you," Mitch said, waving Charlie through her own door.

She listened as he locked her door back up tight—at least he didn't need to be told twice how she liked it—and whoa, her mind skittered to the bedroom before she exorcised that errant thought—and forced herself to face him.

"How did you know who I am?"

He rolled his eyes and huffed out a breath somewhere between disbelief and disgust. "I recognized you. Your disappearance was my case—your face, your smile, every fact and detail, is—unfortunately—embedded permanently in my brain."

"Oh great. Really, this is rich. Of all people to just bump into—" Insane, unhinged sounds wanted to bubble up from her throat. Charlie choked them down and escaped into the kitchen.

She put her hands to her mouth and just stood for a minute, trying to think. She looked around the little space. Only a few out-of-date cupboards, a small basic-model refrigerator, a mini microwave, her single-serve coffee pot, and the vintage *Charlie's Angels* mugs—a set of two so that she could leave one dirty—that she'd found at the flea market. Only moments ago, this place had felt like home.

Charlie took a breath and went to the freezer. She took out the bottle of Tito's vodka she kept on hand, grabbed the shot glass from the cupboard, and headed for the living room couch.

"I think a drink is in order." She gestured for him to sit.

She unscrewed the cap, set it on the scuffed surface of her low table, poured, gulped, grimaced, and handed him the shot glass as he sank down beside her. "I only have one. Dish soap's in the kitchen if you're so inclined."

He took it and the bottle and followed her lead. "Not bad."

"Not bad on the wallet, either," she said, and slumped against the cushions, shutting her eyes, feeling the warm passage of the alcohol's journey down her throat.

Even with the vodka, it was going to be impossible to relax, she thought. His proximity set her on edge. Not only was he lethally attractive, he smelled divine. No heavy cologne, just clean, warm male. How was it that she could be attracted to this man when futures—not just hers—hung in the balance because of him? She slit open her eyes. Mitch was leaning forward, elbows on knees, concentrating on the tipped bottle, lolling it left to right with his thumbs.

He broke the silence. "I wouldn't have guessed you to be a drinker."

"Why not?"

He shrugged. "Not sure. Too serious and uptight, maybe?"

She could take umbrage at that description, but she was too off-kilter at the moment and opted for simple honesty instead.

"I don't drink much, but sometimes it helps me sleep."

He cocked his head to the side, lifting his gaze to hers, and suddenly she realized why his eyes always looked so intense. It wasn't the unusual color, only slightly darker than his sandy hair, or the fact that his gaze seemed to make her pulse race. No, it was because he was always trying to see straight through to the answers he'd been searching for, the secrets she'd been hiding.

"All right." She sat forward. "I can't stand it. No matter what comes next, I need to know." Charlie held his eyes. "Since you know who I am, then maybe you know…how's my mother these days?"

"There's been no change," Mitch said, while Charlie exhaled. "I was just there, and she's the same."

"And the staff? They're treating her well?"

"Seem to be, yes."

"Okay." Charlie leaned back again, then looked directly at Mitch. "Thank you."

He nodded, then shifted on the couch to face her, his knee just inches from hers. She'd never needed anywhere else to sit until now, but suddenly one sofa didn't seem like nearly enough furniture.

"What's your plan?" The not-knowing was killing her.

"My plan?" He arched an eyebrow.

"Yeah. Are you going to, like, call the Blakes Ridge cops and, I don't know, report me or something?"

Mitch laughed so hard he had to wipe his eyes. "Jesus, Charlie," he said when he'd recovered. "There's nothing I'd like more than to call Blakes Ridge and 'report you.'" He did another shot. Then unzipped his sweatshirt and leaned back. His ratty, faded navy T-shirt stretched tight over what appeared to be a rock-hard chest. She saw a stripe of brown leather at his shoulder—a holster, likely with a loaded gun. Reminded exactly who and what he was, she gulped.

"Not a day has gone by since you left"—his voice was hard—"that I haven't ached to drag you in—flesh or bones—and prove to that whole goddamn town that I found you." He pinned her with his eyes. "Did you read the newspapers, after? Do you know you cost me a promotion, made me look like an inept jackass?" He stabbed a thumb at his own torso. "I'm damn good at what I do. It's a given that not every case will be solved, yet somehow I took the fall for yours. I'm still paying for it."

"Why?" Charlie asked. "Why would my disappearance matter that much more than any other case, just some runaway?"

"You weren't just a runaway, once the media got a hold of it. A naive runaway felled by some tragic accident? An innocent teen kidnapped? Murdered?" Mitch shook his head. "In the end, it was 'The Cold-Hearted Teen who Abandoned her Ill Mother and Bested Blakes Ridge's Finest.'"

Charlie blanched and looked away. She heard the liquid slosh again. Out of the corner of her eye, she saw that he held the glass out to her.

The glass was thick, but it looked fragile in his large hand. She took it from him and downed it. Licked her lips. She'd never realized how much better the second shot tasted—smoother, less jarring.

"You can't drag me in," she said, testing her backbone. "Can't arrest me."

He laughed. "No? I'd much rather call every local news station with the breaking story anyway. Photos, video, proof."

"No! Please!" Charlie *had* to stop him.

"Why? Why does it matter now, so many years later?"

"I can't be found!"

"But you are," he ground out.

"Only by you, though!"

He barked out a sound—neither laugh nor growl. "Yeah." He leaned back on the couch and rubbed both hands over his eyes. "And I can't do a goddamned thing about it."

She held her breath.

Mitch ran his hands through his too long hair and set them carefully on his thighs. "It's hysterical, just too friggin' funny. Here I sit, with you on a platter—all I wanted for years—and I barely care." He turned his head, his cheek pressing against the cushion, to face her, but his eyes were flat. "Not while Tiff is out there. I have to find her, Charlie. I have to bring her home." He closed his eyes for a moment. "My mother—she's tough, but we lost my younger brother, to a hit-and-run. My dad died only a few years later, making things even worse. Eventually, she remarried briefly—to a real loser—but she at least got Tiffany out of that deal, even if she did have to raise her alone. Tiff was an unexpected blessing. Such a good kid, so cute and full of energy. My mom started to really live again, to smile. Hell, she didn't have time to wallow with Tiff tearing up the place."

Charlie noted Mitch's small smile and knew he was lost in memories. Soon, he frowned.

"I—I should have been there more. If I had I might have seen—"

Charlie reached out her hand, but hesitated, unsure, and set it back down beside her. "You can't blame yourself for Tiffany's choices."

Mitch moved slowly, settled his warm hand over hers and squeezed hard. "I know it—logically—but I keep thinking that if I hadn't been undercover, if I'd been around, paying attention, I could have intervened before it came to this. I— forget it."

He squeezed her hand again and then let go to run his hands through his hair in frustration. "There's only one thing I can do for them now. Find her and bring her home."

She felt for him, for them. And she craved more of that

touch, that warmth and strength, so she reached out and this time, put her hand over his knee.

"I'm asking you, Charlie," he said, his eyes sliding from her hand on his leg to her face, "if you have any inkling, any clue…"

She shook her head. "I truly don't know where she is or who she's been with. I've been over it and over it, because I was worried about her, too, even before you showed up. I've only ever seen her at Glide." Charlie sat back, moving her hand to her lap. "The only thing is to maybe show you the corners where they deal, the worst streets, point out the other shelters. I've already checked them, but you could hit them again."

"The dealers play dumb. I've been to all the shelters and soup kitchens. No one has seen her for days."

"I'm sorry. I don't know what else to suggest."

Mitch got up and began to pace the area between the door and the coffee table. Only a few strides and he had to turn around and do it again.

She stood, too. "You should go now," she said.

He stopped and looked at her. "I'm not ready to go."

"I just told you that I don't know anything about Tiffany." Her voice raised of its own accord. "And you said you didn't care about exposing me anymore."

He smirked. "I said I didn't care right now." He took two steps, getting right up in her face. She moved back, connecting with the wall to the kitchen. "I still care, very much," he said, taking another step forward.

"Let it rest, until you find your sister," she said, "or for good."

He smiled—a feral gleam full of warning—and her heart skipped in her chest.

"You'd like that, wouldn't you?" he asked. "Plenty of time to run again." He leaned forward, bracing his hands beside her shoulders.

His lips were so close. A shock of heat rocketed from her hairline to her toes. "You should leave."

He shook his head, a chunk of hair sliding down over one eye. "I have unfinished business here."

CHAPTER 13

WARNING BELLS WERE going off in Charlie's head even as she licked her lips in anticipation. She shouldn't want this—him of all people—and yet she did, at her very core. Mitch wanted her just as badly, that was clear. The chemistry was palpable. If she followed the attraction through, she might gain the advantage.

Sex almost always had an agenda beyond simple desire. Sex often smothered better judgment under the onslaught of a hormonal rush. In Mitch's case, hopefully intimacy would soften his hardline moral code.

"This kind of unfinished business?" she asked, raising on her toes to touch her lips to his. Maybe, just maybe, he'd become entangled enough to let her and her whereabouts remain a secret.

He froze and murmured against her mouth, "Questions."

"I don't like questions," she said, and sucked just a bit on his lower lip.

He groaned, grabbed her face to kiss her hard and hot, and pressed her against the wall with his body. Charlie pushed back, her breasts and pelvis seeking more as her arms wound around his back, exploring hard muscle. She pushed his sweatshirt off his shoulders. He yanked out his arms and dropped it to the floor. Her hands wandered over defined ridges that hid under a soft T-shirt, which was pinned to him by the straps of his holster.

His hands roamed, down her sides, back up to her breasts. She whimpered, worked a hand up and around his head, into his thick hair. She pulled his mouth harder against her own. She couldn't get enough.

He squeezed her ass, and she lifted her legs to wrap around his waist.

"Jesus." He thrust her against the wall, grinding, their clothes the only barrier.

He curled, dropping his mouth to her breast. Not enough. She grabbed her army-style tank top and thin bra and pulled them down, freeing one breast for his mouth. He didn't waste any time, sucking her nipple into a wet peak and then scraping his unshaven cheek across it.

At some point, he wriggled out of the holster and reached behind him to place the gun on her low table. She barely registered the fact. His hands and mouth felt like pure heaven—electrified. She moaned, "God, that feels good."

"Bed?" he asked.

"Couch," she said, and he lifted her and spun, taking two large strides before he turned around again.

While one of Mitch's big hands cupped the back of her head, the other supported her from below, keeping her pressed tight against him. Their tongues tangled even as he sank to the couch, as if they'd choreographed the scene.

Charlie straddled him as if it were the most natural thing in the world. She squirmed, seeking harder contact through her jeans. Her knees dug into the wedge behind the cushions but she barely noticed.

She focused solely on Mitch, sliding her hands into his

hair and angling over his mouth, wanting this connection, needing to bind him to her, perhaps her only way of protecting herself in the long run.

Judging by the tension in his body, not to mention the hard length of him pressing against her, he was as turned on as she was—an aphrodisiac in itself. Her body temperature skyrocketed and she arched, rubbing her breasts against his chest and rising up above him.

Mitch growled—a sound purely male.

She smiled into another kiss, and slid both hands down to his chest. He was rock solid, much more fit than the loose T-shirt led a girl to believe. She traced his pecs, then his abs. Yes, he was like steel everywhere, including the length of him, pressing up against her, while she ground down.

His hands slid into the loose waistband of her jeans to untuck her tank and skim up under it, smoothing strokes along her hips, her ribs, until his thumbs brushed the undersides of her breasts.

Charlie arched again, and couldn't help an "mmmnn" escaping from her lips.

He cupped her then and left her mouth, bending her backward, and this time it was he who yanked at the top and bra, teasing each nipple until she thought she could stand it no more. She crossed her arms and pulled both layers up and off.

Mitch groaned. His hands straddled her sides, digging in, while his eyes swept over her. "I don't want to like you, but Christ, I do."

Charlie froze, still as stone and cold as a clear winter night back home. She pushed against his chest, wriggling backward off his lap. He started to sit up, reaching for her, slow to register her retreat through his own lust.

The backs of Charlie's knees bumped the edge of the coffee table. She stopped, horror lodged in her chest. How many times had she had that kind of thought? How often had she sagged in defeat because her body had betrayed her? Physically responding one way when you felt the opposite emotionally?

That had been Thomas Weihle's thing. He'd known, of course, that she didn't want to be there. Didn't want him, didn't want to react. But he knew her better than she knew herself. He knew what was important to her and exactly what to offer to keep her coming back. He knew precisely where to touch her, the perfect amount of pressure, the rhythm her body couldn't deny. Always, she had fought against it, hoping to deny the sick bastard his satisfaction—except he'd refuse to stop until she came. Eventually, in order to hasten the process and escape him temporarily, she'd retreat into her mind, to fantasies she could barely admit. Entrenched in thoughts of worthy partners and the triumph of true love, she'd allow her body to heat, respond, and explode—even as tears had seeped from her eyes, and her heart had shriveled in shame.

That old adage, mind over matter, was bullshit. A woman's body was built to respond. With enough coaxing, enough secrets revealed, and enough leverage in your enemy's hands—you were powerless.

Charlie blinked and found that Mitch watched her through narrowed eyes. A muscle ticked along his clenched jaw. Otherwise, he leaned comfortably back on the couch, arms spread wide along its back, knees apart in a classic male sprawl. If she didn't already know better, he'd pass for relaxed.

Regardless of the level of tension in the room, he certainly remained in control—in control of his body, obviously, and of his mind too. Strong, solid, sure of himself, caring, and, she'd bet, brutal when he felt it was necessary. He made the right choices and rarely had regrets, she was sure.

She bent and retrieved her tank top, slipped it back over her head. The bra she tossed on the table.

Yes, at first she had sought to control him, had hoped the heat between them could be flamed enough to keep him from hurting her. And no, he'd never qualify as a man under her thumb.

But leading him on so that he'd be torn enough not to expose her when the time came? Binding him with her body when he "didn't want to like her." No, she couldn't live with trickery or deceit—especially perpetrated by sex. She'd never willingly put another person in the kind of emotional conflict she'd been forced to endure, no matter the cost to herself.

"Something I said?" he asked, looking up at her.

"I just remembered"—her voice shook—"I don't do casual sex." When, in fact, it felt like anything but.

"How about serious sex?" he asked, eyeing her, still assessing her abrupt one-eighty.

"Very funny," she said.

He rose and moved behind the couch. Restless again, she thought.

"Before you distracted me so smoothly," he said, and she felt the heat of shame creep up her cheeks, "I was about to get answers."

Charlie put her hands on her hips. "I see no reason to answer your questions."

"No reason? Compassion for a guy who tried so hard to find you, originally just to make sure you were safe?" He watched her. "Maybe sympathy? Because I've now got another runaway eating at my soul—my own sister?"

He braced his hands on the back of the couch, glaring at her.

"How about this," he suggested, "you answer my questions, or we go back to having casual sex."

"There's nothing casual about it!"

"Why not?"

"It's loaded with complications."

"It's just you that's loaded," Mitch said. "I'm very what-you-see-is-what-you-get."

He rounded the couch and plopped down on it. Lying down and settling in, he threw his legs up over the end of the sofa and crossed his ankles. "For instance," he said, "I get answers, or I stick around."

"You can't stay here bothering me!" She stamped her foot.

"Only way to make me leave is to tell me what I want to know." He put his hands behind his head.

"Sex is sounding better and better," Charlie mumbled, crossing her arms.

"Mmmn. I do like that idea." He looked her up and down. "But I'll still have questions afterward."

"You're impossible!" She grabbed her bag from the floor, spun, took two long strides, and yanked at the apartment door, but it didn't budge. His palm had landed against the metal before she'd even flipped the first lock, his body boxing her in from behind.

"You're not going anywhere," he whispered into her ear.

She shuddered—with desire, not fear—and turned around.

"You are going to talk to me."

"I don't want to." She ducked under his arm and pushed past him.

"I need answers."

"There's too much I can't tell you, can't talk about."

"Then tell me what you can," he insisted.

She dropped her bag and sat on the couch, elbows on knees. She braced her forehead on her palms. Maybe a few answers would get him off her back. "What do you want to know?" she said into her lap.

The cushions beside her sank as he settled beside her. She waited. The silence heightened the fact that she could smell him—crisp, fresh, and clean, like a bar of Irish Spring soap.

"So many questions, and you can't even remember one?" she snapped.

"I'm trying to pick one you might actually answer," he said. His fingers tapped a rhythm on his thigh, then he began, "All right. Did you plan to run away or did you just go unexpectedly?"

She sighed. "Both."

Mitch raised an eyebrow.

"I had started the wheels turning to make some changes, but I had to go in a hurry—abruptly."

"How did you get the black eye and split lip?"

Charlie pressed her fingers into her eyes. "An experiment gone wrong."

"An experiment?"

"Of sorts."

"Who did that to you?"

She didn't answer, and he blew out a frustrated breath.

"When you left, were you planning on coming back?"

"No."

"Not ever?"

"Never."

"You weren't ever planning on seeing your mother again?"

"No," she whispered.

"How can you live with that?"

She glared at him, but her voice shook. "Cold-hearted teen, remember?" She moved off the couch, grabbed the shot glass and bottle.

"Why did you run?" Charlie moved into the kitchen. Mitch followed. "Was someone harassing you? Threatening you? Beating you regularly?"

"Stop it, Mitch. I can't do this."

"Come on, it's not that hard."

"Easy for you to say." Charlie opened the freezer to put the vodka bottle back. Took it out again when she realized it was empty.

"Then make me understand," he insisted from the door-way. "I've been over and over it, a million scenarios." He scrubbed his hair with his hands and moved past the cabinets. "Was it really all you? I mean, a sixteen-year-old girl, getting your mom in a home, coming up with that kind of money, managing to disappear without a trace?" He shook his head. "It's impossible." He pinned her with a look, his eyes calculating. "You had help."

She laughed—a dismal, flat croak of a sound. "I had no one."

"Where'd you get that kind of money?"

"I didn't rob a bank, if that's what you're after."

"That I know. We checked all the local businesses for sudden loss of cash." He stepped further into her space. "If it wasn't illegal, why don't you just tell me?"

Charlie pressed her lips into a flat line, turned her back on him, and practically threw the empty vodka bottle into the sink. She gripped the basin and tried to calm her breathing, but gasped when Mitch set his hands on her shoulders. He forced her to face him.

One hand remained on her shoulder, his warm fingers

kneading her tight muscles. The other tipped her chin up, making her meet his eyes. "Was it that awful, then, with your mom that you just had to get out?"

She snorted, a harsh exhale. "I would have given anything to stay with her." She shook her head. "But that wasn't possible."

"Why? What could possibly have forced you to leave her?"

"Not what," Charlie whispered, shutting her eyes. "Who."

CHAPTER 14

IN CONTRAST TO the excitement of watching the Hudson home, Thomas had come to dread his thrice-weekly visits to Rolling Meadows. Ellen Macnamara's poor company and the dull surroundings of the place chafed. Regardless of his irritation, it wouldn't do to disturb her schedule until it became imperative, especially now that Laura would soon be home.

Ellen sat—slumped, really—in the rocker today, facing the window that looked out, unfortunately, at the asphalt of the parking lot. But that was the room you got when your daughter wasn't around to advocate for you.

"Hello, dear," he greeted her, and set mugs of late afternoon tea on the small table. He used to stop at the local coffee shop; however, he'd been frequenting the facility so long that the nurses had invited him to make use of their kitchenette. He brought them specialty teas quite often—presenting them as little gifts for the staff. In truth, he couldn't abide the wholesale brand they stocked.

He settled in the opposite chair and set his folded newspaper on his lap. "Watching the sunshine today, hmmn?"

The weather was beautiful. How he itched to be out in it, rather than stuck in this medicinal, fluorescent prison. The landscaping at the facility left something to be desired as well, Thomas thought as he gazed out the window. All those dull, maintenance-free shrubs.

He looked at Ellen, who stared blankly. She certainly didn't mind Rolling Meadows' halfhearted attempt to shield the residents from the view of the blacktop.

He sighed. Already his own yard suffered from lack of attention this spring. The peonies desperately needed to be staked, drooping as they did under their weight. Thomas also itched to pinch back his roses. He despised the small multiple blooms that grew naturally, preferring instead to harness the stems' energy in developing the larger single-rose buds that truly showcased their perfection. The clematis had climbed right off the trellises, and the brown-eyed susans and purple coneflowers were choking out the other perennials—both of which drove him to distraction. Furthermore—he gripped the arms of the chair—he had yet to plant the fill-in annuals.

Meanwhile, he had to log time at his job, too. Although the work had become tedious long ago, regular use of the lab facilities was a must. Of course, his priorities had shifted when Mackenzie appeared to him, so he simply had to come to terms with letting his property go a bit. He reached for his handkerchief, wiped his forehead, and concentrated on calming himself. It wouldn't do to let his emotions get the better of him.

Thomas sat quietly, listening for a few moments. Convinced that Yvonne, the nurse who had greeted him upon his arrival, had wandered off, he slipped his hand into the pocket inside his blazer, unwrapped a small paper packet, and took a few small tablets between his thumb and forefinger. He rose, slipped a finger in Ellen's mouth, and lodged the pills just under her tongue.

He dipped a finger in Ellen's cup to rinse off her saliva, then picked up the mug. "It's not hot, have some." He held her chin, helping her to just a sip. "Another? It's good, isn't it?

Thomas regarded her. "Feel better now? Yes, I imagine you do." *Or at least*, he thought, *you feel nothing at all, which is just the way you like it, depressed soul that you are.*

He shook his head and returned her drink to the table. "That was my fatal mistake, you know—keeping you so far under that our Laura lost hope you'd ever recover."

He steepled his hands. "If I'd stopped bringing your treat regularly, would you have perked up? And if you did, would she have come back? I imagine she kept tabs on you, yet I had no way to be sure. That horrid Mrs. Leonard simply refused to be helpful."

He glanced at the door, then continued, "Now that I've taken care of that little problem, I don't believe Laura has a confidant here. She might never know if you improve—or even if you died."

Thomas leaned forward. "I've found your granddaughter, Ellen." He grinned. "And, I daresay, she'll be much more of a draw than tired old you. Those fools who have been caring for her believe I'll let the child remain with them." He glanced at Ellen. "She'll remain safe, just as I promised. Safe with me.

"I'll give the mail a few days—they know where your errant daughter is, did I mention that?—but I can't watch the couple constantly. I'll need to remove Mackenzie soon. God forbid they should panic and attempt to flee." He grimaced, then cocked his ear toward Ellen.

"Kidnapping, you say, Ellen? Certainly not. She's my flesh and blood, after all. And once my Laura joins us, it will be just as it should have been all along."

Thomas heard footfalls squeaking in the corridor. He folded the newspaper, gathered the mugs, and stood. He bent, leaning close to Ellen's ear as if kissing her goodbye, and whispered, "No family reunion for you, though, poor woman.

Between Officer Saunders and the Hudsons, we'll have no choice but to relocate immediately."

No, he thought, as he strode out of Ellen Macnamara's room at Rolling Meadows for possibly the last time, *I won't tolerate distractions while I'm getting to know my daughter and reacquainting myself with Laura.*

———

Mitch's hand tensed on Charlie's shoulder. Not what, but *who*, she'd said.

"Thomas Weihle," he said, with all the loathing he felt.

Her face, flushed earlier with so many emotions—fear, pleasure, outrage, guilt—drained of color. Shit, he'd been right all along.

Charlie blinked at him, her blue eyes—colored lenses—wide with shock. "What do you know?"

"I don't know much. Still, I've suspected all along that he had something to do with your disappearance."

She shook her head and turned to the sink, leaning over it. "You okay?"

"I'm either going to throw up or pass out, so no, not really," she said into the scratched stainless steel basin.

He set his hand on her back and rubbed, attempting to provide a measure of comfort. Like his mom used to do when he was a little boy hanging over the toilet bowl, retching from some bug.

Jesus, he thought, thank God her common sense had kicked in sooner than his and they'd avoided sex. Things were unbelievably tangled already, especially for her.

After a few minutes of just resting there at the sink, she turned on the tap and splashed her face with water.

"We need to talk frankly, Charlie," he said, handing her the dish towel.

She patted her face, set the towel on the counter, and then looked up at him. "Just because you know about Thomas Weihle doesn't mean things have changed."

He felt his blood pressure rising. "The hell they haven't."

She pushed past him, heading for the living area, insisting, "I still can't tell you anything."

"Charlie, for Christ's sake!" he exploded, rounding on her. "My sister knows Weihle, too!"

She gasped and stumbled back.

"Don't tell me that doesn't change anything," Mitch ground out.

Charlie lowered herself to the sofa, brought her hands to her face, pulled up her knees, and began to rock.

Mitch sat beside her. "Do you see now? You have to talk to me. You just might be able to help Tiffany."

She snuffled, wiped her face with her hands, and turned her head on her knees to look at him. Her nose was red, her eyes flat.

Mitch reached over to stroke her chunky blond hair. No matter that they seemed to be constantly at odds, the urge to touch her never wavered.

"It won't be the same," she said.

"What do you mean?"

"Tiffany's situation. Whatever he's done."

Mitch frowned and stilled his hand. "Why?"

"It'll be tailored to Tiffany's fears, needs, desires... He knows things, somehow. He finds a way to make you do what he wants."

Mitch shook his head. "Kids never think they have resources, they don't realize—"

"*You* don't realize. He's always one step ahead of you. His control is so absolute, there's no escaping him."

Mitch scowled. "There's always a way."

"That's so easy for a cop to say." She rolled her eyes. "At what cost, Mitch?"

"You tell me, Charlie."

"More than you can possibly imagine." She looked up at him, eyes watery. "I escaped with my life, but in the end, he won."

"How can you say that?"

She rolled her shoulders back. "Listen, I don't know what hold he's got over her—"

"It has to be the drugs. He's supplying her. She referred to him as 'boyfriend,' but her friends tagged him as a dealer."

"I can't picture Thomas selling drugs"—she shook her head—"or buying them, for that matter. He'd consider it beneath him."

"He's a scientist at a pharmaceutical company," Mitch said. "He's making them. Or has somebody doing it for him."

"That's possible," Charlie admitted. "He's incredibly smart." She rubbed her arms and looked at Mitch. "He'll be... he'll be making her do things. Things she doesn't want to do. If she needs a fix bad enough, she'll do them. He'll make sure of it."

Mitch shut his eyes, trying to block out images of past cases, pedophiles, children, sick, twisted...

"Mitch," Charlie said, "you need to find her."

"Tell me something I don't know."

"If she left him, he'll be very angry because he lost control over her."

"What else?"

"I don't know, I just don't know," Charlie said, rubbing her eyes. "It's after midnight, I'm exhausted, and I'm working the breakfast shift at Glide tomorrow."

Mitch put his hands on his knees and stood. "Okay. I'm going."

Charlie extended one hand in a halfhearted gesture for him to stop, and mumbled, "I can't believe I'm going to say this, but…" She looked up at him, all big eyes and tousled hair, her lips set in a frown. "It's a rough neighborhood, and people don't know you. You can sleep on the couch if you want."

"Thanks, but I can take care of myself," he said. "Besides, I slept earlier today so I could be on the streets again tonight. Better chance the night crew will recognize her."

She nodded. "Be careful."

"You got a pen and paper? I want to leave you my cell phone number. In case you think of anything, hear anything."

She retrieved the items from the kitchen.

He scribbled down the numbers and handed both back to her.

Mitch went to the door, unlocked and opened it. Then he turned around and looked her in the eye. "You will call if there's anything that might help?"

She walked up to him. "I promise you, I'll let you know if there's anything."

Mitch leaned down and rested his forehead against hers with his eyes shut. "Thank you."

Charlie whispered, "There's no way I want that monster to find her before you do."

CHAPTER 15

TIFFANY SCOTT TROMPED up the stark stairwell in the eerie glow of the fluorescent overheads that always lit up exit routes and lavatories in the shelters. Which one was she in tonight? Oh, who cared, as long as she got to lie down.

She reached a landing, decided this floor was as good as any, and pushed open the heavy metal door.

Tiffany stumbled as the door picked up speed and swung free, smacking the wall behind it with a loud crack. Some kid jumped off the windowsill. She tried to focus on his face, but his dark, thick eyebrows wiggled like furry caterpillars. Did she know him?

"Hey, dude," she said, giving him her sweet smile. "I got turned around. Can't remember which room I'm in."

"Not my problem," the boy said, and turned back to his window.

"Wha's your name?" He didn't answer. She pulled a chunk of hair forward and put it in her mouth. "We've met 'fore, right?"

He made a sound she didn't much like and turned around to stare at her like she was a freak. "We've met. I'm Ian."

He didn't look very nice—such a mean look. She tried not to sway.

"Oh," she said, "Ian."

He rolled his eyes. "You're Tiffany."

She brightened and beamed at him. "Right." She sidled up to him and tugged on his sleeve. "Hey, Ian, you got anything good on ya?"

He blanched. "Nope. I'm clean."

"Oh come on," she cajoled. "Maybe you have some friends."

"No friends. Not the kind you're looking for, anyway."

"You're no-o fu-un, you're no-o fu-un," she singsonged, and tried to lay her head on his shoulder even though he was shorter than her. It'd feel so good to lay her head down for just a minute.

He averted his face and slid away, returning to his half perch on the sill, one leg braced on the floor.

She moved to the wall and leaned her back against it.

The boy picked at the frayed bits of a hole in the knee of his jeans.

She explained, "Getting low, man. Really…" Was she slurring?

The boy stopped picking and glared at her. His eyebrows were still. The caterpillars went to sleep. She giggled.

"People are looking for you," Ian said.

"Me?"

"Yeah, Charlie, in the dining room. Remember her? She wants to know if you're all right."

"I'm great. I feel really good."

Ian rolled his eyes. "And your brother, too. He's looking for you."

"My brother's in Pennsylvania." She pushed off the wall to walk away.

"He's here. I know where he is."

"He should stay out of my life." She flopped her hand back and forth to brush the topic away.

"He wants to help you."

"Help me what? He wants to lock me up!" She laughed so that she wouldn't cry. "So does my mom." She shook her head. "I'm not going back to that place."

"I can take you to him tomorrow, when lockdown's over."

"No way."

"Tiffany, listen, your brother came all this way, you should at least talk to him."

"Don't tell him you saw me. I just wanna be left alone." She shook her head and mumbled, "Just…fuck you."

She walked down the hallway, past a few closed doors, and then turned around. Maybe this kid could help her.

"Sorry, dude," she said. She forced her lips into a sweet smile and swung her hips. "Hey, you must know somebody."

"Yeah, I know your brother."

"No, silly, somebody willing to share, to party."

"I don't," he said. "Not anymore. Besides, you're already pushing it."

She didn't respond. What was he griping about now?

"You shouldn't be getting high in here. They don't hand out beds to junkies," he said.

Just then, the door swung open again with a loud bang. Ian jerked, nearly falling off his perch. Tiffany laughed at him, then turned.

It was one of the aides from downstairs. He sported a ponytail of thin hair, lots of tattoos, and wore all black. All these places were like prisons, like rehab, with fucking patrols appearing out of thin air.

"You almost made him fall. Scared us," Tiffany said, trying to enunciate clearly.

The man narrowed his eyes. "You guys are supposed to stay in your rooms," he said.

"I know, Aaron, sorry," Ian said.

"Trouble sleeping again?"

"Yeah."

"You'd better go give it another try," Aaron said.

Ian nodded and stood, as Aaron crossed his arms over his chest and settled his gaze on Tiffany. The boy skirted them and headed for his room.

Aaron said, "You were warned last time you were here. No alcohol, no drugs, nothing."

"Look," she said, spreading her arms, "I don't have anything on me."

"It's not what's on you, but in you." He sighed. "Come on, let's get your stuff. You're gonna have to leave."

"Oh come on, dude," she said. "You're over…overreacting." Yeah, that was the word.

"You had your chance." He reached for her elbow to lead her toward the exit door.

She pulled back, planting her feet. "I'm not going," she said, her voice getting loud.

"Yes, you are," he said.

"No!" she yelled, and ran. She'd barricade herself in that Ian kid's room.

She got only about two steps before Aaron grabbed her arm and yanked her around to face him.

"Listen," he said in a tight voice, "you go calmly, it just is what it is. You freak out, and I'm going to have to call the cops. Then it's something bigger, something I'm guessing you don't want."

"You'd throw a girl out onto the street?" she shrieked.

"I don't like it, but that's what's gonna happen," he said. "Besides, somebody clean is out on the streets tonight because you took their spot."

"Oh for Christ's sake, throw me out, then. It's so lame in here." She wrenched her arm free and stomped through the door to the stairs. "Don't touch me, you pervert!" she yelled. "I can do it myself!"

Fucking everybody was always in her face. When the hell would it stop?

———

Mitch woke suddenly, body tense, and senses alert. He'd removed his shirt, shoes, and socks, but had only unbuttoned the fly on his jeans before crashing. A beam of early morning sunlight slashed across the denim at his knees. There was a significant crack of space where the curtains in his bargain room at the Motel 6 didn't quite join. He could hear sounds of life out on the streets, but his room was quiet.

Then a rap on the door.

In less than a second, Mitch was peering through the peephole. The kid from Glide, Ian. He swung open the bolt, then the door.

"What happened?" he barked in a scratchy voice.

"Sorry to wake you."

Mitch held up a hand and shook his head. "Not a problem."

"I saw Tiffany last night."

Mitch's knees felt weak with relief. "Thank God," he said.

He motioned Ian in, grabbed a T-shirt, and popped it over his head. Adrenaline surged.

"Where is she?" he asked, as he reached for his holster.

Ian grimaced. "I don't know. I'm sorry, I couldn't get out of lockdown."

"Fuck." Mitch grabbed his head in his hands, shut his eyes, and bit down hard to keep from exploding. Not the kid's fault he'd jumped to conclusions.

He let his arms drop and took a deep breath, then motioned for Ian to sit in the side chair by the window.

"She was at Glide last night," Ian said. "Saw her in the hallway, trying to find her room. She was…"

"It's okay." Mitch sat on the foot of the bed and braced his elbows on his knees. "Tell me straight."

Ian shook his head. "You're not going to like it."

———

After he split from young Ian outside the doors of the motel, Mitch's feet ate up the blocks to Glide. He knew he must look like hell bearing down—working on about two hours' sleep with fury radiating out of him like laser beams—because everybody he passed scurried out of his way.

While he'd been trying to pry answers out of Charlie about her disappearance—and, oh yeah, mauling her against the wall of her apartment—Tiffany'd been shoved out onto the street, intoxicated and alone.

He was disgusted with himself for losing focus, and mad as hell at Aaron—Ian didn't know his last name—the night watch at the shelter.

He yanked open the heavy church door, scanned a sea of people—some still eating, some cleaning up—and spotted the man he wanted in the back, heading through a rear door.

He jogged around the edge of the room and slipped through the door only a minute behind him into a utilitarian hallway, with lots of doors leading off in different directions.

"Hey!" he called, and Aaron stopped in his tracks ahead.

"Oh, it's you."

"Yeah, it's me. I hear you had a little run-in with my sister last night."

Aaron stroked his ponytail, which hung over one shoulder. "Yeah, I did."

"And?" Mitch scowled at the scrawny biker dude.

Aaron put his hands on his hips, elbows out. "And I had to put her out, okay?"

"You put a young girl out, alone, on the streets in the middle of the night?" Mitch's temperature was rocketing. "Why wouldn't you call the cops? Why didn't you try to find me? You knew I was looking for her. For Christ's sake, I flashed you her photo just the other morning!"

"Chill out, man, it's policy. They can't stay if they're high or causing trouble, and she was both. I didn't call the cops, because…" He shook his head. "I guess I didn't feel like it was my business. I've been there, man, and lockup is no safer than being out on the streets."

"If you've *been there*," Mitch said between clenched teeth, "you should be an advocate for playing it tough."

"I was, I put her out."

Mitch stuck his fingers in his hair and squeezed his head hard, so he wouldn't hit this guy.

"You should have called me."

"Charlie didn't seem to like you the other day"—he shrugged—"so I wanted to see what she thought before I bothered."

Mitch looked up at the ceiling, trying to gather his patience. "Do you know where my sister went? Did you give her any direction? Did she tell you anything useful?"

"No, man. By the time she left the building she was ranting and raving about what a dickhead I was."

Mitch seconded that sentiment silently.

Aaron continued, "I did tell her you were looking for her here. All she said was, 'Yeah, no shit.'"

"Damn." Mitch blew out a breath. "Listen, if you see her again, at the shelter, anywhere, call me." Mitch dug out his wallet and handed him a card, his cell phone number already scrawled on the back. He looked Aaron in the eye. "Please."

Aaron raised one eyebrow.

"Check with Charlie," Mitch said. "She and I have reached some common ground. I guarantee, she'll tell you to help me."

CHAPTER 16

MITCH HAD BEEN on his feet for hours. He'd walked the meanest streets in the dead of night talking to anybody who'd let him approach—same as he'd done every night since he'd arrived in California. To blend in, his posture telegraphed a don't-give-a-shit attitude, and his hooded sweatshirt—a common look—both cast his face in shadow and concealed his sidearm. The fog, hanging thick and damp, also provided cover, yet it lent everything an eerie air.

A few guys he'd pegged right off as dealers. Although he swore he was only out to locate a missing person, they'd sooner suffer detox themselves than rat out a client, or a potential client.

He showed Tiff's picture to plenty of prostitutes. Usually the working girls were happy to give somebody up—one less young, beautiful thing infringing on their turf—but none of them recognized Tiff. A relief, really, because it meant that things hadn't come to that, at least not yet.

A couple of addicts said they might have seen Tiff, but they were so stoned they could barely focus on her picture. Getting concrete information from them was like trying to squeeze water out of the soupy air that had rolled in from the bay.

Unfortunately, juvenile records were sealed, so even if

there'd been a recent arrest logged for Tiffany, the National Crime Information Center wouldn't be any help. Besides, misdemeanors weren't necessarily listed anyway. So, in addition to the original APB Mitch had sent out—adjusted to include the entire state of California—Carson, from his desk in Pennsylvania, had faxed the local precincts a couple of photos that Mitch's mother had supplied. Hopefully somebody would pin her face to a bulletin board instead of sticking the printout in a drawer.

Mitch had personally visited all the precincts in the shadier areas of town, flashing the picture he had, the first day he'd been canvassing. He'd been covering all his bases, even though he knew the office day shift wasn't the crew he needed to be talking to.

About two a.m., Mitch stopped trying to blend in, and started approaching cruisers. Showing his badge, making nice, passing around Tiff's photo, and asking the officers to contact him if they saw her. The local law enforcement had their own cases, their own priorities, though they had been forthcoming with information on where he should concentrate his search. So he covered more ground, through more of the worst neighborhoods.

He headed back to the hotel close to four a.m.—frustrated, discouraged, worried, and friggin' terrified. No one had seen Tiff—not since Aaron had thrown her out of the shelter. But how far could she have gone in twenty-four hours? How could she have just up and disappeared when she'd been right here in this neighborhood?

He couldn't shake the sickening notion that he ought to be checking the morgue.

————

Tiffany walked down the street like a ghost sliding through the fog that had rolled in earlier that evening. She felt as if her feet barely touched the ground and like her head floated somewhere above her. She reached behind her to pull up the hood of her sweatshirt. Maybe if it was up, it would keep her head from slipping away like a balloon.

She heard a voice, muffled in the fog and muted through her sweatshirt, though comforting to her all the same. Then she frowned. Her brother's voice. Her feet stopped, but her head kept going until she shook it and gathered herself. She slunk forward slowly, straining to see. Yes, Mitch was on the steps talking through the door to somebody. Those shelter guys were right. Her brother was really here in this miserable city.

She knew this building, but not that guy at the door. Mitch sounded angry. She squeezed herself. She always hated disappointing him.

His foot braced the door open, and then he put his shoulder to it and went inside.

"Hey, man, easy. There's no girls here at all," somebody said.

Tiffany needed time to think, but it was hard with all the fog. She turned right and went down a few stairs. She crouched beside a garbage can near a basement door.

The little girl side of her wanted to run to Mitch, bury her face in his chest, and sit forever with him stroking her hair.

Except it wouldn't happen like that. He'd insist she had a "problem," drag her to counseling, or worse. He'd never let up. He was one of the most determined people she knew.

Good thing she was leaving for home tomorrow—no, today now—anyway. She was only out tonight, getting enough stash to get her through. No bus this time. Still, bumming rides should be easier than scoring a decent fix.

At home, it'd be simpler. She knew what was expected of her, and as long as she was willing, old Tommy'd keep her high as she liked. The only trouble would be that he probably wouldn't let her bunk at his house. He was too intense, anyway. She'd never stay with him.

She'd live her life the way she wanted. She was sick and tired of everybody trying to make her do things she didn't want to do—the school, the courts, her mom. God, even her friends had started nagging her before she left. And Tommy, the pervert, he asked a lot.

The only people that never asked her for anything were the old ones at Rolling Meadows. They were just happy to see her, to have company or someone to listen to their story.

Tiff sniffed and wiped her nose on her sleeve. She put the strings of her sweatshirt hood in her mouth and chewed and chewed them.

Mitch came out and took the steps down two at a time. He went all the way down the row of buildings, in and out of each. Every so often, if he stepped inside, she'd move to another basement landing, staying well behind him, just close enough to hear his voice. Back when she was still small enough to fit on his lap and press her ear to his shirt, she could hear that deep, strong voice rumble somewhere behind the *thump thump thump* of his heart.

When Mitch crossed the street, she stopped following. Someone had a lawn chair on this lower landing, and she was so tired. She sat, put her head down on her knees, stuck her hands—which were suddenly like ice—in near her stomach, and shut her eyes.

She'd have to be a little more careful. That nurse, the other night, had scared her a little bit. Not because of what she'd said, but because Tiffany had felt like she'd almost wished it had really happened.

When his voice drifted away in the fog and she could no longer hear him, she whispered, "Bye, Mitch."

———

Charlie forced herself out of bed at five a.m. Sunday, groggy and out of sorts. She'd tossed and turned most of the night worrying—about Tiffany, about Mitch, and certainly about her own fate.

She believed she was safe for the moment. Mitch had to focus on finding his sister. He was here, not in Blakes Ridge. Plus, she'd seen compassion in his eyes. Maybe, just maybe, once Tiffany was found, he'd let things lie.

She rested her forearms on the porcelain sink in her six-by-six bathroom—tiny stall shower, sink, toilet—while she swished with some water. As she brushed her teeth, she eyed her tired self in the medicine cabinet mirror.

"Don't get complacent, girlfriend," she said around her toothbrush to her reflection. She spat. "Your days here could easily be numbered."

She twisted the knobs in the shower, then shuffled into the kitchen to brew her little pot of coffee. Back to the bathroom. The water should be warm now. And she'd have a hot cup of joe waiting when she was done.

Through her quick morning ministrations, she went over an escape plan. She didn't have much stuff, and thank God, this time she could live on the cash she'd saved for quite a while before she had to find another job. She had new identification and a new look to match all ready to go—a girl in hiding always did. The sticky bit would be transportation. She didn't own a car. Besides, she'd never learned to drive. She could rent one anyway, but learning on the fly could attract attention—a poor plan for remaining under the radar. She sighed. City buses to start, one town to another. Maybe a train at some point. Not much choice.

But the most pressing question was: should she take off right away or wait to see what happened? If she left today, Mitch—or somebody he called in, if Tiff was still missing—would be on her tail in no time. Surely she should wait at least until he left town with, she hoped, his sister in tow.

Charlie stared at her reflection—wet hair and somber brown eyes—and felt her past creep forward. She yanked open the cabinet door so she couldn't see herself any longer. With brisk movements, she mussed her short hair with gel and popped in her blue lenses. Charlie wrapped her torso in a towel and headed for the coffee.

By the time the caffeine kicked in, she was feeling more like herself. She hit the bedroom and dressed quickly. Comfortable black cargos from her favorite army-navy store and a fitted black tee. Large hoop earrings, as a nod to something feminine.

She'd start with a double shift at Glide, then do a shift at Cleo's. She gulped. God, how'd she'd miss them if she had to go.

But not today. Today, she determined, would be a regular day in the life of Charlie Hart.

CHAPTER 17

WHEN CHARLIE ARRIVED at Glide just after six, Henrietta threw up her hands in relief.

"You're late," she scolded, "of all days!" She bustled Charlie toward the dining room. "That boy Ian's waiting for you. Has some news about your girl."

Charlie's pulse picked up, and so did her step as she headed toward him. *Good news, please.*

Henrietta had set Ian up with some biscuits and butter, which he looked to be plowing through, otherwise the giant room was empty—they didn't open the doors until seven but started work far earlier, especially today because of Sunday services.

"Ian." Charlie slid in next to him at the first table. "What did you find out?"

Ian swiped the back of his arm over his mouth. "A girl at the shelter heard that another girl OD'd—" Charlie gasped, and Ian put up his hands. "Wait—supposedly she's all right. Had her stomach pumped or something and was turned loose."

"Are you sure it was Tiffany?"

"Pretty sure. I asked a lot of questions, and I think I know one of the EMS guys that had her. He mentors at the youth center but works the night shift with EMS. So if you want, I can take you over there, find out for sure. Or maybe I should take that cop?"

"He'll definitely want to know." Charlie dreaded passing on this kind of news, even though it could lead to a break.

"I can go to the Motel 6 and get him. I know which room." Ian pushed back his chair.

"How do you know what room?" Charlie narrowed her eyes.

"Uh, I went there looking for him the other night. Tiffany surfaced."

"And you didn't think to tell me?"

"There was nothing you could have done."

"How do you know? I asked you to let me know if—"

"Chill. I'll fill you in, but right now we need to hurry. The night shift ends soon, probably at seven."

"I have Mitch's cell phone number in my bag. Let me go to the kitchen and use Glide's phone, then we'll start walking. I've got to tell Henrietta that she'll have to do without me for a while, anyway."

"Just use your cell on the way, it'll be faster," Ian suggested.

"I don't have one."

"But there was no phone in your apartment," Ian stammered.

Charlie shrugged. "Nobody to talk to." And it was safest, too.

———

The trio found Ian's friend at Saint Francis Memorial Hospital at the tail end of his shift, just as he was about to leave the emergency bay.

Donny, a fit African-American man with a shaved head

who looked to be no more than thirty years old, hopped down from the cab of the ambulance. He and Ian exchanged a complex handshake, and then Donny slapped Ian on the back.

The fog had burned off, and the bright rising sun belied the serious nature of their call.

"So what's up, dude? You doin' all right?"

"Yeah, man," said Ian, "everything's cool. We're here about a friend." Ian introduced Mitch and Charlie, and then explained, "I think you had Mitch's sister on a call last night. Blond girl, pretty? OD'd? Named Tiffany?"

Donny looked at them, then leaned into the ambulance. "Yo, Ricky, I need a minute, okay?" He turned around and faced them. "Yeah, I remember that one, but it was two nights ago, Thursday. And I never did know her name, because that girl was beyond speaking."

Charlie saw Mitch shut his eyes. She squeezed his arm, then asked the question she suspected he couldn't. "Did she come through?"

"Yeah. I asked about her the next time I was in. They pumped her, got her straightened out. But the nurse said soon as she was lucid, she was looking for a fix." He turned sympathetic eyes to Mitch, "I'm sorry, man. Some of these addicts are so deep in."

Mitch asked, "Where did you pick her up?"

"Overdose Row. One of the crack dens there."

"Can you give me the address? Maybe she's there now."

Donny looked at the three of them, then shrugged. "Wasn't supposed to tell you anything at all about no patients, so might as well go all the way." He tore a scrap of paper from his clipboard and scribbled the address on it for Mitch. "Keep your badge in your pocket down there, though."

Mitch nodded, then asked, "What's the name of the nurse you spoke to about Tiffany?"

"Ginny. Technically, she can't tell you nothin' either, so be smooth. Don't get her in trouble."

"I won't. Thanks, man."

"Good luck," Donny said, before he turned, hopped in the cab of the ambulance, and slammed the door.

———

"You didn't have to wait," Mitch said as he exited the sliders and spotted Charlie and Ian.

"We wanted to," Charlie said, her brow creased with concern. "Find out anything helpful?"

Mitch relayed that the nurse, Ginny, had said Tiffany refused to list a residence, or any information other than her name, claiming that she was only visiting San Francisco temporarily. The woman surmised that, like many addicts, Tiffany didn't actually have a steady place to live.

"She did have one interesting piece of information, however," Mitch continued. "Apparently, Tiff told her she just wanted to go home, that 'she could get high for free' at home."

Charlie raised her eyebrows, and Mitch nodded once.

"Does she have the funds to get all the way back to Pennsylvania?" Ian asked.

Mitch shook his head. "I doubt it, but somebody could have lent her the money. She certainly didn't ask Mom, or I would have heard about it." Mitch grimaced. He wouldn't share this possibility with his mother, at least not yet. She'd only get her hopes up. "There's somebody else she might have called," Mitch said, and looked Charlie dead in the eye. "Cash wouldn't be a problem for him on short notice."

Charlie nodded in confirmation, then slid her eyes away.

"I've got a friend on the force working Tiff's case at home, so I'll give him the heads-up. O'Dell can check the bus and trains again, even the airlines."

"There's hitchhiking, too," Charlie mumbled.

"Yeah," Mitch said, "there's always that."

"That's what I'd do," Ian said. "Probably save my cash for food, and, you know."

Charlie nodded. "Me too, especially if I didn't want to be found."

Mitch rubbed his fingers over his eyes and then back through his hair.

"What now?" Charlie asked.

"The crack house. If going home was just talk, maybe I'll get lucky and she'll still be there, sleeping one off."

"I'm coming with you," Charlie said.

"So am I," Ian added.

"No, it's a horrible neighborhood."

"No shit," said the teen, over Charlie's, "No kidding."

"It's dangerous. I don't want to be worrying about you two as well."

"If she's not at that address, you'll cover triple the ground in the same amount of time this way," Charlie said. Mitch was shaking his head, but she grasped his chin and made him look at her. "We want to help. Please let us."

Mitch ran his hand through his hair and gritted his teeth. "Fine." He didn't like it, but Tiffany's overdose scare made it crystal clear: he could use all the help he could get.

They took a cab to Overdose Row, and started with the address Donny had provided. Charlie and Ian waited on the street, while Mitch forced his way inside and searched every room. There were people sprawled on the floor. Litter and slop everywhere, huge holes in the walls, windows with no panes. The residents could barely respond to his inquiries. No Tiffany.

Mitch slammed the door behind him, swamped in frustration and disappointment, and met Charlie's eyes as he hit street level. He looked away and dug out two extra pictures of Tiffany. They sort of piggybacked each other up both sides of the block. These streets looked even more dilapidated in daylight than they had in the dark of night. A sheen of sweat had erupted on Ian's face, and his jaw was clenched so tight Mitch worried it'd lock up. He didn't want to risk the kid's hard-earned sobriety.

"Head home, man, if it's too hard."

"No," Ian said. "I'll manage."

Mitch tried to keep his mind focused on gaining entry, sweeping the rooms, listening closely to conversations. He was working overtime to avoid picturing Tiffany with these skeletal people, on the infested beds, using needles and all the other shit he saw scattered around. Charlie and Ian were to only ask questions at the door. If someplace seemed promising, they were to call for him.

Just as he pounded on a door, he caught worrisome sounds in the distance. A yelp, and a scuffle. He spun and saw Charlie flailing. A man had grabbed her.

"Ian!" Mitch bellowed as he leapt all six stairs and hit the sidewalk running. Out of the corner of his eye, he saw the boy turn and knew he'd follow.

"Stop! Police!" he yelled as he saw Charlie's feet disappear into the building as if she was being dragged.

Mitch crossed the street and covered the distance in mere seconds, unzipping his hooded sweatshirt and drawing his gun as he ran. The door of that building hadn't closed, and he flew up the steps.

"Ooof!" came a male voice. "You slut!"

Mitch flattened himself outside against the wall—a split second only to draw a focusing breath. Then he burst in through the half-open door. The door slammed the wall and ricocheted back, though Mitch was already clear.

A skanky twenty-something user held his gut, where, Mitch guessed, Charlie had elbowed him.

"Freeze!" Mitch said, loud and clear, yet the slimebag reached for Charlie anyway, heedless of the gun aimed at his head. She scrambled out of the way, even as Mitch put himself between them and kept advancing.

"Go," he said to Charlie. Then, "What the hell are you doing, man?" Mitch yelled, forcing him backward down the hall.

"Thought she wanted some," the whiny shit said.

Mitch lost it. He hauled off with his right and slugged the guy in the chin. The man's head snapped to the side before he stumbled into the wall and then toppled over. Those multiple thuds sounded like music to Mitch's ears. Even better, he'd heard Charlie's retreating footfalls, fast and sure.

He holstered his gun, bent over the man, and growled in his face, "You'd do well to remember that no woman on the planet would want a shitbag like you."

He took a quick tour of the house, making sure Tiffany wasn't passed out somewhere inside. He slammed his hand against a wall at the thought of her in this guy's clutches.

Mitch left with angry strides and went straight to Charlie, who held tight to Ian's hand. He saw the concern written all over her face before she launched herself into his arms. He held tightly, shut his eyes, sucked in the solid feel of this woman.

"What happened in there?" Charlie asked.

"Barely touched him," Mitch said. "Did he hurt you?"

"No." Her voice was muffled as her face was still buried in his chest. "Idiot, I want to know about you."

"I'm fine."

Physically, he was great. It'd felt so fucking good to hit somebody, and that dickwad had certainly deserved it. Emotionally, he was a wreck. How had he come to care so deeply about this woman in such a short time? My God, the instant and total fear he'd felt...

Mitch placed his hands on either side of her face and tipped it up. He lowered his forehead to hers. "You've gotta go. I can't go through that again."

He pressed his lips to her forehead and straightened, but she didn't let go.

Tears hovered in her eyes. "I want you to come, too. Can't the cops come back with you?"

"No. The residents will scatter like cockroaches."

"Um," Ian said. "I'm pretty sure some window shades got yanked shut after you yelled 'police.'"

"I'll go a block over and come back later," Mitch said.

Mitch rubbed his hands up and down along Charlie's upper arms, then stepped back, breaking the embrace.

"Ian, take her home, okay?" She started to protest, so Mitch said, "Charlie, take Ian home."

Charlie narrowed her eyes; however, Ian looked distinctly relieved.

Mitch wasn't proud that he'd lost control, but anybody who put his hands on Charlie would be hard-pressed not to connect with his fists.

CHAPTER 18

THIS TIME, MITCH used the buzzer outside Charlie's building. He shouldn't even be here, but she'd asked him to let her know what he found out, and—somehow—the woman didn't have a phone.

Mitch pressed the button again and leaned against the door. The early afternoon sunshine warmed the back of his head.

He felt like shit. Had he slept more than a few hours at a time since he stepped off the plane in California? He couldn't even remember.

"Who is it?" came a voice—so static-laced that he could barely make it out—from the box.

"Mitch," he sent back.

Several seconds went by, and then a loud buzz and subsequent click signaled him to enter. Mitch pushed through both doors flanking the eight-by-eight vestibule, then trudged up the dingy stairwell toward the third floor.

If he was honest with himself, he ached to see her and he needed—somebody, something. He was scared for Tiff, frustrated, disgusted, dejected… True, he couldn't actually count Charlie as a friend, yet he felt a connection and was sure she did, too. Besides, she was one of the only people in this city who cared about Tiffany.

Charlie, still in the black getup she'd been in early that

morning, waited in her doorway. She looked hot in black, and he loved the sexy earrings.

She searched his face. He wished he could see her real eyes—not those blue contacts. In her old pictures, they were a gorgeous brown.

"You didn't find Tiffany?" Concern creased her brow.

"No. Overdose Row was a bust." His voice hitched. "It's like she's vanished."

Charlie stepped forward and wrapped him in a hug. Given the turbulence of their relationship so far, maybe he should have been surprised. Instead, the embrace felt like the most real, natural thing. He dipped his head toward her shoulder and wound his arms around her back. The contact made him want to sob like a baby, so he concentrated on the skin of her neck, soft and sexy and mere millimeters from his lips. She smelled incredible. A mix of sweet warmth, citrusy shampoo, and—bacon?

He pulled back. "Lemme guess. You headed back to Glide this morning and served what? Bacon and eggs?"

She grimaced. "Yeah, it tends to linger. And we had Sunday services—a big deal there—so I haven't managed a shower yet. Come on in."

She bolted the door, retrieved a glass of water for him from the kitchen, and sat with one knee tucked up under her on the couch facing him.

"So tell me," she said.

Mitch leaned his head back and shut his eyes.

"They knew her. Said she'd been around about a couple of weeks." He paused. "I forced my way into nearly every building on that stretch, each shithole worse than the next."

Mitch opened his eyes, but stared at the ceiling.

"Half of them in there were passed out, the rest high as

kites. They don't know what day it is, what anyone else's real name is, or even whether they were fucking a blond or a redhead."

He squeezed his eyes shut again.

———

Charlie felt tears well in her own eyes. He'd seen awful things in his job, she was sure. But looking for one of your own in a place like that? This morning, she'd seen only the surface of what he must have seen time and again, and experienced only a fraction of what he must feel.

She shifted over and placed her hand over Mitch's and squeezed. He turned his palm up and laced his fingers with hers.

"Nobody remembers seeing her recently—meaning today, probably yesterday, and maybe the day before. But how can I trust the timeline of people who don't even know if it's day or night?"

He shook his head and turned to look at Charlie.

"Another dead end," he said, then shook his head. "When this nightmare finally ends, I have to make some changes. I'm done working narcotics."

"Seeing Tiffany mixed up in it all makes it too hard?"

"Jesus, no. I'm more determined than ever to get as much shit as possible off the streets. But someone else is going to have to do the dirty work." Mitch looked her in the eye. "I'm not proud to admit it, but undercover work was a way to hide for a while."

"What were you hiding from?"

Charlie watched Mitch become still, and his eyes locked on the far wall. Moments passed before he spoke. "We'd lost my brother to a hit-and-run—case unsolved—when he was only nine. It should've been me."

"You mentioned that. How old were you?" Charlie squeezed his hand.

"Twelve. We'd been riding bikes together. He crossed the street first. My dad never recovered from that loss. My mom either, really, although we both found joy in Tiffany. I was seventeen when she was born." Mitch smiled just a bit.

"My dad died only a few years after my brother. I swear from a broken heart. I tried to be a good kid, make it easy on Mom, but the woman worried over everything—and who could blame her? When she married Bob Scott, though, I really pushed back. He was either absent or combative. Felt trapped, and treated my mom like shit. Wanted nothing to do with me or even Tiffany. He took off pretty quick. I know my mom was relieved, and yet there she was, alone again. I had memories of my dad, but Tiff had a big, fat void where a father should be. I did what I could to fill that gap, but honestly, our family life was incredibly tangled up with sadness." Mitch tore his eyes away from the wall. Glanced at her and then away again as if he was embarrassed.

He said, "Then there was the stress of your case. All this pressure from the community, especially the press. The woman I'd been dating dropped me like a hot potato. I felt like I was disappointing everyone—the force, the chief, the community, your mom, you…but most of all, myself." He squeezed her hand again. "I'm done locking myself away. Family has to come first."

"My mom never recovered after my dad died either," Charlie said. "I think she always battled depression, but losing him broke something major in her. So in a way, I'd lost her before I had to leave her."

Mitch reached over and cupped her face in his hand. He was so tender at times.

"You're right to put them first. Lucky to have them," she whispered, her heart clogging her throat.

"I know I am."

Charlie had to look away. "Have you eaten anything?"

"No. Maybe later, when I can get Overdose Row out of my head."

"Okay," Charlie said, and watched Mitch lay his head back on the couch again. He hadn't had time to shave again this morning, and the afternoon light made his scruff look almost golden. A shudder rippled through him, and his fingers tensed briefly on hers.

She looked down at their hands, hers swallowed in his brawny one. She rubbed her thumb lightly over his, back and forth, back and forth.

Charlie had been exposed to a lot when she'd been on the streets, but she was smart enough—and scared enough—to steer clear of drugs. She hadn't been able to afford to let her guard down, or lose control.

Her priorities had been clear cut when she'd first run. Top of the list was making sure Thomas couldn't find her or discover the pregnancy. Thankfully, she'd found the New Beginnings Maternity Home, a place that didn't focus on your past but on your future, and turned away no one for lack of funds. They provided nutrition and medical services, support and counseling, even education and a part-time job. But most important, because she'd come alone and in fear, they had accepted her lack of identification and hadn't pressed for personal details. Essentially, they had allowed her to hide out for the term of her pregnancy.

Next, she had needed to ensure her baby's future, not to

mention her mother's long-term care. In her naiveté, she'd initially thought that the mortgage money from Weihle—she'd insisted on a lump payment—would be enough to secure Ellen's care at Rolling Meadows for years to come. In fact, that chunk of cash had barely covered the six months that Charlie had stayed at New Beginnings.

Enter Pamela Hudson, thank God. She'd been Charlie's manager at Macy's, and Charlie had known that Pam had suffered numerous miscarriages and a failed adoption. Her boss was the type who wore her emotions on her sleeve. Everybody in the department knew of her ongoing heartbreak.

Although she'd known it was illegal, Charlie had gambled—offering to give Pamela and her husband, Ray, her baby for a price. They hadn't called the police or anything else—in fact, other than taking twenty-four hours to think about it, they'd jumped at the chance, ignoring right and wrong to see their dreams become reality. Even so, Charlie had asked for no more, no less than Rowena Leonard, the director at the nursing facility, had told her she'd need for her mom's care. The Hudsons' payments, one at the promise of a child they'd been so desperate for, and the next when she was handed over into their arms, secured her mother's care for the long haul. Well, that and Mrs. Leonard's willingness to bend a few rules, and keep a secret or two.

Charlie wasn't proud of selling her child—she would have preferred any alternative to that. But try as she might to come up with a better solution, it seemed the only way to take care of her mom and keep all three of them out of the clutches of Thomas Weihle. She felt tears threaten, as they always did when she covered this ground.

She glanced at Mitch. He hadn't noticed; his eyes were shut and his posture relaxed. Although he breathed deeply and his chiseled jaw was a bit slack, a frown remained and his eyebrows pulled together. No doubt his subconscious wrestled with the burden of finding Tiffany even while his body gave up and found rest.

Now that she could look her fill, she discovered that his hair actually held strands of blond, honey, and walnut, which combined to make a warm, sandy mane. His hair curled up just slightly at the ends by his neck and ears—well overdue, she imagined, for a cut. His lashes and brows were darker, the stubble on his face nearly blond, the skin tan and weathered. She had a crazy urge to stroke every color she spotted.

Instead, Charlie scooted closer and leaned her head on his shoulder. His fingers twitched once in hers. She doubted she could sleep, but it wouldn't hurt to sit still for a few moments. He'd never know she sought a bit of comfort from him.

She gazed around at her scrappy little apartment, her eyes scanning the series of deadbolts, the geometric rug she'd picked up, the pot of fake flowers she'd graduated to when she realized she'd never manage to water regularly…

The first few years there'd been only running fast enough, and far enough. But by the time she turned twenty, Charlie had realized that she had to stay put in order to improve her living conditions. When she could make ends meet—feeding herself with her own funds, getting out of the shelters, renting a single room here or there, actually saving the surplus—she chose the area she'd felt most comfortable, and stayed. This bare-bones, low-rent walk-up had come to mean security and serenity, comfort and peace.

Glide had been a godsend, giving her a sense of purpose, and a means to give back. Cleo's Bistro provided a great cash income for a girl like her. Both Henrietta and Cleo had become dear friends, and although she tried not to get too close, she valued them beyond measure, for she ached for family, stability, and love.

Charlie looked back down at their interlaced hands. Mitch's fingers were relaxed in hers. His breathing remained steady, and he slept on.

Idly, she wished that there were some way to have a future with this man. Sexy and handsome, tough but caring, smart and steadfast, fierce and protective of those he loved…well, he was all a woman could want and more.

But anybody she cared about would find danger—or heartbreak—eventually. Because she knew, at her core, that Thomas Weihle would never give up—that she'd either be caught or forever running.

Charlie squeezed her eyes shut, then raised her head from Mitch's shoulder. She slipped her hand from his and forced herself to get up, and away. No good could come from dreaming of a future she'd never be allowed to enjoy.

CHAPTER 19

MITCH STARTLED WHEN he woke, then rubbed his hands over his face. His bleary eyes found Charlie watching him from the doorway.

He smiled, and asked, "How long have I been asleep?"

"About an hour," she answered.

"Not enough to get me through," he said.

"Why don't you go lie down on my bed? I have to go to work in a couple of hours anyway, so until I get back"—she shrugged a shoulder—"the bed's yours."

He lifted an eyebrow. "You're sure?"

"Yep. I'm not using it."

He nodded and moved toward the bedroom. She followed.

"You need anything in here?" he asked, the mattress dipping as he sat and pulled off his boots, sweatshirt, and holster. How weird, she thought, seeing a man in her room, on her bed.

"Nope." She swept an arm in front of herself. "I traded in the bacon and eggs." She smiled. "Not that I won't pick up some more slop at Cleo's."

He smiled as he lay back. "You look tired, too."

She shrugged. "I didn't sleep that well last night."

"Lie with me." Mitch held his hands up, spread his fingers wide, and then made a show of securing them in the front pockets of his jeans.

She raised an eyebrow.

"Come on. Just for a little while."

Charlie gulped, then slid in next to him. He patted his shoulder, just above his chest, so she tucked into him and laid her head there. He was warm and solid.

His arm curled around her back and rested on her hip. Then he lay still, true to his word—or his goofy pantomime, anyway.

She tried to just chill out and enjoy the comforting physical contact. Not happening for her, though. She was ultra-conscious of the muscle under her cheek, the large, warm hand cupping her hipbone, and how good he smelled. Must be some manly-man scent of deodorant, because although it smelled like aftershave, she could feel his scruffy chin snagging in her hair.

She wondered what it'd be like to sleep with this hunk of man...couldn't keep the idea from swirling around her head, gaining steam, and making her most sensitive spots feel hot and restless...the more she tried not to think, the more she realized how good she felt, how right he felt. Until, she thought, why not?

After all, this could be her one and only chance to experience full-throttle, all-out passion. She could never count Thomas Weihle—shuddered even to think of him, her mind closing down the minute any memory surfaced. The only two men she'd taken to bed by choice had been nice and sweet and somewhat average. At the time, she'd been desperate to wipe out some of the damage Thomas had done, had ached to prove to herself that she wasn't ruined forever. She'd needed to experience a *normal* sexual encounter. By design, both relationships had been with men she was comfortable with and trusted not to get intense, and yet nobody she couldn't let go of at a moment's notice, nobody she'd look back and miss, nobody who'd try to entangle her…

Mitch—he was a different sort entirely. She'd have to lock her heart in its own fireproof box to keep it safe. However, the sex would be something for the record books. Something to remember on all the lonely nights ahead. Too soon, she'd be forced to run, or he'd fly home in a hurry with, she hoped, Tiffany in tow. If she wanted to just once grab a taste of real romance, the time was now.

She tilted up her chin, pressing her lips to the exposed spot between Mitch's jaw and his neck, licking him just a bit. His arm tensed around her. Otherwise, he froze.

"I thought you didn't do casual sex?" he asked. "Or was it that things are too loaded between us?"

"I'm not thinking anymore," she murmured, kissing his square jaw this time, beginning beard and all.

Mitch reached up his left hand and tilted her chin up to search her eyes.

Charlie sighed. "This—you—is the only thing that's felt good in so much bad. I just decided, what the hell? No ulterior motives, and no regrets either."

He ran his free hand through her hair, then palmed the nape of her neck, his thumb rubbing up and down. "You think you can hold to that, huh? No regrets?"

She swallowed. "Shouldn't you and I be able to take a little something just for us, just because it feels right, for right now?"

One corner of his mouth quirked up, but she almost missed it, because he wasted no time. His mouth covered hers, hot and hungry.

The hand—the one that had rested so innocently on her hip moments before—slid over the curve of her waist, the ridges of her ribs, and pushed up her breast, thumbing the nipple into a tight bud.

Charlie moaned and squirmed, twisting her hips to press against him. He pinned her pelvis under him and feasted on her jaw, her neck, her collarbone. His kisses were delicious: warm, wet, sweet, and hot all at the same time. She fisted her hands in his hair and bucked, wanting more.

He ground down, kissing her all the while.

She slid her hands up under his shirt, along his broad back, and down his sides.

Off came her T-shirt, though he barely lifted his head from nibbling around the lace of her best black bra.

"Take it off," she pleaded.

He smoothed his fingers just under the top of the bra, just shy of her nipples, working his way to the front clasp. He spread the flimsy fabric wide and traced under her breasts, before his eyes lit back on her face. "So beautiful," he said, before leaning down to press another kiss to her lips.

Charlie felt the blush rise on her cheeks, or was that just more of the heat that infused her everywhere else?

She traced her thumbs inside the waistband of his jeans, felt his stomach muscles clench. Hard, flat muscle, getting harder, reacting to her touch. He switched from the tender kisses he'd been doling out to sucking her bottom lip into his mouth.

Charlie arched her breasts up into his chest, stretching like a cat. Then she smiled around their kiss and worked the button on his fly. He raised his hips some, giving her access, and groaned when she got her hand around him.

He was thick and hard. Wanting better access, she slid both hands around his backside and pushed down his jeans and boxers. She could only reach so far, so she smoothed her hands back up over muscles that felt like steel under her palms. All the way up to his shoulders, the cotton T-shirt stretching as she yanked it over his head.

He hopped off the bed, pushed off his jeans and boxer briefs in one fell swoop.

Wow, she thought, what a whole lot of man. He was built—everywhere—tall and tapered, his muscles defined but not bulky, sandy hair coating his legs, nesting his cock, and yes, some on his chest. All male—rugged, smokin', and way ready.

When she finally looked up at his face, he was grinning at her, a playful light she hadn't seen before sparkling in his eyes. "Your turn." He crooked a finger at her, so she scooted over.

He pulled her up and proceeded to give her some of her own medicine. He traced the waistband of her black jeans and took his sweet time with the zipper before finally sliding a thumb under her panties, where she was already swollen with desire.

Charlie's hands flew to his shoulders as her hips leaned forward, instinctively seeking the pressure he was withholding. "Not so fast," he said, and started kissing his way down her front as his hands pushed off the tight denim. When he'd gotten them to her knees, he toppled her to the bed and used his teeth through her thin black panties. Lord, but this was hotter than anything she'd ever experienced.

"Oh, yes," she hissed, and he released her knees from her jeans. She spread wide for him, and he ran his hands along her legs before stripping her entirely. He kissed her thoroughly, his tongue dancing with hers, all the while stroking her senseless where it counted.

Dear God, she was going to come already if he didn't stop. "Mitch, please." She reached for him, sliding her hand up and down the length of him, teasing his balls, then grasping the base of him tight and guiding him toward her.

"Wait," he said with one last kiss, and bent to the floor to paw through his jeans.

"Came prepared, did you?" She smiled, scooting farther onto the bed.

"After last night, when I nearly combusted, I dug through my bag," he admitted.

"I'm gonna be glad you did," Charlie said, and Mitch laughed out loud.

She watched his big hands make quick work of the prophylactic. "Is that the only one?"

"Yeah, I didn't really think…" He trailed off as he climbed over her on hands and knees.

"We'd better make it last, then," she said, and gave him a shove onto his back so she could take charge.

———

They lay as before, her head on his chest, but this time they were naked and his hand cupped her ass instead of her hip. She had her knee thrown up over his thigh. Her breasts pressed against his ribs.

Mitch traced circles on her soft skin, and somehow she tucked in closer. The sex had been, Mitch thought, as amazing as Charlie herself. So friggin' hot, sexy and fierce, bold, and yet occasionally vulnerable—a combination he found both intoxicating and irresistible.

Charlie shivered even though late afternoon sunshine peeked through the curtains. The sweat they'd worked up had now cooled. Mitch reached behind her to flip the spread up over them, even though they had collapsed on top of it. He yanked up his side, too, so that the edges overlapped, cocooning them in between.

"It's strange," he said, "but I no longer think of you as Laura."

"That's good," Charlie replied. "Because I left her behind years ago."

They were quiet listening to the city sounds from the street below drifting in through the open window—a car zooming by, the beeping of a vehicle in reverse, a raised voice now and then.

"I didn't really mean to lose parts of who I was then. It's just… I ran for so long and grew up so fast"—she lifted a shoulder in a half-shrug—"that Laura just got left by the side of the road somehow."

"Tell me what it was like—being on the run, so young and alone. How did you manage?" Mitch asked.

"Like being on a never-ending treadmill. Not just covering distance, but getting enough food, finding safe places to sleep and wash, staying alert for danger—all without money. It was…terrifying, exhausting, awful."

Mitch tightened his arm around her and kissed the top of her head. Her tousled hair tickled his nose.

"I'd find a crappy job, for cash. And as soon as I had another nest egg started—or sooner, if I got spooked—I'd move again. Town to town, city to city. Every time, I'd change my hair, my look, my name…"

Mitch waited while Charlie traced patterns on his chest.

"You still want to know why I left?" she asked.

"Yes."

"Because of Thomas Weihle. He made me a deal. He'd pay our mortgage for the rest of the year, ten months' worth, if I let him beat me."

"Jesus," Mitch said, fighting to stay calm so she'd keep talking. "And you actually agreed to that?"

Charlie finally looked into his face. Her eyes mirrored her soul—vulnerable, miserable, full of guilt and shame, old fear and new.

"You have to understand," she said, her voice wavering. "I'd been supporting us entirely on my own. I couldn't keep us afloat. If I'd tried to sell the house or stopped paying too many months in a row... I was terrified state services would separate my mom and me, kick us out, put her in a loony bin. Thomas knew all of that. So he knew I'd agree to almost anything in order to be able to stay with her and keep her safe."

She shifted, sliding her leg down parallel to his, tucking the arm she'd flung over him into her own chest. "When I was in second grade, my dad got sick with cancer. When it became clear he wouldn't make it, he insisted that my mom put him in a hospice facility. He didn't want to burden her. I'm not sure she ever forgave him for stealing our last months as a family, no matter how sad or hard. He was everything to her. She fell apart without him—starting the minute he was gone from the house."

Mitch felt her shudder before she continued, "Lots of families have good things to say about hospice, but this one was horrid. I'd heard stories about purgatory, and I was convinced that facility was its first stop. I simply couldn't risk my mother ending up in a place like that. She was all I had left. Thomas knew that and used it."

Charlie would no longer meet his eyes. "At first—well, I was so naive. I blamed myself. If I hadn't agreed to that first kiss, if I had told someone right away, if I hadn't been so ashamed...maybe it all could have been avoided."

"Charlie—"

"I know, Mitch. I really do. I'm the victim. He's the fucking pervert who'd been playing me for years. Setting the snare, planning his strategy, blocking all possible escape routes, ensuring my long-term compliance before I even realized I was trapped."

She raised big cornflower-blue eyes to him. "I got brave a few times, thought I could end it, make him stop."

Mitch could barely force out the words. "He punished you somehow, but didn't beat you."

"Oh no, that wouldn't have made me complaisant for long. The boy I'd been dating—back when I still ached to pretend I was like any other regular teenager—" She broke off on a harsh laugh. "Billy was knocked off his bike and beaten to within an inch of his life with a baseball bat. The night after I'd stood up to Thomas."

Mitch froze, his fingers digging into the blanket over her hip. He remembered that kid. They'd never found the perp.

He forced his grip to relax. "And the next time?"

"Usually Thomas picked me up outside Macy's after work, but he'd said he had an 'engagement of the utmost importance.' I was relieved to bum a ride from a coworker, until we neared our neighborhood, and she slammed on the brakes suddenly and skidded. My mother was standing in the middle of the main road. Naked and barefoot. We almost hit her."

"Fucking bastard," Mitch said. He was rigid with fury, but lay still as a rock.

"Yeah," she said. "Hell of an obedience school, huh?"

"My God," Mitch said, stroking her temple and looking into her eyes. "I'm so sorry—for all of it."

"Me too. But I'm not done yet. I want to tell you how I left."

"After the sick fuck beat you."

"Yes. He'd…escalated over time, often causing me pain

during sexual encounters—but this was different entirely," she continued. "He'd been waiting for this one for a long time. He swore he wouldn't touch my face. He relished my building fear and fed on the anticipation. So he scheduled our 'special date,' as he referred to it, a month out. When it came time— the look in his eyes was so twisted, so scary. I knew it was going to be bad. He totally lost control."

She shook her head. "The fact that he broke his own rules terrified me more than anything. I knew then I had to leave— immediately. Or he'd somehow end up killing me before I could get us free of him."

Mitch hugged her to him, tight as he could without crushing her. He'd pummel the sick fuck when he got a hold of him, prayed he'd be given a reason to take him out. My Lord, all that she'd endured. And Tiffany? What had Weihle put her through? If she was in Pennsylvania right now...

When he trusted himself to speak, he asked, "So the money he gave you got your mom into Rolling Meadows?"

She nodded. "I insisted that he give me all ten months' payment at once—it was the only way I'd agree to it. I didn't have much bargaining power, except that obtaining my agreement was always important to him. Somehow, my...consent, I guess, got him off."

She cleared her throat.

"So, because I knew he'd give me the money when it was over, I'd already talked to Rowena Leonard. It wasn't enough— because I wanted only the best for my mom—but when she saw my face looking like mincemeat..." She shrugged. "She was a good woman."

"Then you know she died."

Charlie nodded. "That's why I had to ask you how my mom was. Once Rowena was gone, I could no longer call

Rolling Meadows asking about Ellen Macnamara without giving myself away."

"You know Weihle visits her regularly?"

He felt a shudder ripple across her, and then she nodded.

"That's why I can't trust anyone there. I don't like it, but there's nothing I can do. He's keeping close in case I try to contact her."

"You made three payments to Rolling Meadows. The first was Weihle's money. Where did you get the rest?"

Charlie shook her head and raised her head to look at him again.

"I'm sorry, Mitch. That's something I just can't tell you about."

"Maybe someday," he said. Because even though the odds were against them, he wanted to spend more time with her, a lot of it—enough that she'd come to trust him.

CHAPTER 20

MITCH SKIRTED THE LINE and snuck into Glide via the kitchen door.

"Hey—" some guy started. Henrietta waved him off with a giant spatula. "Charlie's not here," she said to Mitch, one hand on a hip, the other still brandishing the utensil.

"She's at Cleo's, I know. I'm actually looking for Ian."

"Uh-huh," she said, eyebrows raised, "and you think you're so special you get to sneak in the back door?"

"Not so special. Hoping maybe I've got an in with the woman creating all these good smells back here." He winked and gave her the smile he always used to butter up his mom.

"Hmmph," was all the answer he got, but he saw her crack a smile before she turned away. "Go find the boy, then, but come see me after."

"Yes, ma'am."

Mitch picked his way through the patrons into the dining room and spotted a head full of short, sticking-up black hair bent over a tray, like an animal trapping his prey.

"You're easy to find," Mitch greeted him.

Ian looked up with a mouthful of food.

"All I had to do was look for the biggest pile of grub on the tables."

"Ha ha. At least you're not paying this time." The kid grinned and slugged some milk.

"Amen, brother." Mitch let his smile slip. "You heard anything new?"

"Nope. Nothing."

Mitch ground the heels of his hands into his eyes. Shit. He was running out of options, and his luck tanked empty at every turn.

"Guess the crack house was a dead end?" Ian said as he forked a giant bite of meatball. Apparently, there was no conversation that arrested the boy's appetite.

"Yeah. They'd seen her, but nobody there can keep track of themselves, let alone somebody else."

Ian grimaced. Hard to believe, Mitch thought, that this good kid had been part of that nightmare, too.

"I appreciate you coming to me with the information."

"No problem. I'll keep an ear out for you."

"Thanks." Mitch flattened his hands on the table. "Other than getting enough to eat—which you seem to have covered—you okay, kid? You need anything? Money, a ticket home, or whatever?"

Ian's gaze dropped to his food, and he shook his head. "Naw. I'm okay."

"If you're not—at some point—I'll do whatever I can." Mitch slid his card along the table until it stuck under the kid's tray.

Ian didn't reach for the card, but he met Mitch's gaze with a direct look of his own. "Thanks, man."

Mitch clapped the boy on the shoulder, then pushed up from the table and headed back to the kitchen with heavy steps. Either his baby sis had gotten damned good at hide-and-seek, or she'd flat out disappeared.

Henrietta took one look at him and shoved an apron at him. "Come on. God's work is good for the soul."

She steered him to the dishwasher, encasing them both in a cloud of steam when she yanked it open. "Unload into stacks, then carry 'em over there." She pointed to the start of the serving line. "We're low, so get a move on."

He reached for a plate. "Yow!"

Mitch shook his hand, throwing a scowl over his shoulder at Henrietta; however, she'd moved back to her position of queen bee. He saw some thick rubber gloves near the sink and wriggled into them, snapping and pulling until his fingers were encased and he couldn't help but think, *A helluva lot less fun than rolling on a condom.*

Mitch shook his head, thinking of the time spent bedding Charlie. All long limbs and lush curves, slender but strong, and the blush on her cheeks, the swell of her lips—she was downright gorgeous. That was a given. But also, man, she'd been amazing. At turns laughing and serious, needy and giving, comfortable taking charge and even letting him lead.

Considering all she'd been through, Mitch found that astounding. Hell, he'd known plenty of women with perfectly normal backgrounds who had sexual issues out the wazoo. He'd wanted to ask Charlie about it, yet he'd been hesitant, not wanting to bring up more bad memories for her.

He unloaded, shifted stacks, loaded again, slid the next basket through, and so on.

Maybe it was the time spent on a simple task or perhaps the comforting clatter and hum of a kitchen—albeit a restaurant-sized one—but after a while, he felt slightly better. Maybe, too, it had nothing to do with helping out at Glide and everything to do with replaying sex with Charlie in his head.

"Hey," Mitch heard, just as he felt a poke in his side and jumped. "Where you been, in la-la land?" Henrietta said right beside him.

"Something like that." Hopefully his tongue hadn't been lolling out.

"Well, come back to earth. I wanna talk to you."

"About?"

"You know damn well what about," she huffed. "I wanna know what your intentions toward my girl Charlie are."

Henrietta glared, and Mitch worked hard to keep a straight face. He hadn't been grilled over a girl since he was eighteen. Still, he appreciated that Charlie had somebody watching over her. He put down the hose and faced Henrietta, who stood waiting with her hands propped on generous hips.

"Your girl Charlie probably wouldn't want you butting in." He let the corner of his mouth turn up a bit before turning serious. "It's complicated."

Henrietta's jaw set and her eyes narrowed. "A cop-out from a cop."

"It's not a cop-out. It's the truth." He started to run a hand through his hair, but then remembered the rubber gloves. "I like her, Henrietta, a lot, and I…care for her." He rolled his shoulders, trying to loosen some tension. "I'm not out to hurt her, but my sister's welfare has to come first. There's no way around that. I've been frank with Charlie." He shook his head. If Henrietta only knew the kind of hurt he could dole out to her girl.

"You know about her past?"

Mitch nodded. "Yeah, most of it. You?"

"She hasn't told me a thing, but I know all I need to know." Henrietta crossed her arms over her chest and stuck out her chin, as if challenging him.

Mitch smiled. "I'm with you there."

Henrietta seemed to relax a bit at that. She nodded. "Did you eat before you came over here?"

"No. Sleep trumped food this afternoon."

"I could feed you here"—she gestured to the serving line—"since you helped out and all, but food's mighty tasty over at Cleo's."

Mitch raised his eyebrows. "That right?"

"Mmmn hmmmn. Fresh seafood, nice ambience." She bobbed her head, like a perpetual nod. "And Cleo's tends to be slow Monday nights. Bet you could sit awhile."

"You don't think that pretty waitress would be mad?"

"I think," Mama Bear said, "she could use somebody to see her home safe."

Mitch grinned. "By curfew, right, Ma?"

"If you're smart." She swatted him with a towel. "Now take off those gloves. You look ridiculous."

———

Mitch peered at his reflection in the glass of a storefront and ran his hands through his wet hair. He'd hustled to the motel after leaving Henrietta for a quick shower and shave. He tried not to feel guilty for taking a timeout. The reality was that the evening was too young yet for Tiffany's counterparts to be roaming around. He planned to hit the streets again late night, with his holster on. At present, he wore his leather jacket, instead of his bulky sweatshirt, as a nod to the restaurant.

Ridiculous to be prepping for a date, when it was quite possible—even after what they'd shared yesterday—that Charlie'd send him packing. Just because she'd said no regrets, didn't mean she'd be able to keep them at bay.

He strode another twenty feet uphill and spotted her, a wine bottle gripped in one fist and two goblets in the other hand. She wore big hoop earrings that hung out from that messy, sexy hair, and a black T-shirt that scooped wide and low. He'd love to slide his lips over all that exposed skin and nibble on her sexy collarbones.

Get a grip, man. You can't walk in there with a woody.

Mitch pushed open the door just as Charlie set the glasses upright on the table of an older couple.

She froze, just for an instant, and he wondered if she'd ever stop reacting that way to him. She raised her eyebrows pointedly, but spoke to the couple as she fished a corkscrew out of the deep pocket of her black apron.

Mitch leaned against a high, antique-type hostess station that stood sentry just past a heavy velvet curtain that sectioned off a makeshift entryway from the small restaurant. There were two attractive black women sitting toward the back, laughing and talking animatedly, but Henrietta had been right. Cleo's was slow.

Charlie made easy work of the cork, poured for the gentleman and smiled when he tasted, then nodded. She poured the woman's wine, then back to the man's glass, before setting the red on the table.

"Would you like a few minutes before you order?" They answered in the affirmative, and she flashed a brilliant smile. "All right, then, enjoy."

Her hips swung under the crisscrossed straps of her server's apron as she wound her way through empty tables toward him. He'd never seen baggy cargo pants look so good before.

Mitch looked up and realized Charlie's eyes were actually warm. She smiled, a bit shy. They hadn't seen each other since yesterday afternoon when he'd zonked out in her bed, naked and satisfied like he hadn't been in—well, ever. He was so out that he hadn't even heard her leave for her shift.

"Hey," she said.

"Hi." He smiled like a kid, and had the silly thought that if he were a puppy he'd be wagging his tail.

"Looks like the sleep served you well."

He pushed off the desk and rubbed his chin. "Could be you've just never seen me clean-shaven before."

"I like it." Her eyes twinkled. "I'll have to test out the feel of it later, though."

He itched to grab her and plant one on her right here, right now, so he let her see in his eyes the heat that engulfed him at that comment.

"That must mean I'm welcome in this establishment for dinner."

"You wound me. I'm not that cruel."

He smiled. "You seem to have sheathed your claws for the time being."

"I guess I have. Pick a table. But I get to select your meal."

"Deal."

———

Charlie plopped down across from Mitch just after ten p.m. with a small glass of red wine from a bottle her other patrons had left.

"So"—she eyed him over the rim of her goblet—"what'd you think?"

He smiled, teeth bared, and a wicked glint appeared in his eyes. "I think I like watching you work a room."

A blush crept up her cheeks. "I meant, what did you think of the food?"

"The steak was perfect and the onion tart was damn good.

And I don't know what Cleo did to those vegetables, but they didn't taste like greens at all."

"She's quite a chef."

"Best meal I've had in ages—tell her so, if she doesn't come back out before I leave." Mitch glanced at the kitchen door in the back corner. "She seems to like you."

Charlie shrugged. "We respect each other. Hard work, women alone, all that."

"Between her and Henrietta, I feel like I've spent the day in the station's interrogation room." His lips quirked up, and Charlie had the craziest urge to kiss that corner of his mouth. She eyed the level of vino in her glass—no, she hadn't downed it. Mitch was the intoxicating factor here.

She cleared her throat. "Well, I don't know how you fared with Henrietta, but you nearly charmed the pants off Cleo." Charlie rolled her eyes.

Mitch grinned. "The question is, have I charmed you?"

"Well, as I recall, my pants actually did end up on the floor."

Mitch threw his head back and let loose a hearty laugh.

Charlie joined him, and then wondered if she'd ever been as comfortable with a man. There hadn't been many, and admittedly, they'd mainly been experiments on her part. She had chosen wisely—meaning her other sexual encounters had been, in large part, a relief to her emotionally, enjoyable certainly, but free of romantic entanglements or long-term possibilities. With Mitch, however, she suspected she could easily become enamored and addicted, risking the hard shell surrounding her heart.

"About last night," he said as he swirled a now-watery gin and tonic he'd been nursing all night. "I had a good time."

He rolled his eyes at himself. "Well, obviously I had a good time."

Charlie leaned back in her chair and braced herself. Was she about to hear a big "but"? Or was he aiming to get her horizontal again? What?

He shoved the drink to the side. "I mean," he said, looking her square in the eyes, "I like you, even without the sex—which, granted, was mind-blowing—but also last night, this evening, too…"

Mitch shrugged. "It's good—being with you. Even when we're just"—he lifted a hand—"sitting here."

Charlie's heart did a flip-flop of joy inside her chest, even though it was crazy, totally nuts, for her to be involved with this man. Should she remind him of all the reasons they shouldn't be together?

No, she'd made her mind up yesterday. They'd take what they could, before the short fuse they'd been betting against burned down and blew up in their faces.

"I like you, too," she said, "and the sex wasn't bad either."

He grinned, stood, leaned forward, and planted one on her right there in front of the plate glass window, his hand cupping the back of her head hard.

"I owe you for that one," he said, nose to nose, and then sat back down, smiling. "It was no less than great."

"You're right," she said, and laughed, but she was still reeling from that kiss.

The heat in his eyes made her feel giddy. She licked her lips and watched his eyes shift to her mouth and darken.

"Are you headed out there to search for Tiffany again tonight?" she asked.

His mouth settled into a grim line as he looked out the window. "Yeah. As soon as I see you home."

"Don't worry about that—"

He held up a hand and shook his head sharply. "Don't even say it. I'm walking you home."

"Okay," she said. She felt silly and pampered and out of her element, but he'd touched her heart, too—this handsome, capable man wanting to take care of her.

She swirled her glass, watching the red gain some legs, then looked up, suddenly feeling shy.

"I hope you'll find her tonight, but if you don't...would you like to crash at my place? I mean, it'd probably be nice not to be alone after that, and I'd like to hear more about Tiffany and the search."

He reached across the table and put his hand over hers, enveloping it in his warm one. "Thanks. If I can, I'll be there." He smiled and squeezed her hand, but she could see he was already combing the crack houses in his mind.

"Don't wait up, though," he said. "If there's a lead, I'll follow it until it's dead."

———

Mitch rapped on Charlie's door at 3:20 a.m. Charlie knew the second she laid eyes on him that the night had brought him no closer to finding Tiffany.

He reached for her, dug his fingers into her hips, and buried his face in her neck. She heard him inhale—long and deep.

Charlie spread his jacket and slipped her hands up under his shirt. His back and shoulders felt tight with tension. When she bumped into his gun, she froze for just a second, her fingers stiff, and her breath tight.

He scowled, then tore off his jacket, dumping it on the

floor. He unbuckled the holster, set it more carefully on top of the coat, then turned to flip her locks.

As she cupped his face with her hand, running her thumb over his cheekbone, she noted the haggard look that hung over his features. He shut his eyes and let out a heavy breath.

Charlie slid her hand around the back of his head, stood on tiptoe, and kissed him like she meant to devour him.

Mitch groaned and grabbed her, plastering her against him. Her feet lifted off the ground, and he carried her to bed.

They tasted, touched, and explored. He'd been fierce and hungry at first, trying, she knew, to erase all the fear he felt for his sister. Later, he'd been so tender that he'd brought tears to her eyes. He'd fallen asleep exhausted just before dawn. Charlie fought slumber, aching to imprint this time with Mitch on her mind, for she knew they'd be torn apart sooner or later.

CHAPTER 21

TIFFANY SCOTT EASED the creaky kitchen door to her home open. The key had been in its usual spot, under a stepping stone she'd made at a pottery place a few years ago with Carrie. Most of the paint had worn off the Mother's Day present, although originally it had read *Home Sweet Home.* The colorful little squares of mosaic winked up at her out of the sandy gray concrete, reflecting the morning sun. She smiled, because they seemed to greet her.

Carrie—her best friend once upon a time. Forever ago. Carrie might have some booze or weed. Nah, Tiffany needed a stronger hit, and fast.

She'd used her meager stash crossing the country. Sharing it here and there, to bargain for rides. She'd kept plenty for herself, but wasn't sure where it had gone. Maybe that last dickhead stole it after she'd conked out in the passenger seat. Why every guy thought they were entitled to a piece of her was beyond comprehension.

God, she hoped her mom wasn't home. She so didn't want to deal. Didn't have the energy for another friggin' battle.

Tiff managed to keep the screen door from slamming and set her backpack on the indoor mat. She headed directly across the room, goal in mind.

"Shit," she said when she bumped her leg on a chair and caused it to drag a foot along the worn wooden floor. She reached the drawer where her mom kept emergency cash and yanked it open.

She'd walk to old Tommy's if she had to, but it'd be so much faster to pay for a cab. Just a little money from her mom's drawer. The woman worked. She wouldn't even miss it. Tiff would take some for the next fix, too. Just in case Tommy wasn't home or was being an asshole.

Where the hell was the money?

"Come on," Tiffany said, and rifled harder, things tipping out of the drawer.

Maybe in the jars, she thought, grabbing for one.

"Tiff."

Mom. Tiffany spun, and the sugar canister fell from her hands and hit the floor. Deirdre's hands were wrapped around the cordless phone and her face was white. She didn't blink. Didn't even look at all the mess, just stared at Tiffany.

Her mom took a step forward, one hand now reaching toward her, the other cradling the receiver to her ear. Tiff stumbled backward, slipping in the white crystals. Could she snort sugar? She dropped to her knees and grabbed a fistful.

Then Tiffany froze, panicked—she couldn't think like that around her mom. She lifted her head, humiliated, and found herself level with her mom's knees. Pajama bottoms and the hem of her robe.

"I woke you," she mumbled. "Why aren't you at work?"

Deirdre whispered, "Insomnia. I overslept."

"911. What's your emergency?" Tiffany heard above her. She scrambled to stand, as fear pounded her chest. "You've reached 911. Is there an—"

"No. Sorry," Deirdre said, eyes still glued to Tiffany, then pressed a button, silencing the woman's voice with a beep.

"M-Mom," Tiffany said. "I just need some money." She

needed way more than money, she thought, starting to freak. She couldn't get stuck here—it'd be bad.

"Okay, baby." Deirdre nodded. Slowly, she moved to set the phone on the counter to her right. "Come here, sweetie. You look like you could use a hug."

Tiff pushed her hair out of her eyes, but didn't move.

Deirdre stepped forward, moving slowly, and wrapped her arms around her. Tiffany stiffened. She tried not to shake. She wanted to run, but needed that cash bad. Her hands lit a second on her mother's shoulders, and then she pulled away.

Tears glimmered in her mother's eyes, and Tiffany was reminded again of those mosaics. Deirdre had really blue eyes, just like her own.

"How about a nap?" Deirdre asked.

Tiff shook her head.

"You probably haven't had a good meal. I'll fix your favorite. Scrambled eggs with cheese."

Tiffany edged toward the door. "I just came for some of my things. I'm gonna go."

"No!" Deirdre said. "You just got here. Stay. I just want to know you're safe, okay, hon?"

"I'm f-f-fine, Mom. But I have to go."

Tiff bent for her bag, but Deirdre was still talking. "How about a shower? It will give me a chance to find you some money, okay? I can't remember where I hid it last time I went to the bank."

Tiff looked aside, and then to her mom. For real? Or was this a trick?

Still, there could be money she'd missed up in her room. She'd cleaned out the piggy bank long ago, but maybe in a pocket, or under the bed.

"All right. A quick sh-shower."

Deirdre nodded and carried the bag for her, leading the way upstairs to the bathroom by her bedroom and Mitch's. Not that he'd lived at home much during her lifetime.

"This way you'll have your whole closet to choose something clean. We should get you a new backpack, though. This old-school one has certainly seen better days. Here, take a fresh towel."

Tiffany went into the bathroom, fidgeting, waiting for a chance to search, while Deirdre fluttered around.

"Well, nothing's changed in here, so…" Her mom turned to go and then stood in the doorway a moment. "Baby, I just want you to know, I'm here for you, no matter what. It doesn't matter what kind of trouble you've gotten into. Okay? I love you."

Tiffany nodded, but couldn't look at Deirdre. It did matter, and love wouldn't solve anything.

Her mom left, shutting the door behind her. Tiffany locked it, and then turned the water on full blast. She pressed her ear to the door and listened. Crying. From right outside. Her mom hadn't even gone downstairs.

Tiff gritted her teeth. She couldn't stand to be caged like a bird. Was her mom going to stand guard? Fuck this shit. She paced the tiny room and chewed on a finger. Her eyes lit on the window. She'd climbed out before. It wasn't easy, but if you hit the exhaust cover for the kitchen hood right with your foot, it was all good from there.

No money, though. Damn. She should have had that guy take her all the way to Tommy's, but she'd been anxious to ditch him. Whatever. She'd come cross-country with almost no cash; surely she could get across town.

Tiff frowned as she worked the lock. Didn't used to be so complicated. If only she wasn't shaking from inside… Finally, it gave, and she pushed the sash up as quietly as possible. God, but her head hurt after all this.

When she turned for her bag, she spotted the mirror over the sink. She'd always loved smeary fingerprint letters squeaking through steam. Her mom used to complain about cleaning off smiley faces time and again, but Tiff had never thought she had really minded.

She drew a big smiley face, concentrating on putting the eyes in the right place. Underneath, she wrote:

I LOVE U, MOM.

Tiffany stood back to admire the drawing, but the lines filled with new steam too quickly. So she leaned out the window, tossed her bag into a bush, and her leg over the sill. She gulped a big, sweet breath of freedom, but she still felt trapped.

———

Charlie hadn't set an alarm, yet woke early anyway. She had no Glide shift until lunch on Tuesdays, so she lazed in bed, watching Mitch sleep, her heart twisting with feelings that were foreign to a hardened soul like her. She sought a distraction and slid her palm over his hipbone, cupped him, got a rise out of him almost instantly, then decided he probably needed his sleep more than she needed him.

She tucked her hand back under her pillow and hooked her leg over his, content just to soak up his presence.

Too late. His eyes—heavy-lidded and hot—watched her.

"Don't stop," he murmured, and rolled over to pin her and capture her lips in his.

And they didn't, not for quite a while.

Finally spent, they'd considered showering together, but Charlie's shower stall was like a broom closet. So Mitch had taken a quickie, she went next, and by the time she was dressed, he was out cold again. He'd sprawled facedown on her bed, under the covers this time, the sheet barely covering his rear end. Broad shoulders, smooth and solid, brown hair—darker when wet—curling just a bit over his neck. She'd offered him her razor, but he'd said he was too tired to care.

Out of nowhere—a tune blared. Charlie jumped at the side of the bed where she'd been watching him. Mitch bolted upright, then scrabbled for his cell in the mound of clothes on the floor.

He pushed a button, put the phone to his ear, and faced her. She realized he was sticking up like a tent pole, and widened her eyes at him. He grinned back.

"O'Dell, what's up?" he said. In mere seconds, his expression turned serious and he looked dark and foreboding again, just like when he'd entered her apartment that first night he'd called her Laura. "Jesus, where?"

He stuck the phone between his ear and his shoulder and shoved his legs into his boxers, then his jeans. His boots were on before he said, "No, she did the right thing calling you first. I'm friggin' two time zones away." He got one arm in his T-shirt. "If you find her, bring her in—I don't care for what, just get her off the streets until I can get there."

He listened for a moment. "If she's underground, get a warrant for that prick Weihle's house." Another pause. "I've got proof. Tell Marcone to trust me."

Charlie's heart seized and a rushing filled her ears.

Mitch turned to her as his head popped through the neck hole of his shirt. As he rounded the end of the bed, he shoved the cell phone into a back pocket. She retreated.

His expression darkened. He stepped forward and grasped her upper arms to keep her in place.

"Tiffany's in Blakes Ridge."

"I'm glad," she whispered. "Maybe she'll go home—to your Mom."

"She's already been there. Wouldn't stay." He scowled. "You and I both know she's headed for Weihle, for his drugs."

She looked away, but he grabbed her chin and forced her to face him.

"Come with me," he said.

"No." She shook her head free of his hand. "No way. I can't."

"You can. It's different now. With your help, I can land him in jail. Keep Tiff away from him."

"No!" Charlie could feel hysteria rising in her chest. "I'm only safe if he doesn't know I exist—if he can't find me."

"I'll keep you safe," he insisted. "If you talk, we can nab him for pedophilia."

She twisted out of his grip. "You don't understand! For one thing, I *let* it happen."

"Bullshit! No matter how it went down, what he made you feel or believe, he's the criminal! You're the victim!"

She tried to put some distance between them, but her bed took up the whole damn room. "Mitch, I can't go back there. You don't know what he's capable of. He'll use my mother—and there are...others who could be hurt—against me."

"You have to be fucking kidding me, Charlie." Mitch was in her face again, intimidating with his size and fury. She backed against the wall, upset, but he didn't truly frighten her.

"Think about someone other than yourself!"

"I am!"

"Not my sister," Mitch growled.

"There's nothing I can do for her!"

"How can you say that?" Mitch slammed his palm against the wall beside her. "If you talk, he's locked up."

"If I talk, the cops will insist on knowing *everything*. Then he'll have more leverage against me. Lives will be destroyed."

"What can he possibly do to you from behind bars?"

"I don't know." She shook her head. "If he finds out I'm alive, there's no telling what he'll come up with."

Mitch's face was suffused with disgust. He pushed off the wall and stalked around the bed.

Charlie's heart twisted in pain to see what he thought of her now. Respect, tenderness, and passion had been wiped out by disbelief and loathing. But it wasn't her who was the monster here. Like him, she was fighting tooth and nail to protect the innocent.

When Mitch reached the door of the bedroom, he turned. "I really don't want to hurt you, but you and your secrets leave me no choice. Even if it only buys me a few hours of Weihle in jail," he said, "I'll expose you to save Tiff."

At that, the vise squeezing Charlie's heart released, plummeting her into a vacuum of fear.

CHAPTER 22

AFTER THE DOOR SLAMMED behind Mitch, Charlie sank to
the bed. For a few minutes, she hugged herself, frozen with
dread and numb with blind panic. Finally, she forced herself
to snap out of it and take action.

She moved to her bedroom closet and dragged out her
worn duffel. She'd been through this scenario many times,
but always before she'd still been living out of a bag and had
already been poised to leave.

Even the first time, she'd been ready to leave for so long
that packing up had barely been a factor. Charlie snorted at
herself. Pack up. What a joke. She'd slipped one of Thomas's
own sleeping pills in his tiny glass of high-end scotch—his
preferred post-sex drink. He never drank enough to lose
control—although given the throbbing mess that was her face
and body, he didn't need alcohol to lose it. So she'd taken matters into her own hands. She'd no idea whether it would just
make him drowsy or zonk him all night, so she'd worked fast
the minute he'd let her return home. Begged Rowena Leonard
to come to the house. Bundled a few nightgowns, a robe, slip-
pers, thick socks, underthings, and hairbrush into a kitchen
garbage bag for her mom. She'd added a fat envelope of
cash—almost the exact amount Weihle had already given her
to have his sick fun. She'd prayed Mrs. Leonard would take
pity on them, would break her own rules. Very carefully, she'd

laid the picture that had always sat at her mom's bedside, her and her parents on moving day, between the folded clothes.

After the Rolling Meadows director had left with her mom, she'd blocked her mind to the knifelike pain of sending her off. She forced herself to move, terrified that Thomas might somehow have woken and seen Mrs. Leonard's car. She'd intended to quickly pack a single change of clothes—something she'd never worn in Thomas's presence and something that he hadn't provided her. Except there'd been nothing that still fit that hadn't some association with Thomas Weihle or her falsity of a childhood. She'd considered taking a practical outfit of her mom's, until she'd caught a light flick on at Thomas's house out of the corner of her eye. She'd grabbed a snapshot of her six-year-old self and her parents at Niagara Falls, frame and all, and stuffed it under her coat and into the waistband of her jeans. Then she'd slipped out the back door and into the woods.

She still had the photo, tucked into an envelope with some more recent ones. It was the only picture she had of her parents, plus it was the only vacation she'd remembered them taking. Charlie smiled, thinking back.

They'd splurged and stayed at a fancy hotel. She remembered tipping her head back and spinning underneath the chandelier in the lobby. Her dad had caught her under the armpits before she could topple over from dizziness.

"Easy, Squirt," he'd said from above her with a wide grin. She'd giggled, and then stopped, eyes widening in awe. She'd spotted a beautiful blond woman with diamond earrings and a fancy hairdo—called a chignon—doling out orders in French. The woman hadn't raised her voice and wore a kind smile, yet all the other employees scurried to do her bidding.

Maybe, Laura had thought, her gold nametag and navy blue skirt and suit jacket signified her as someone important.

"Who's that Daddy?" she'd asked.

"I believe that's the manager."

"Manager of what?"

"This hotel."

Her mother had piped up. "At home, she'd be called a hotelier. Here, it's *hotelier*." She twirled her hand with a flourish as she affected the French accent. They'd cracked up.

"I want to be her when I grow up," young Laura had declared.

"And you can be, Squirt," her dad said, kneeling down to force her to look at him. "You can be anything you set your mind to."

Hah, she thought now. Only one semester of French in high school, no diploma, no chance to go to college or forge a career path of her choosing. Instead, Thomas Weihle had forced her to live a shadow of a life. Always careful to stay under the radar, searching out jobs that didn't require a background check and paid in cash. Avoiding telephones, credit cards, paper trails, or ownership of any kind.

Charlie bit her lip as tears sprang to her eyes. That was why Glide and Cleo's had been such a blessing. For the first time, she'd held not one, but two steady jobs. Fantastic jobs that she'd actually enjoyed, where she'd excelled, and had even been valued. And Henrietta, who'd not only given her this apartment to live in, without ever asking for a signed lease or a reference or even a driver's license, but who'd also acted as a surrogate mother. To some degree, Henry had inadvertently filled the dry well that had always left Charlie so thirsty. God, what blessings she'd found here in the Tenderloin.

This time, she thought as she hoisted the duffel onto the bed and unzipped it with a jerky pull, leaving was really going to hurt.

Right on top was the six-by-nine manila envelope of pictures the Hudsons had sent over the years. And one that the New Beginnings den mother had taken soon after delivery—during the brief time when Mackenzie was hers and hers alone. Charlie remembered that day like it was yesterday.

She'd held her precious baby every one of those minutes, and tried to get her to nurse. The doula said it was important for the baby to have the colostrum if nothing else. Her tiny lips latched on and sucked with more power than Charlie had imagined possible. She had been shocked at that pull—pleasure and pain intertwined—and the way it reached all the way to her womb. She still felt that sharp tug physically sometimes when she thought of Mackenzie. That and her cherished photos were all she'd ever have of her daughter.

As long as Weihle couldn't reach Mackenzie, that was enough.

Charlie set the envelope on the bed next to the bag. She believed she had enough time to double-check her carryall. Mitch had only just left, and his first priority would be to get home. Sure, he could call someone, tip off the police to a now-found missing person, but she didn't think he would—at least immediately.

Her toiletry case had everything she needed, but she went to the bathroom to swap a few things out. She'd gotten pickier about brands since she'd been stable. Besides, she'd paid for them, so she might as well take the bigger bottles. And other than some ibuprofen, some Neosporin, and a few Band-Aids, there weren't any medicines in her bag. She yanked open the medicine cabinet and scanned the contents.

She'd take the juice and vegetable capsules that Henrietta had pushed on her. Fresh foods would be harder to get on the road.

She passed over the box of Clairol Nice 'n Easy Born Blonde Maxi. Her duffel already held a Ziploc bag with a long red wig—kept for just such an emergency—along with some artsy black-framed glasses. They'd do in the short term.

Goodbye, Charlie, she thought with a pang.

She went back to the bedroom and pawed through the duffel. There were some durable, comfortable clothes that wouldn't show the dirt—all pieces she'd never been seen wearing around here, like khakis and a stylish cropped canvas jacket. None of the clothes were black, though—that'd be too similar to her usual look here in the Tenderloin.

She eyed her closet. When had she acquired so many clothes? None of it could come. She shook her head, both at the tug of longing she felt and at her capriciousness in spending on clothes, humble though they were, when she knew damn well they wouldn't travel.

It was all just stuff, after all. And Charlie knew from experience she could live with very little.

Charlie scanned the living room. Nothing to bring there either.

In the kitchen, she grabbed a hunk of cheese from the fridge and a box of Wheat Thins she'd recently opened from the cupboard. Her bag already held a Ziploc of some peanut butter single serves, packets of nuts, and various protein and granola bars. They might be stale; however, she figured that was an easy price to pay for getting too comfortable, too lax.

Last but not least was the money she kept in the duffel—her savings—always ready to go. Some stashed in a deep pocket. Some in socks. And a belt that wrapped around your middle, filled with small bills and—another—fake ID. The picture showed a red-haired woman, Joanne Strinner. Glasses, brown eyes.

She'd wait until she got out of the Tenderloin to ditch her blue lenses. While she was here, she should still be Charlie. Too many people knew her too well. Easier to pretend she was taking a couple of days off than to explain why she'd dressed in disguise.

She should go to Henrietta and to Cleo and spin that tale, buy herself a few days before folks started asking questions. Family emergency? Emotional breakdown? It would give her a chance to say her goodbyes—of sorts—anyway. They'd still be hurt when they realized she was gone for good, but she'd have to hope they'd understand and realize she'd done what she could. Ian, too—maybe she could pass a cryptic message to him via Henrietta, or an old-fashioned note.

Tiffany still haunted her, though. She couldn't shake the feeling that she had to do something for her, but what? Going to Blakes Ridge was suicide. Talking to the cops? Not an option.

If it was only her, maybe. But there was no chance in hell she'd endanger Mackenzie. And if she came forward, the girl and her parents would inevitably be exposed and therefore at risk from Thomas.

Charlie sank onto the couch to think. The pad where Mitch had scrawled his number was still there on the table. She picked it up, smoothed her fingers over his name. The other contact info she needed—Rolling Meadows' phone and the Hudsons' address—was in her head. She tore the sheet off, folded it a few times, and crammed it in her pants pocket. She'd never use it, but couldn't leave it here.

She picked up the pen and scribbled a quick note.

Ian,

Tiffany's been seen at home & her bro's gone back, so don't worry.

I have to take some time. Stay out of trouble in the meanwhile—I know you can!

Always,
Charlie

She tore it, folded it like the other sheet, printed his name on the outside, and jammed it in the opposite pocket.

Charlie twirled the pen and considered. A letter was a decent way to impart information without having to answer any questions. She glanced at her watch. Whether she could afford the time or not, she had to do this.

To: Detective Sergeant Mitch Saunders
Blakes Ridge Police Dept.

If it helps, share the following:

Thomas Weihle and I first kissed Halloween night, only a few weeks after I turned fourteen. To my intense regret, I agreed to let him to give me my first kiss. He made me swear to keep it a secret—and, later, everything that came after. As a girl, I felt guilt, shame, and responsibility. Now, as an adult, with counseling, knowledge, and distance, I know that he broke the law, crossed boundaries, and is one sick mother.

Weekly "tutoring" in the art of kissing gradually turned more sexual.

*He told me I couldn't teach a boy to make me come
unless I knew how myself. He insisted I learn, with his
instruction. That was spring. Soon after, the "lessons"
focused on making him come.*

*He'd give me extras—shoes that actually fit or
a winter coat that didn't show my wrists—if I'd do
extra...like sneaking over in the middle of the night and
waking him naked, or doing a striptease in front of an
open window, or other things like that.*

*He made me trick-or-treat to his house on
Halloween—our "anniversary"—in the costume I'd
been wearing when we first kissed. He celebrated by
fucking me for the first time.*

*I had to come to him once a week, or he'd tell my
mother everything—what a slut I was, and more. She
was so fragile by then, and I was terrified news like
that—no matter how much of it was untrue—would
send her over the edge. That was before she became
so comatose. It seems crazy now, but I was grateful
Thomas didn't require me more often.*

*Thomas thrived on making me do things I didn't
want to do—which was everything. When I was
desperate enough, he bought my cooperation with
money or necessities. When I tried to stand up to him,
he'd use fear and threats—usually against people I
cared about more than myself. Always, he found ways
to ensure my silence.*

*Thinking back, it must have been easy for him.
I was the perfect target, right next door, with my
father dead and my mother completely out of it. I was
responsible for us both, and what little money we had
had long since run out.*

*He always insisted no one would believe my word
against his. I hope like hell he was wrong, and that you
can use this letter to nail the bastard.*

Charlie blinked and stared at the page. Her stomach felt
crampy and she felt sweaty all over.

She'd purposely left out that final beating. She didn't want
any more attention drawn to Rolling Meadows than necessary. And it had been hard enough telling Mitch.

She put an arm over her stomach and leaned her head
back. What she'd said to him before he left was old stuff—
deep guilt, humiliation, and shame rising up and out.

When she was thinking straight, logically, she knew that
the only one at fault was Weihle—a master manipulator and
bona fide pedophile. The counselor at New Beginnings—who
didn't know details but had her suspicions—had pounded it
into young Laura that none of it was her fault. Bad people
were out there, bad people did bad things, sometimes inno-
cents suffered for it. She learned, little by little, to stop blaming herself and recognize the situation for what it was.

Still, seeing it all written down like this was—horrifying.
She'd worked hard to eradicate her past, not just literally, but
emotionally silencing it as well. But this, this felt like a violent
volcanic eruption from somewhere deep inside her psyche.

When Mitch read this, would he still find her sexy? Or
would he cringe—thinking he'd screwed a tainted whore? If
so, then he wasn't the man she'd thought.

She squeezed her eyes shut and clenched her fists. She
couldn't worry about that now. She'd never see him again
anyway. She'd be gone and untraceable long before this letter
arrived and came to light. Plus, having this out there wasn't as
bad as not doing what she could for Tiffany, or the next girl.

Charlie read over the letter to Mitch once. The account was just as hard to read as to write. Purging secrets took far more time than one would imagine, she thought, glancing at her watch. Past time to get a move on.

She signed her name—Laura Macnamara—added the date, her birthdate, and her disappearance date for good measure. Would the letter and Mitch's corroboration be enough?

She yanked a couple of hairs out of her head, wincing. Maybe the department still had old evidence in her case file that they could do a DNA test against.

Stamps weren't something she kept on hand. She'd have to buy one at the post office. But the trip would allow her to close out her mailbox as well. That way if the Hudsons sent something before she had a new address, it would be returned "undeliverable"—a smoke signal courtesy of the US Postal Service, alerting them that she was on the move again.

And who knew? Maybe she'd get lucky and her little black hole would hold the latest news of Mackenzie.

CHAPTER 23

MITCH HAD BOOKED the first flight possible by phone as he'd hustled out of the Motel 6. Then, at the airport counter, he'd flashed his badge at the pretty—but tame compared to Charlie—ticket agent, cited an emergency on a case, and was reasonably sure she'd manage to bump his name to the top of the standby list for the earlier flight. Worst case, he'd twiddle his thumbs and stuff himself with food court preservatives until he could board the red eye. Best case, he'd be on United Airlines flight 760 departing at 1:45 p.m. With the layover in Chicago and the time change, he'd arrive in Allentown just before midnight. From there, a forty-five-minute drive to Blakes Ridge.

Either way, he had hours to kill in the airport. He'd already talked to O'Dell—who'd entered a revised APB for Tiffany targeted to the entire state of Pennsylvania—and his mom, who was in pieces.

After being escorted through security with his locked sidearm box—he'd rendezvous with the pilot to hand over the case just before boarding—he paced near his carry-on. While the inability to do anything concrete tortured him, Mitch's frustration level soared to an all-time high. Sitting in one place on a cramped airplane at an air traffic controller's mercy would surely drive him insane.

For a drug-addled teenager, Tiffany was awfully hard to

keep track of. She'd always been smart; however, you'd think the drugs would have made her foggy or careless. Instead, she seemed to hold all the cards, always one step ahead of him.

He dialed Marcone next. With Tiff on the loose, they needed surveillance on Weihle's house, at the least. He hoped the information that he'd gleaned from Charlie would produce an actual warrant, and fast.

"Chief, it's Saunders."

"Mitch, I heard the news—good and bad."

"Yeah, a real mixed bag. Listen, Chief, we need to get a car over to Weihle's house pronto and a warrant ASAP."

There was an infinitesimal pause, then, "The link is a little weak, son. I don't think the judge'll grant you the warrant."

Mitch gritted his teeth and shoved a hand through his hair. He hadn't told Marcone about finding Charlie—instead granting her a temporary pass—and now he was paying the price.

"It isn't weak, Chief. Laura Macnamara is alive and living here in San Francisco. I was right about Weihle. He's not just involved. He's all of it. He's a pedophile." Despite his fury, he lowered his voice and bent for his bag.

He'd take this conversation over to the corner near the floor-to-ceiling windows.

"Laura Macnamara's out there? That's huge for you—wait, why the hell didn't you tell me?"

"It's complicated."

"It wraps up a case you've been raked over the coals for, and it's complicated?"

Mitch could just see Marcone sitting behind his desk shaking his head with bafflement.

"Believe me," Mitch said, "right now, I'm wishing I had told you, and that we already had the sick fuck in custody, but for one, I was trying to honor Char—Laura's wishes, and two, my focus was on finding Tiffany. I thought there'd be time to deal with the Macnamara thing. Never imagined Tiff would head home."

"All right. Is Macnamara coming in to give a statement?"

"No, she's refused. She's terrified of Weihle. But I've got the whole story—or nearly all of it. Also snapped a few pictures of her on my cell as proof."

"Mitch—"

"Chief, you wanna hear the whole story now, or shall I save it for the judge?"

He heard a sigh from his boss, who said, "I believe you. I always have, but I'm warning you, on your word alone, no witness, I'm not so sure the judge'll go for the warrant." He cleared his throat. "It's common knowledge around here that your focus on the Macnamara case borders on obsession."

"Fuck that," Mitch said, "I'm telling you. It's all related. And Weihle's got everything to do with it! He should already be in for questioning!"

Mitch pressed his fists to the plate glass, wishing he could smash it into zillions of jagged pieces.

Marcone's voice was filled with sympathy. "I'm on your side, Mitch, and I haven't given up. So calm down."

"Would you calm down if it was your sister?" Mitch shot back. Then he straightened, shoved his hand in his hair, and paced a tight circle. "Even if you take them as separate issues, I should have my warrant." His voice was tight, but level now. "Tiff is missing, and Weihle's admitted she's been to his house. Her friends will confirm that. They dropped her off. Rolling Meadows connects them as well. That should be enough when we're talking about a missing girl." The points flew off his tongue like arrows hitting a mark. "But add in

Laura Macnamara pegging him as a pedophile? It's a friggin slam dunk. Tell the judge," he ground out, "I'll swear under oath."

"I'll tell him."

"I know O'Dell has talked to Weihle's boss, but I want a warrant for the workplace, too—lab, office, wherever he spends time at Novatru."

"Of course."

"Chief, I believe Tiff will go to Weihle the first chance she gets."

"Why would she willingly return to a pedophile?"

"I believe he's been supplying her with drugs."

"Kinda off type."

"He's a chemist. He's making them."

"Hmmn. Possible. Well, we've got a few good selling points for the warrant. The trouble is going to be reaching Judge Abrams—big fishing trip, you know."

"Shit," Mitch said, recalling that it was officially trout season. And Harry Abrams was passionate about fishing—and hunting, for that matter—and just as manic in his hatred of being disturbed while enjoying his free time.

"Don't worry, son," Marcone said. "I'll put on my waders and go see him in person if I have to." Mitch knew Marcone despised the great outdoors. He didn't give a shit.

"You might well have to, Chief." Mitch rested his forehead against the cool glass and shut his eyes. "He might already have her."

"No," Marcone said, "we've got patrols driving by. There's been no activity reported."

"That's not enough. I need eyes on that house every minute, preferably unmarked cars."

"Mitch—"

"Chief, I'm telling you, Tiffany will show at Weihle's for a fix—if she isn't already holed up in there."

"All right. I'll order constant surveillance. Anything else?"

"Not that I can think of. Keep me posted."

"Likewise."

Wishing he had a better feeling about all this, Mitch stabbed a button on his phone to end the call. Then he scrolled through the digital menus for the pictures of Charlie. The best one he'd taken at Cleo's while she'd been focused on a customer. Guilt threatened to surface, but he shoved that feeling aside. He couldn't afford to care right now. Not while Tiffany was wandering around Weihle's backyard.

He'd been hoping to avoid it, for Charlie's sake, but he wasn't playing wait and see any longer with Tiffany at risk. Time to ramp up the hometown pressure.

Mitch dialed 411 and asked for WKDB, the local news station. Once he was connected, he requested Veronica Braun. She'd been like a dog with a bone on the Macnamara disappearance six years ago—her bleached incisors clamped down tight and her loud bark creating a helluva ruckus. Her focused and relentless coverage had created more of a big deal than there should have been. He'd felt venomous toward her then, but he could accept that she was only doing her job—too thoroughly, perhaps, for lack of any other exciting news.

"Veronica Braun," she said, sounding distracted.

"It's Mitch Saunders from—"

"I know who you are, Detective, but I will say—I *am* surprised to hear from you."

"I'm sure you are." He had her full attention now, he knew. He pictured her brunette helmet head and made-up face. "I've got the tip of a lifetime for you."

"Ooooh, do tell."

Imagining drool spilling over her bright red lipstick, he smiled. "I need something from you first."

"I knew you wouldn't call me with no strings," she huffed. "Like what?"

"You got some kind of sister station or something in California? San Francisco, to be exact?"

"You're calling me to bypass me on a story?"

Mitch wanted to growl. Reporters always kept numero uno front and center.

"I'm giving you the *local* exclusive, but you can't get to San Fran in time. Trust me, you'll get a bigger story in the long run if you play nice with another station."

She didn't hesitate. "There's no station there directly affiliated with WKDB, but I've got a friend out there I can call. What's up?"

"Remember the Macnamara case?"

"Of course."

Mitch sensed Veronica actually holding her breath.

"I've found her. Laura Macnamara."

"Whoa. Dead or alive?"

"Alive."

"And she's in San Fran?"

"Yes. Here's what I want you to do. Call your friend. Explain the background, and then have them get a crew to this address: 105 Eddy Street, apartment number two. That's the building she lives in." He checked his watch—nearly noon. Was she working the breakfast or lunch shift today? "If they don't catch her there, she volunteers at Glide, it's a mission. They'll know of it. If they haven't found her by evening, they could check Cleo's Bistro. It's a restaurant on Jones, the cross street is Post."

"Is she willing to talk with the press?"

"No, they'll have their work cut out for them. She doesn't want to be found." Mitch cringed. "I'm betting she'll attempt to disappear again. So hustle on this."

"Wow. So she actually left voluntarily?"

"Out of self-preservation. She'd been molested regularly for years."

"By whom?" Veronica broke in.

"I can't tell you that yet."

"Come on, Detective. You're giving me half the story?"

"Details on the perp are yours as soon as we have him. It's tricky, Braun. I've got to force the issue, but there needs to be some question marks. I don't want him to run or go underground. Plus, my ass is on the line for tipping you off. Got it?"

"Yep. She was abused by 'someone close to her.'"

"Good. I'm going to send you a few recent pictures of her I got on my phone—she looks like a different person now—that way the news crew will know who they are looking for. You should use them, too, until they pass you some live footage. Dig up some old photos from your archives, as well, okay?"

Veronica didn't respond right away. Then, "Detective…I need to know why you are doing this. If you just wanted to exonerate yourself, you'd have gone to any other reporter here other than me."

"You're the loudest."

"Thanks," Veronica said, laughing, "but normally you'd give anything to have me silenced."

"Means to an end. I need this guy in custody, and I need a warrant for his property. I'll get both faster if Judge Abrams is feeling the pressure." Veronica didn't need to know a thing about Tiffany.

"Nobody around here knows better than you what a pressure cooker the media can be."

"True. Listen, keep Laura Macnamara as unscathed as possible. I know you need the visual and the rehash for this to work—just be sensitive. She's the victim here. She doesn't deserve this kind of onslaught, but I've run out of options." And the clock was ticking fast.

"I'll do what I can," she said.

"Give me your email address so I can send you these pictures. By the way, she goes by Charlie Hart now. Don't waste any time."

"It's not in my nature to sit around doodling, Detective."

"Yeah, that's another reason I chose you."

Mitch hung up with a gripe in his gut. He squeezed his eyes shut for a second, then forced his fingers through the motions of forwarding the photos of Charlie to Braun. Once they were sent, he shoved the phone in his back pocket. He felt sick about the maelstrom that would soon be unleashed on Charlie, when she'd been so adamant that she remain anonymous. He wished she had more faith in him. He would have kept her safe, one way or another, but she'd refused to work with him, to trust in him.

Although he hadn't actually betrayed her—he'd been upfront about his position—it didn't matter. She'd never forgive him for this.

CHAPTER 24

WITH HASTY MOVEMENTS, Charlie set her duffel on the floor, tucked two envelopes and a note under her arm, and put the key to her apartment door for the last time. She placed her palm on the cool metal, bowed her head for only a moment, then bent for the bag. As she turned to climb the stairs, Henrietta cleared her throat. Charlie jumped and spun, a hand slamming to her chest, as the letters dropped to the floor.

"Good Lord, Henry, you scared me. What are you doing standing there, catching your breath?" She tried a smile, though it came off shaky at best.

"Uh-huh," Henrietta said flatly.

Charlie squatted and gathered up the mail. When she stood, she joked, "You really should put in that elevator and make it a real penthouse."

"In this old building? Fat chance." Henrietta's mouth tipped up on one side. "I'd use the fire escape like a slide first. Wouldn't the grandkids get a kick outta that." She smiled, and Charlie eased—until Henrietta clucked her tongue. "I heard a lotta shouting from you and that cop awful early this morning."

"Oh, I'm sorry, Henry."

"That's all right." She inspected her nails then raised her eyebrows. "I'm more interested in the quiet between the other night's brouhaha and this morning's brawl."

"Henry!" Charlie couldn't keep the flush from her cheeks.

"Just tell me, was he as good as he looks?"

"Henrietta—"

"Oh shush." Henrietta swiped a hand through the air. "I'm just playing with you."

Charlie shook her head as Henry hitched her purse strap back up.

"Let's move on," the older woman said as she crossed her arms over her ample chest. "What you up to, girl?"

"Oh, this." She glanced at the bag over her shoulder. "I'm just going away for a few days."

"Going away for a few days? You?"

"Don't look at me like that. I'm due for some time off."

"Oh, no doubt about that, child, but it ain't like you to take it." She looked Charlie up and down. "Are you going with Mitch?"

"Certainly not."

"Hiding from him?"

Charlie's face blanched, and Henrietta narrowed her eyes.

"He hurt you? Threaten you?"

Charlie dropped both bags and moved to lean her forehead against the doorframe. "Not like you think, Henry. He's a good man, but it's complicated."

She felt Henry approach. Sheesh, but the woman's footfalls were quiet now that she'd finally, at Charlie's insistence, traded in her pumps for a pair of sneakers.

Henrietta's hand rested on Charlie's back and began to make slow circles. She said, "I know that you been through a lot—" Charlie started to open her mouth, but Henrietta stopped her. "Uh-uh. Let me say my piece. I don't care where you come from, what kinda horrors, because there ain't nothing you could have done that I would judge you for."

Charlie turned her head toward Henrietta. "Henry—"

"I'm not done. I don't know what kind of trouble this man has brought to your door, but you are a grown woman now: smart, capable, tough. It's gonna be okay in the end. You gonna make it all right, somehow, someday. But you can't do that if you're always running away. Sometimes you have to stand still and face things down."

Charlie straightened then and regarded the older woman, tears in her eyes. "Oh, Henry, this I can't win. For me, running is the only safe bet."

Henrietta shook her head. "You're leaving for good, then?"

Charlie nodded. "I'm sorry. I hate to leave you, leave all I've found here." She spread her arms wide. "I wish I thought I could come back, but…" She shrugged. "That's about as likely as Glide running out of hungry mouths."

"Well, the apartment will wait for you."

"No, Henry, you've got to rent it. You need the money." She held out one of the envelopes she'd been holding. "This is next month's rent, so you have time to find somebody you like."

Henry shook her head. "Don't worry about the apartment. It'll keep. I want you back."

Charlie took Henry's hand and pressed the envelope into it, though her heart squeezed with pain. "I won't be able to come back, Henry." Her voice caught. "I'm sorry."

Henrietta looked at Charlie with tears welling in her own eyes. "Feels like losing one of my own…" Her grip tightened on Charlie's hand. "You know I'm always here if you need me?"

"I know. Thank you, Henry. I just wish I could offer you the same."

Charlie wrapped her arms around Henrietta. They rocked from side to side, both holding on tight while they still could.

Finally, Charlie pulled back. She swiped her arm across each cheek to dry the tears, then reached in her pocket.

"Will you give this to Ian for me?" she asked. "And maybe a word to Cleo, with my apologies?"

Henrietta sighed and shook her head.

"I'm making a quick stop at the post office, and then…" Charlie shrugged.

"It's not right, leaving this way."

She had no idea. "I don't like it any more than you do." Charlie frowned. "Walk with me to the post office?"

Henry nodded, and Charlie matched her pace as the descended to the first floor. Tenants lived there too, a young family with two children, all sharing a bed. They didn't speak English and kept to themselves, but they were clean and polite and, according to Henrietta, paid the rent on time so far.

When they'd reached ground level, they passed into the small, worn vestibule where the mail slots were—not that Charlie had ever used hers. As she yanked open the heavy metal front door for Henrietta, quiet erupted into chaos—blinding pops of flashbulbs and multiple shouts from reporters.

"Miss, miss," they called. One was front and center, louder than the others, shouting, "Laura Macnamara? Or do you prefer Charlie Hart?"

Charlie stood stock still for a split second, then she slammed the door in their eager faces.

She felt her face drain of color and knew her eyes were as round as saucers. She froze, like a thief caught cornered in a dead-end alley. Henrietta stood dumbfounded, purse clutched to her front.

They both stared at the fat metal knob as it started to turn. Charlie sprang back and yanked Henrietta with her through the inside door, which locked automatically.

"They found me," she whispered. "It's too late now."

A camera lens appeared flush against the wired-glass pane alongside the door.

Henrietta grabbed Charlie's arm and pulled. "Come on, child—get away from the window. Let's go upstairs."

Charlie zipped past her, taking the stairs two at a time up all three flights. She squatted, back against the wall and hands pressed together, just past the landing on the top floor near Henry's apartment, and tried to think.

When Henrietta crested the last step, audibly cursing every pound that had taken up residence on her short frame, Charlie said, "He sure didn't waste any time, did he?" Her voice sounded unsteady.

"Who?" Henrietta asked with a bit of a wheeze.

"Mitch—you know the one I threw away my better judgment for?" She laughed, a harsh, mean sound, and stood. "He sent those reporters."

Henry didn't say anything, just fished her key ring out of her pleather handbag and opened the door, motioning Charlie in ahead of her.

"Settle in. Looks like we're going to be here a while."

Charlie tensed. "No. I have to leave. I can't hole up here. I'll be like a sitting duck, for God's sake."

"Charlie. I said sit down," Henry said with a fierce, mothering expression on her beautiful brown face. "You are not going to panic. You are gonna to tell me what the hell's going on, and then between the two of us, we'll figure a way out of it. Okay?"

Charlie nodded.

"Now sit, I said."

She forced herself to comply, sinking into the worn sofa with shaking knees. Henry closed the curtains in the living room, got them both glasses of water, then sat down beside her. She took Charlie's hands in her own.

"Okay, spill."

———

Charlie paced from wall to wall in Henrietta's apartment like a caged animal. She had to get out of this building before her face ended up on national news. Californians probably wouldn't care much, but in the eastern half of Pennsylvania, she'd be big news. She needed to get far, far away, and fast— well before Thomas had a chance to pick up her scent and track her footsteps.

Henrietta rested with her feet up on the sofa, quietly sipping a cup of tea. Charlie marveled at her calm. Then again, if Charlie's sordid history hadn't ruffled the woman's feathers, probably nothing could.

The phone rang, and Charlie sprang toward the sound. "It's Ian," she said as she read the caller ID. She'd asked him to create a diversion because she'd remembered some of his stories. Apparently, the kid was an old pro at escaping "the Sentinels," which was his name for the staff employed by his father to keep tabs on him.

"Answer it, then," Henrietta said.

"Ian, it's me, Charlie. I'm putting you on speakerphone."

"I got what I need," he said. "I'll be there in ten."

"I'm almost afraid to ask." Charlie gripped the phone hard.

"Don't worry," Ian said. "I begged some Black Cats from Aaron at Glide."

"Black cats?" she asked, picturing a squirming, hissing sack thrown over Ian's shoulder.

"Firecrackers," he explained. "That dude's a sucker for the red, white, and blue holidays."

That's right, Charlie thought, Memorial Day was coming up at the end of the month. Glide's menu showed burgers and potato salad.

"Aren't fireworks prohibited in California?"

"Yeah," Ian snorted, "all but the tamest consumer fireworks are illegal." She could hear the excitement in his voice, and rubbed her forehead with the tips of her fingers.

"Don't you already have marks on your record or something? Maybe I should figure something else out."

"No way. I'm all in for wreaking havoc toward a good cause. Besides, I'm way overdue for some fun."

"Ian, if you get caught—"

"I won't. Trust me." She heard the conviction in his voice, and looked to Henrietta.

The woman nodded and said, "I'll watch out for the boy."

"All right." Charlie sighed. "What's the plan?"

———

After a second tearful goodbye and a hug she'd try to remember the feeling of forever, Charlie closed the door behind Henrietta.

It'd take a while for the older woman to descend the flights of stairs. Charlie wiped her eyes and nose with a tissue. Next, she checked her red wig in the mirror, buttoned the cropped jacket, and added a looped scarf. She set a pair of black-rimmed glasses on her nose and slung the strap of her satchel crossways over her chest. Cripes, but she hoped all this paraphernalia stayed on through her escape.

Charlie let out a shaky breath. There was nothing else left to do.

She peeked out around Henrietta's homemade curtains at Eddy Street below, where Ian looked as if he was pretty much set up. He crouched in the entryway of a closed-up shop, well hidden from the angle and the bags of trash that stood in a bulging tower at the curb. On the cement in front of him, he'd lined up strings of firecrackers.

Charlie, too, was more than ready. In fact, she felt like she was about to burst out of her own skin. She poked her hands through the curtains and worked to push the painted sash up.

She crossed to the windows on the side street, where Henrietta would exit the building. There were loads of people blocking the door. One guy in a tie with a full head of blond hair spoke into a microphone and gestured at the building. The cameraman appeared to be filming footage. All the other bozos stood to the sides or behind the camera, but they seemed to pay close attention, as if they needed a news briefing themselves. There were no less than five station-affiliated vans parked along the street.

Charlie moved again to watch for Ian's signal. He seemed to be paying close attention to the activity in the street. Suddenly, she saw him grin and then bend down to light a fuse. Henrietta must have arrived on the scene.

Ian poked his head up over the trash bags and hurled a rocket across the street. Charlie ran to the other window. She couldn't see the firecracker, but the hissing fuse must have been audible, because one or two reporters swung their heads to look. Just as quickly, they focused again on the blond guy who was holding court.

Charlie had just begun to worry that Ian's firecrackers were duds, when she heard the first *Pow!* and then *Pow-Pow-Pow!*

Reporters spun around, frantically searching for the source of the noise.

The second rocket went off and they dove into action, ducking and running for their respective vans. Again, Charlie darted back to Ian's side of the building, and tossed her bag out onto the fire escape. She swung out one leg and then the other, put the duffel on as if it was a backpack, and clambered down the steps. Nobody but Ian seemed to notice. His grin stretched from ear to ear as he waved at her, then heaved another string. Charlie saw this set skim along the blacktop of the street.

In the pockets of quiet between explosions, Charlie heard Henrietta hollering. She was supposed to act like she'd been frightened out of her mind, clutching at her chest and yowling like she'd been hit or maybe was having a heart attack. She must be doing a damn good job of it, because reporters backtracked *toward* the firecrackers, shouting and waving at their cameramen, not willing to miss a good story. Charlie could just imagine the headlines: *Woman Caught in Crossfire of Gang Shooting!* or *Teen Prank Responsible for Woman's Cardiac Arrest!*

She reached the ladder one level above ground and swung around onto it. The rickety thing slid surprisingly fast but jerked to a stop well above the cement, jarring her whole body. She couldn't see the reporters or camera crews. They must be gathered in close to Henrietta at the side door. Charlie couldn't help but smile thinking of Henrietta and her fifteen minutes of fame.

Charlie braced her feet on the bottom rung and worked her torso down until she hung like a punching ball. Gripping tightly with her hands, she lowered her legs so that her feet hung only a few feet off the ground. She shut her eyes and let go. Because of the extra weight on her back, she landed hard with a woof, then tipped right over backward. She wriggled her arms out of her duffel, then jumped up.

Ian waved, and Charlie took the moment to blow him a kiss. She scooped up the bag and hugged it to her front. Then she turned and ran down the street away from the commotion. She thanked her lucky stars for friends like Henrietta and Ian, and sent up a wish that they'd both emerge from this incident without repercussions. Even though her heart wrenched in protest, she prayed, too, that she'd be able to disappear again, her trace as fleeting as a wisp of smoke from one of Ian's firecrackers.

When she reached the block that housed the post office, Charlie—huffing and sweating—debated for only a moment. Was stopping to check for a picture of Mackenzie still worth the few minutes it'd cost her? Yes. And closing the post box so that any letters from the Hudson's would bounce back? Definitely yes.

Yet even the bell on the post office door made Charlie's muscles tense. Adrenaline had pumped through her, intense and hot, as she'd climbed down the fire escape. Although she'd put a few blocks between her and those swarming reporters, her anxiety level remained sky high.

Not only was she damp and sticky, Joanne Strinner's wardrobe had that yet-to-be washed stiffness. Plus, she felt overly conscious of her long, bright hair—the red seemed startlingly fake. She shifted nervously as she spoke to the postal worker, but he didn't give her a second glance as he stuck the stamp on her confession letter. He couldn't take the envelope since it lacked a return address; however, he pointed to the out-of-town slot.

"Complete this in full." He slid her the form to close out

the PO box. "You only get your fee back if you turn in your key."

Charlie nodded and took the sheet full of minuscule type and little boxes, along with the envelope addressed to Mitch Saunders, Blakes Ridge PD—which felt like a ticking bomb. She crossed to the out-of-town slot. Her hand hovered there for a moment, then she gulped and shoved it through. She hadn't planned to tell a soul—ever—about those years with Weihle. Yet here she was baring all, first to Mitch, then Henrietta, and now her hometown police precinct—a written account, no less, irretrievably entered into the US postal system. Unreal.

She'd warred with herself on the way over. Furious that Mitch had sold her out, she'd been tempted to rip up his letter out of spite. Except she hadn't written it for him. It was meant to help Tiffany—and who knew how many other young girls. Sending it couldn't hurt her—she'd never set foot in Blakes Ridge again. Despite Mitch's stunt, in her ugly wig and new clothes, she'd already put distance between her and Charlie Hart—yet another roadblock set up on the long path that led back to Laura Macnamara.

She sighed. It had been a long time since she felt like Laura, but Charlie would be harder to shed. Volunteer, employee, friend—no matter how unintentional—to Henry, Cleo, and Ian…and even brief lover to that snake Mitch. Charlie Hart had become a real person—not just an assumed role—that had felt just right to her starved, wayward soul.

She straightened her shoulders, hauled up her duffel, and crossed to the back, where rows and rows of PO boxes stretched from floor to ceiling. Charlie had pulled her key off the ring to turn it in and close the box. But first, she wanted to make sure nothing had come from the Hudsons.

She dropped her big bag to the floor with a soft thud and squatted down.

She smiled when she saw the envelope. Hurrying with excitement, she snatched it up, shut the box, and stood. But just as she started to tear it open, she noticed that the handwriting wasn't Pamela's. Ray's, maybe? Also, it felt thin like a letter, not stiff like a picture. She hoped Pamela was okay. Charlie frowned and stuck her finger inside, ripping it slowly with a sense of dread. One sheet of lined yellow paper.

Dear Laura,
Mackenzie's true father has come to us, insisting
that you return home where you belong.

Holy mother of God, Charlie thought, leaning against the banks of silver boxes for support.

Hurry, for the child's safety depends on you.

It was Pamela's writing inside, but not her voice. Charlie tentatively raised the envelope to her nose and sniffed. Thomas's cologne assailed her.

Her little key clanked on the hard floor, then the form she'd not yet filled out floated down beside it. Bile surged up into her throat.

Weihle had finally found her.

Worse, he'd found Mackenzie.

God, how? She'd been so careful.

In a daze, she hoisted her duffel again, staggered out of the post office, and stood in the sunshine. Tears streamed down her face. The sickening letter was crushed in her fist.

Any choice she'd had in the whole matter had just been ripped from her.

She registered a series of clicks and realized a scruffy man with a camera and another wearing a tie hustled toward her. She spun, back into the post office, and flew through it toward the door in the back marked "emergency exit only."

She ran a block at full throttle, her duffel suddenly feeling heavy, as if she'd packed Glide's whole stockroom of flour sacks. She waved down a city bus as it approached the corner, and hopped up onto the stairs, panting.

The double doors snapped shut behind her. She bent to look through the side windows. The two men a half a block behind threw up their hands and turned away. She dug out her wallet, paid, then slumped into a seat near the rear door. Her hands shook as she read the letter over again, looking for clues.

She didn't know where this particular bus was headed, but make no mistake, it was the first leg of her journey back to her own personal hell—courtesy of Thomas Weihle.

CHAPTER 25

THOMAS WAS MERELY PUZZLED when he saw the cab, but his temper flared the moment he realized just who stood on his stoop. Tiffany Scott, the little whore, had turned up—on his porch, of all places—at the worst possible moment.

Thomas approached the taxi on the passenger side, gritting his teeth as he seethed. He had far more important goals today than getting rid of a sniveling addict. My God, he'd already prepared the ideal living space—days ago, because it'd been even easier to secure than he'd expected. And it was all going to be so fitting, so perfect…

No, he wouldn't postpone, he'd waited too long. He'd take care of this new wrinkle.

"How much?" he said to the driver. He leaned his forearms on the open window and hoped his custom-made dress shirt wouldn't be ruined.

"Twenty-four," replied the grungy, bearded driver. Shaggy hair, too. Looked bored to death.

Thomas made a point of looking at the dash where the man's photo hung.

"William A. Benson of the On Time Cab company," he read. The man's cab number and license plate, as well as his driver's license number, were listed there plain as day. "Do you prefer Bill?"

He shrugged, hands still on the wheel.

"Mr. Benson. Here's one hundred dollars, on one condition. You dropped someone—I don't much care who—at a different house. You never saw this girl."

William/Bill Benson raised shaggy eyebrows, but reached out for the money and said, "I got it, mister."

"See that you do, Mr. Benson. I tend to overreact when agreements are broken, and"—Thomas smiled and looked pointedly at the cab company information again—"you'd be so very easy to find."

"Easy, man." The cabbie held up his hands. "I never saw her—or you." Then he shoved the gear shift into drive and peeled away with a screech—drawing even more attention to them, the imbecile.

Thomas turned toward the house and sneered.

Tiffany had started down the steps toward him. The last thing he wanted was a gooey homecoming right here in the middle of his property. Not after that detective—Tiffany's brother—had cornered him at Rolling Meadows. Worse, he'd recently seen a man drive by and eye up his house. A plainclothes officer? Both counts incensed him. Tiffany had already proven to be a huge mistake.

"Hey, baby," she said. "Thanks. I wasn't sure how I was going to pay that guy if you weren't home."

The cab had finished its haphazard k-turn in the middle of the street and zoomed off, braking hard at the stop sign.

Thomas ground his teeth. "You know I despise pet names," he said, and walked right past her. He waited until the cab turned left and zipped out of sight, then turned his key in the lock.

"Get inside," he barked, and motioned for her to enter.

"I've missed you," she said, and attempted to look flirty. Thomas rolled his eyes. She couldn't pull it off while she was shaking for a fix. Besides, she looked drawn, filthy, spaced out, and jittery—thoroughly unattractive overall—a poster girl for drug addiction.

She attempted to place her hands on his chest as she entered, but he slid aside and swallowed his revulsion, glancing out the door for a sweep of the neighbors' yards—all clear—before closing and locking it.

He should have poisoned her like the bad weed she was when he had the chance. Instead, he'd banked on the fact that her voracious appetite for drugs would create an inability to return home, or perhaps even end in overdose far, far away in California.

Certainly, he knew better than to leave matters to chance.

Time to pay the piper, he thought, then smiled. Actually, he'd pay only in inconvenience, while she'd pay the ultimate price all by herself.

"Tommy, what are you thinking about? Something I c-c-can do to make you happy?" Tiffany stuttered. She wrapped her arms around herself, but couldn't stay still.

"You cannot possibly make me happy," Thomas said, and focused again on the matter at hand.

He needed to get rid of this nuisance quickly. Besides the fact that her brother was actively searching for her, he had a very important date to keep tonight. And truly, that doll shouldn't have to wait for his attention, ever.

Oh, how he'd love to don a pair of gloves, reach out, grasp Tiffany's scrawny neck, and squeeze. He smiled, imagining the way her eyes would widen with shock, then change, from confusion, to fear, to horror, to resignation, just as her skin would change color from lack of oxygen.

But no—as much pleasure, as that would give him at this moment, he suspected he wouldn't relish the memory in the long run. Strangulation was simply so unimaginative. Besides, it suggested a crime of passion, which this most certainly was not.

"Please, p-please…I'll do whatever you want," she begged, her teeth chattering. She crossed her arms and grasped the hem of her T-shirt as if to pull it up.

"You disgust me," he said, and strode toward the kitchen. "Keep your clothes on. We both know it's not me you need."

Tiffany sobbed, a small mew, and then he heard her padding along behind him. Just as well. He certainly didn't want the mangy bitch anywhere near his living room furniture.

First things first. He still had some of her special synthetic stash in an old prescription bottle. Just enough to make her malleable, while he decided how best to remove her from the equation once and for all.

Just as he pulled down the bottle, she pressed herself up against the back of him, her lips instantly closing on his neck.

He spun, his shoulder shoving her off balance, and backhanded her.

She staggered, even as her hands flew to her cheek, eyes tearing. She scurried backward to the opposite side of the kitchen, out of his reach. Whimpering, she sank to the floor, then cowered in the corner against the cupboards.

He felt his lip curl in disgust. The skin on his neck crawled and he felt an overwhelming urge to shake like a wet dog.

He went to the sink and washed his hands with scalding water and hospital-grade antibacterial soap, then wiped his neck with the same.

"I will give you what you need on one condition." He spoke in clipped tones, tamping down his fury. "Do not touch me. Do not attempt to disrobe. Do not even speak." He raised his eyebrows.

She nodded, and only the smallest sob escaped.

He held out a box of tissues, waited for her to take and use one. Then he shook out two tablets and set them on the floor in front of her. She scrabbled for them on all fours like the bitch she was, shoving them into her mouth with incredible speed. She leaned her head back against the cabinets, wrapped her arms around her knees, and shut her eyes.

In mere minutes, the shaking stopped, her features relaxed, and color suffused her skin. She smiled, slowly. Although her lips were chapped and purple circles hollowed her eyes, he was reminded, once again, of the stunning beauty, full of life and light, that had first attracted him.

She had been an angel with the old geezers at Rolling Meadows, yet Thomas had easily discovered her troubles and had known she could be tempted to be a very bad girl with the right motivation.

Ah, but the chase and draw had been exciting. The first few times he'd had her, he'd surveyed the private war raging behind her eyes. Excitement, a bit of fear, perhaps even loathing, certainly pleasure—against her will initially, of course—but always, in the end, capitulation. He'd been so satisfied, so pleased. And for her part, ultimately, she'd found relief, because she could sink into an oblivious high.

Unfortunately, her growing appetite for a deeper high and the constancy of her need made her too easy—a true whore, one whose conscience had deserted her, one whose backbone had crumbled like chalk. In no time, she ceased to arouse him no matter what fantasy he devised, and finally, he'd been unable even to stand the sight of her.

But helping her run off to California had been lazy on his part—an unfortunate error he now must rectify. There was no question of simply letting her walk away again, especially here in Blakes Ridge. She'd continue to turn up, infesting his life like a dandelion invasion, requiring his attention and constant management, at a time when he would need all his focus on sweet Mackenzie and her errant mother, Laura.

He glanced at Tiffany, still tucked up in a ball but recovered now, her head swaying slightly to a tune only she heard. Thomas snapped the childproof cap onto the plastic prescription bottle, then turned it round and round with his fingers.

Certainly, the most obvious solution would be to send the wastrel into overdose—entirely believable, even probable. Although, feasibly, that would create quite a mess to clean up—something he'd prefer not to have to deal with today of all days. Plus, there was the body to consider. If only she had done herself in—

The perfect plan crystallized suddenly in his mind, and Thomas laughed.

CHAPTER 26

MITCH TURNED ON his phone the minute the flight attendants announced that electronic devices were once again safe to use. He'd never felt so friggin' impotent in his life. Trapped in a tiny window seat miles away from where he needed to be, unable to receive calls, hands tied in terms of helping Tiffany…

Four messages. One from Carson O'Dell, two from Chief Marcone, one from his mom.

The cabin had come alive at their descent. Right on time, they should land by eight p.m. Mitch ignored the rustle and bustle, listening closely to the voicemail messages.

Marcone's voice first: "It took me all day, but I tracked down Judge Abrams. All the way out in some goddamn stream in Carbon County—without telling anyone his destination. How a man of his position thinks he can go off without a cell phone is beyond me…" Then, finally, "We got the warrants. Teams are setting up."

Mitch breathed a sigh of relief.

His mother had Marcone and O'Dell keeping her updated; she'd only wanted to check in with him. Her voice sounded raw, her nose congested. She'd likely been crying most of the day. He blanched and angled himself toward the window. Privacy was for shit on these tin birds.

Carson confirmed that they'd entered Weihle's house. For

a second, Mitch felt a surge of elation, only to have it crushed flat. "Weihle's nowhere to be found."

"Fuck," Mitch mouthed. His fists clenched so hard that he was surprised the phone continued to work.

The last message was Marcone again. "Somehow the press found out about Laura Macnamara. Know anything about that?" Mitch winced. "We've got mothers from four counties tying up the lines, demanding the pedophile be put to justice. We'll hold a quick press conference with WKDB to calm the waters. You should be able to view it from their website when you get service back."

Mitch exited the plane and beelined for the first empty corner of the Chicago airport he saw. He probably had about a half an hour before his connection boarded. His Blackberry couldn't pull up WKDB's website fast enough. Finally! The headline read, "Molested and Missing: Local Teen Found Alive after Six Years."

There was a picture of Charlie in the foyer of her building, blond hair as crazy as ever, her gorgeous face shell-shocked, blue eyes wide and disbelieving. Braun's friend had found her.

Damn, I'm sorry, Charlie, he thought, squeezing his eyes shut.

He felt sick. There'd be no stopping her from running now. She'd believe she'd have to leave that neighborhood, Glide, Henrietta, and Cleo. Probably already had. He hoped she'd find peace again soon. He'd lock up Weihle forever, ensuring that she'd finally feel safe wherever she landed next. He'd find her again, get word to her when it was done, make sure she knew he was no longer a threat…

For Charlie and for Tiffany. He'd fucking nail the bastard if it was the last thing he did.

There was a video, too.

Marcone, in flak pants, boots, a windbreaker, and a police-issued ball cap, his face serious, front and center behind a podium and microphone. Judge Abrams, to Mitch's surprise, stood to the side. He didn't fit the judicial stereotype. Instead of balding and potbellied and draped in robes, he was tall and lanky, with a heavy salt-and-pepper beard covering a perpetually tanned face. He wore outdated eyeglasses, dark green waders, an olive shirt with rolled-up sleeves, a khaki vest sporting multiple bulky pockets, and a hat with numerous pins and feathers attached. He looked stressed and harried. Mitch knew the guy hated to be interrupted while enjoying his sport. Almost as much as Chief Dominic Marcone despised the great outdoors. Mitch felt a flicker of amusement: he'd have liked to have been sitting in a duck blind watching the exchange when these two met in the woods.

Focusing, he strained to hear the sound via the phone's tiny speaker.

"Please," the chief said with his hands out, "stay calm. We do have a good idea who the perpetrator is, but we have to go through the proper channels. Any arrest must hold up in court, if we want this person off our streets for good." Mitch saw Abrams nod in agreement in the corner of the screen.

The camera switched to Veronica Braun, heavily made up and not a hair out of place. Her expression reflected the perfect amount of concern, mixed with a determined, business-like demeanor. "The man's name, Chief?"

"That's information we cannot share at this time." There was a murmur from the crowd, and other reporters lobbed questions as if they were tomatoes.

"How can we keep our children safe if pedophiles are being protected?"

"Has Miss Macnamara come forward?"

"When do you expect to have the man in custody?"

"How was Laura Macnamara found?"

Marcone held up a hand to silence them, and answered only some of the many questions. "I'm not yet at liberty to divulge the whereabouts or willingness of Laura Macnamara. The judge"—he looked at Abrams—"has personally issued the warrants we need. Our officers strive every day to keep our children and our citizens safe, and today is no different."

Braun's voice again: "Did Detective Saunders really work this case for six years? Did the department give up on him too soon?"

The chief's eyes narrowed. "I'm glad you asked that question, Ms. Braun." He looked out at the swarm of microphones held by hungry reporters. "The department never forgets about a cold case, but is sometimes forced to table them temporarily to deal with fresh ones that have a higher chance of being solved. Detective Saunders, himself, never gave up on the Macnamara case. He is one of our most dedicated officers."

The judge leaned forward to be heard. "A good man. We never doubted him."

Mitch shook his head.

"Where is Detective Saunders now? Is it true his sister has disappeared?"

"Unfortunately, yes, Tiffany Scott is missing. The community's help would be greatly appreciated in this matter. Anyone who has knowledge of her whereabouts is urged to call the precinct." Marcone held up a hand. "Thank you. That's all for now."

Mitch lowered the phone. Every muscle in his body was tense. He'd been successful, to a degree—they'd gotten warrants. He'd hope a tip would come in about Tiffany. However, he feared Thomas would bolt, or do something drastic. And the guilt was swamping him, as his heart bled for Charlie.

God, for so long he'd cared about nothing more than getting answers to the Macnamara case, clearing his name, reclaiming his dignity, plowing ahead in his career. Seemed fucking ridiculous now. He couldn't give a shit.

The only things that were important were finding Tiffany and helping her to get well. Proving that Weihle deserved to be locked up forever. That would allow Charlie, too, to move forward, to live freely and fully without always looking over her shoulder. And his mom, God. She'd endured enough loss. If he could ease her suffering, give her back her daughter...

Mitch registered the voice over the PA system: "Flight 6146 to Allentown, Pennsylvania is now boarding." Shit, what gate number? He whipped the boarding pass out of his back pocket. Good, just across the way and a nice, long queue forming. He had time for a call.

"Mitch?" Deirdre nearly shouted, and Mitch realized there must have been a delay in the connection.

"Mom, it's me."

"I know. Have you heard anything new? Have they found her?"

"No, I'm sorry, Mom. I just checked messages. You probably know as much as I do."

"Oh." Her voice was fragile now. "I hoped, when I saw your number..."

Like the dark falling fast outside O'Hare's floor-to-ceiling windows, Mitch felt heavy and smothered—if only he could *do* something for her.

"Where are you?" Deirdre asked.

"At the airport in Chicago—a short layover. About to board again. I land in Allentown at midnight."

"So late?"

"I know. It's killing me, too. But Carson and the chief are doing all they can."

"But it's not enough! She's still out there somewhere, doing God knows what! I can't help her I can't protect her when she's—" Deirdre broke off on a sob.

"Mom—please. They'll find her."

"But Mitch, you don't know—so much of this is my fault. If I'd handled her differently…"

"Mom, you did everything right. We got her into rehab, you did everything you could. Very few kids ever get help unless the people they love play hardball with them." He knew his voice sounded hard and angry, but he was ticked. Fucking pissed that his mom was going through this. "Do not blame yourself."

Deirdre sniffed, loud and messy-sounding.

"I feel just as responsible for not being there for the both of you more," he said. "Maybe I would have realized where this was headed sooner."

"No, it's not your fault." She exhaled. "And if I can't blame me, then you can't blame you."

Her voice was tremulous at best. Both she and Mitch knew they'd each carry the weight of this no matter what they spoke aloud.

There was more, however. He cleared his throat. "I need you to know, Mom. Tiff is…well, she's really far gone. She nearly overdosed in California."

"Go on," she whispered, and he imagined her holding tight to the kitchen counter or lowering herself into a chair.

"I talked to both the paramedic and one of the nurses at the hospital. She was looking for another fix as soon as she came to. She wouldn't hear of entering a program."

"So, although she didn't manage to kill herself yet, she still might? Is that what you're saying?" Deirdre asked.

"Yes," he said, his voice gruff. "What I'd tell any other parent in this situation is that even if we can get her off the streets and into rehab, it would be forcible, with no guarantee she'd actually get well. We'll keep at it"—he gulped—"but she may well slip again. Tiff has to want it. Addicts often have to hit rock bottom—and we'd be amazed at how low that bottom is—before they'll fight to climb up and out of the hole they've dug. Sometimes, they don't ever fight."

He heard her blow her nose before she spoke. "And what are you telling me, your own mother?"

"That we won't give up. You or me. And we won't let Tiff give up either."

Deirdre didn't respond. He figured she was trying to get a hold of herself.

"There's something else," he said. "Have you seen the news?"

"No. I couldn't concentrate, so I turned the TV off."

"I shouldn't tell you, but this isn't a case I'm working, this is Tiffany, and you have a right to know." He drew a deep breath. "Remember that teen runaway case I landed a while back? Laura Macnamara?"

"Of course. The girl with the comatose mother? The case that's been hanging over you all these years?"

"Yes. I found her. In California."

"That's great, Mitch. But what does this have to do with—"

"It turns out, this neighbor of Laura's was sexually abusing her, threatening her…" He fucking hated having to tell her this. "Mom, Tiffany knows this man, too."

Deirdre gasped. "No!"

"I don't know for sure what their relationship involved,"

he continued, "but I suspect the worst. And I believe he was supplying her with drugs—tailor-made just for her."

"Dear Lord," she breathed.

"Yeah," Mitch said, "so you've got to stop blaming yourself. Tiffany didn't just wander down this path. She was led—by a monster with an iron grip."

CHAPTER 27

"TIFFANY, CHILD. You must be so tired," Thomas cooed, as the girl swayed on her feet, flirting with the quarry's precipice.

Any other time, he would have enjoyed this little scenario immensely, drawing it out to savor in full.

Instead, the dust from their ascent had barely settled, and he felt rushed—conscious of every minute ticking away. He refused to reschedule tonight's momentous event, and yet so much needed to be accomplished between now and then.

Thomas brushed the sleeves of his pullover off with his hands, although it was likely pointless. He'd had to carry Tiffany—in a fireman's hold—the last hundred yards or so to the crest of Stone Hill. She was malodorous and greasy— her hair lank, her clothing grungy. He shuddered. Really, who knew where those garments had been? Purposefully he sniffed, hoping the heavy scent of the pines behind him would clear his nose.

"I'm cold and tired. I want to sit down now," she whined.

"Remain standing. Recall, please, that I gave you what you needed a few hours ago, but didn't ask anything of you in return." Thomas took a breath and consciously attempted to put aside his anger at the girl's abysmal timing. Then he put great effort into softening his voice. "Well, this is what I had in mind. A nice hike, beautiful scenery. Allow the fresh air to clear your mind, the breeze to cleanse your soul."

She turned to face him, puzzled, yet too zoned out to follow the inconsistencies through.

"Don't fret, sweet Tiffany. Today is different. You'll keep your clothes on, and so will I. We won't even touch. See how far away I am?"

He spread his arms wide just as the wind surged then calmed, and moved back another few feet toward the tree line. He stood now about ten feet from Tiffany, well away from the edge himself.

"I want nothing from you now. We're here only to talk things through, for your own good."

"I'm not good," she said. Her lip wobbled and her voice sounded querulous, like a young child on the verge of tears.

"You're right, sweetheart. You haven't been very good at all. Your mother, and your brother too, would be so disappointed to see what you've become." He shook his head.

Tiffany sobbed once.

"You came home, but didn't want to face them, did you?"

Tiffany started to buckle into a sitting position.

"No!" Thomas barked, and she was just enough used to following his commands to pop upright again.

Except he didn't want to just order her off the edge. Where was the fun in that?

"Do not sit." He'd have to speed this up. "Turn around. The sun will feel good on your face."

She turned, stumbling a little on the uneven rock beneath her feet.

"Step to the edge, Tiffany. Can you feel the sun?"

"Mmh hmnh. But I want to go now."

"You are tired, so tired, because you are weak."

"I tried, really…it's so hard."

"So hard to stay clean? To please everyone? To stay

strong?" He tsked with his tongue. "I'm afraid your addictions are so great now that you might never manage to control your urges."

She swayed. "I know. I only get worse."

"It must be terrible."

"It never goes away; it grows like a monster."

"What kind of monster?"

"Ugly. Mean. Like a nightmare, all dark. Bigger and bigger, always looming over me."

"Can you fight this monster?" He smiled—thrilled—feeling all he'd been missing for so long.

She was crying now, softly, but her shoulders shook. "No. It's inside me, screaming and thrashing and clawing me everywhere."

"You *can* fight him, Tiffany. You can silence him once and for all." This was it, Thomas thought, as the power rose within him. He stood tall, legs spread, shoulders back, chest out, cock engorged. "You can end it."

Her head hung low already. Now she shook it slowly back and forth. The early evening sunlight seemed to wrap around her thin frame, as if the light pulled her toward its source.

"You can end the monster's control, and all the pain and fear and need with just one step." Thomas held his breath, exhilarated by the special power he wielded—the ability to see inside another soul, the pull of his own voice, the weight of suggestion, and the twist of will. "It will be so much easier this way."

"It won't hurt me anymore?" she asked.

"No, sweetheart, it'll be all better, finally, all better for you."

"But my mom…"

"She just wants you to be at peace."

"She loves me no matter what."

"No matter what."

"I'm so tired." She looked back at him.

"I know, but you don't have to be anymore."

She nodded, turned back to the precipice, and murmured, "The monster will have to sleep, too."

"Yes," Thomas whispered.

Tiffany spread her arms wide, looking for all the world as if she could fly. Thomas, too, felt as if he could soar from the rush of power.

She teetered for a moment in slow motion, her open sweatshirt billowing behind her, then fell forward, away from him. In a mere fraction of a second, maybe less, she'd disappeared.

Thomas tilted his head. He heard a muffled thud from far below.

"Sweet dreams," he said with a grin, and strode toward the trees.

———

The name "Laura Macnamara" jumped out at Thomas from the six-o'clock news radio report in the rental car, where he sat watching Mackenzie's home, shuttered though it was. He spun the dial hard to increase the volume, flooding the car with sound, even as he registered the fact that the announcer had actually said, "...a break in the 2006 case of missing teen Laura Macnamara."

Thomas was still flying high after Tiffany's demise. Adrenaline surged anew and he held his breath. Now what?

"She's been found, alive and well," the voice recited, "in San

Francisco, California, having disappeared of her own volition. Stay tuned for updates to this breaking story."

Thomas's hands clenched the steering wheel as he considered the ramifications of Laura surfacing publicly—just when he'd expected to be able to enjoy her presence in secret. Had she even received the Hudsons' letter yet? Would she return to Blakes Ridge, or attempt to disappear again without ever checking her post box?

Thomas reached for his iPhone, sitting in the rental's cup holder. He needed more information. Indeed, the local news affiliate had more detail on its website, including shots of Laura with a horrendous haircut—bleached blond—that completely overshadowed her natural beauty. New evidence pointed to abuse, the site read, by someone close to her. It was now believed that she had disappeared out of self-preservation.

He'd thought the police presence camped in front of his house was a result of Tiffany's return to Blakes Ridge and her brother's meddling. Now, he realized that wasn't necessarily the case. There was another explanation.

Laura had talked. Broken her silence and their secrets. Named him.

He seethed, his blood pulsing with the need to vent his rage—preferably on her, the bitch. The sedan suddenly felt claustrophobic.

Another picture showcased the little snitch in a red wig, also heinous. Were those tears in her eyes? She'd never been one to fall to pieces. He'd squinted at the tiny picture on his handheld, then enlarged it as far as technology would allow. Painstakingly, he moved the photo around, trying to see the background. He was nearly sure she stood in front of a post office. Anticipation surged within him.

Tear tracks were evident on her still-smooth skin, and shock dulled her expression. He noted two bags over her shoulder and scrolled down…a piece of paper—yellow-lined—was clutched in her fist.

Thomas punched the air, leaned his head back on the seat, and let a smile take over his face. He couldn't believe he'd actually toyed with delaying tonight's excitement by twenty-four hours because of the Tiffany interruption. Oh no, not now. He laughed.

There was no time to waste, for he'd see his Laura in the flesh, very, very soon.

CHAPTER 28

MITCH HAD BEEN WAITING for the nose of the plane to tip slightly, signaling descent into Allentown. When it did, he immediately turned on his cell, rather than waiting for an announcement. Missed calls from Carson O'Dell and Chief Marcone. Lots of them. But no messages. Only one text from Carson: *Call me as soon as you land.* Mitch tried, but the phone kept cutting out. No steady service yet. It was nearly midnight. The flight was on time—thank God, because Mitch couldn't stand another second of being cooped up.

He retrieved his bag early from the bins overhead and sprang out of his seat the second the ding sounded. Another text had come from O'Dell. *Meeting you at airport.*

Bad news or good? Mitch's truck remained here in the airport lot, so Carson wasn't here to offer him a ride.

He clambered down the metal stairs to the tarmac, where the pilot handed him his gun case. Mitch ran for the doors and found Carson pacing just inside the terminal. He strode toward Mitch as soon as he spotted him.

They grasped hands in a shake, and Mitch got a bad feeling from the stoic expression Carson wore.

"You don't have him in custody yet?"

"No. We've looked everywhere. He took time off from work, hasn't been to Rolling Meadows. Isn't home. He's friggin' vanished. Mitch—"

"Tiffany—is she safe?"

"No. She's…" Carson shut his eyes and audibly gulped. Mitch felt his heart drop out and land with a deafening thwack on the hard tile.

"A hiker called in a jumper out at old Stone Hill— descriptions match Tiffany and Weihle."

Mitch felt his vision start to go black as his chest squeezed. No. No! He sucked in air. "A jumper? But two descriptions? What the hell are you saying?"

"We don't have positive ID yet," Carson was saying. He squeezed Mitch's shoulder.

"But you think…" He couldn't voice it.

"I don't know." Carson shook his head. "It doesn't sound good."

The urge to yell and pummel and rage through the terminal consumed Mitch, yet he couldn't mourn her yet. It wasn't definite. He had to hope.

"Details," he managed, and began to walk. He had to move.

"The hiker says he saw two people on the east ridge of the quarry. Man and a young woman, judging by the clothing. Just talking for a while, and then the girl…jumped." Mitch felt Carson look at him, but he focused dead ahead toward the exit. Carson added, "The man didn't try to stop her, just walked away."

———

Mitch skidded to a stop, billows of road dust enveloping the truck. He shoved open the door but left the lights on—it was after one a.m. and pitch black out there. He ran for the officers just off the lot in a patch of scrappy grass. O'Dell pulled his own vehicle alongside before the dust had stopped swirling.

Officer Carmen Amenilo met him halfway in the twin beams of light. "Mitch, the CSI team finished on the east ridge. Search-and-rescue went around to the quarry entrance for the most direct access. They'll head up from the base." She scrambled to keep up with his pumping strides. He aimed for the older man half sitting on a large boulder.

"This is Max Danning," Amenilo said, "your witness. Max, Detective Saunders."

"Detective," the man said, as he stood.

He fit the baby boomer age frame—probably technically AARP, but obviously fit. He had a hiker's walking stick, a tan bucket hat, and a compact backpack. He wore cutoff khakis, wool socks pulled up to mid-shin, sturdy boots, and a faded Led Zeppelin T-shirt. His face was partially lit—the beam from Amenilo's cruiser hitting him square in the chest. Mitch could see that Danning looked kind, with blue eyes and a direct gaze, and that he was way tired. He would be. His 911 call had come in at 6:30 p.m.

"Thank you for waiting."

"Yeah, no problem. It seemed...important."

"Max, this girl you saw"—Mitch had to clear his throat—"could very well be my sister."

"Oh, man, I hope not."

Mitch clenched his teeth and nodded once. "I need you to walk me through it, every detail."

Danning nodded. "I crested the south ridge, and sat in my favorite spot to watch the sun set, and to hydrate. I was facing west, so I didn't realize at first that there were people on the eastern side. A reflection, maybe from a watch or something, caught my eye."

His gray brows lowered. "Two people, male and female. They talked for maybe ten minutes, but I don't know how long they'd been there. I wouldn't have paid much attention, except the girl was rather close to the edge and the man stood back."

"How far back?"

"Probably ten to fifteen feet."

"So he didn't push her."

"No, never touched her. At first she faced him, with her back to the edge. After a while she turned to face west, as if looking out over the quarry. From their hand gestures, I figured they were having a conversation. Too far to see their expressions. I assumed he was maybe afraid of heights."

"The gestures, were they angry? Agitated?"

"No, the man was calm, but expressive with his hands. She was more still, looked maybe sad. Hung her head at one point. They certainly weren't arguing or yelling. That's why I was so shocked—completely dumbfounded—when she went over like she did."

Carson jumped in: "Physically, what did they look like?"

"She looked young. Jeans, tight all the way to the ankles. A white shirt and a big zippered sweatshirt—or maybe sweater, but that shape—over her top."

"Hair color?" Mitch held his breath.

"Blondish. Long, and loose, midway down her chest." Max gestured to his own chest.

"And the man?"

"Also blond. Short hair, although long enough to blow in the wind. He had reflective sunglasses on. Loose pants—probably slacks of some sort the way they flapped around—and a windbreaker—navy, like the type golfers wear. Didn't look to have a hood."

Carson raised his eyebrows at Mitch, and he gave a curt nod—the descriptions certainly matched.

Mitch asked Max, "What happened just before she jumped?"

Amenilo, who'd been furiously scratching in her note-book, paused and looked up.

"Nothing, man. She just spread out her arms and tipped forward, almost in slow motion."

"What did the man do when she jumped?" Mitch asked.

"Before she…went over…he just stood there. In the same spot, still as stone." He shook his head. "After? I don't know. My eyes were on her. I was so shocked. I couldn't believe what I was seeing."

"But he didn't try to stop the girl or yell for her or anything." Mitch spoke through a clenched jaw.

"No. And when I looked up, he was gone."

"How long until you called in?" Carson asked Max.

The man grimaced. "I'm afraid it was about a half an hour. I'd left my cell in the car. I considered heading the other direction to find the girl, but I'm not familiar with the inside of the bowl. Wasn't sure there'd even be a path.

"I decided the best bet would be to get down as fast as possible and call for help, and then I planned to go back up the path I suspected the guy would have come down. I don't know what I would have done with him"—he shrugged—"but I at least wanted to get a description. So I ran down the path as fast as I could, called 911, and hustled over to the east side, but there were no cars in that lot."

He shook his head. "I was fast, but had a lot more ground to cover than he did." Max Danning looked directly at Mitch. "I'm sorry. I really hope she's not your sister."

Not the man's fault, but fear and enormous frustration battled in Mitch. He felt as if his skin was close to busting apart with a giant kaboom. He, too, prayed it wasn't Tiffany, and yet his gut told him he'd lost her. Only his iron will, and unreasonable shards of hope, kept grief from geysering up before stone-cold facts.

"Amenilo," Mitch said, "how far's the drop from the east precipice?"

"Unless she managed to hit an ledge, about two hundred feet." She put a hand on his arm. "I'm told the face is fairly smooth." At that, another of those shards he'd been holding on to shattered.

"Max, make sure this officer can reach you." He nodded at Amenilo, and turned his attention to Carson. They walked about fifteen paces away before Mitch spoke, fighting hard to keep his voice to loud, rather than raging.

"Weihle should have been in custody *before* this happened. I want him—now." He scowled, and his hands fisted. "He's eluded you so far—but he's obviously here somewhere. From what I learned in California, this"—Jesus, he could barely think it, let alone voice it—"talking someone off a cliff thing matches his MO." Mitch ran his hands through his hair in frustration. "It has to be him."

He refused to admit to himself that if the man on the cliff had been Weihle, the chances of the girl being Tiffany were… "So he's got a hideout—somewhere you haven't looked, somewhere local. Find it." He pinned O'Dell with his eyes, barely restraining himself from taking his friend by the lapels. "Fucking find him."

Mitch ached to complete that order himself, his very cells surging at the call for action, but he had to see about Tiffany first. "I'm headed for search-and-rescue," he shot over his shoulder as he headed for his truck.

Because he *had* to know. Was the girl who'd plummeted to certain death Tiffany, or—*please, God*—not?

CHAPTER 29

FLASHING LIGHTS BOUNCED off each other in a bizarre dance of color from patrol cars, an ambulance, and even a fire truck. All over Thomas's property, people swarmed in and out of spotlights that broke up the blackness of night. Far more police presence than he'd expected. Impossible, yet clearly happening. Laura would pay dearly for this.

Thomas tore his attention away from the action and sat up a bit in his seat to check his appearance in the rearview mirror. No cause for alarm. He did, indeed, look just like his neighbor Tony Silvia, with his bulky, hooded sweatshirt, Phillies ball cap, and longish dark hair. Thomas had even conceded to a tasteless gold chain at his neck.

No matter about his abused yard or his invaded home. Although he'd certainly never planned to bring a child to his own residence—talk about a beacon for the law—he had originally counted on being able to access his things. He gritted his teeth, but tamped down his ire. Indeed, there'd be much he'd be giving up soon; however, the gain would make any sacrifice worth it.

He glided to a stop near the officer who stood in the road and pushed the button that rolled down his window. The chill of the cool spring night flowed in, disturbing the warm cocoon he'd made of the car.

"Officer, what's happened?" he asked, neighborly concern dripping from his voice.

"I'm not at liberty to say. Where are you headed?"

Thomas had planned for this middle-of-the-night arrival. "That's my house, there." He pointed out the windshield, then hooked a thumb to the back seat. "We're just getting home from the airport—flight delay. First Disney trip." He smiled, then put his hands alongside his head in the classic sleeping pose.

The cop cupped his hands to the glass of the back window. He would see exactly what Thomas intended for him to see. Two duffel bags on the seat, the oversized slumbering princess doll—he'd been pleased with the appropriateness of that—and the exhausted child tucked safely into her car seat, head lolling to the side. Little did the cop know, she slept far deeper than a typical REM cycle normally allowed.

The cop straightened and returned to Thomas's window.

"Is my neighbor all right?" Thomas asked. "Can you tell me that much?"

The officer's head wagged back and forth under his formal cap. "Sorry, sir. I can't tell you anything at all," he said, and waved Thomas through.

As he pressed gently on the gas pedal, Thomas eyed his rearview mirror again, this time watching for any movement by the patrolman.

The fool didn't suspect a thing.

He swung into the driveway and executed a quick k-turn where it opened up in the rear of the house. As he hit the remote for the garage door, he chuckled. His plan had been flawless, as always. Even the improvised parts, like the Tiffany complication, had gone seamlessly.

Home sweet home, he thought, as he rolled the car inside. Only one task left before all his preparations bore fruit. To wait.

But if he knew Laura, and he did, they wouldn't wait very long.

CHAPTER 30

THE SPAN OF TIME between one thirty a.m. and the break of dawn had been the longest, most agonizing hours Mitch had ever passed. No other young blond girls had been reported missing from Blakes Ridge, or any of the surrounding areas. He'd been forced to accept the fact that they searched for his sister. Tiffany.

Mitch had spent hours contacting neighboring departments, but to no avail—none of the local precincts owned heat-seeking infrared equipment. Night-vision goggles were all that was available. Regardless, search-and-rescue had deemed the black hole that was the bottom of the old quarry simply too dark and dangerous to be traversing without nature's help. The fact that the inside face of the quarry was prone to occasional avalanches didn't help. Mitch's protests were overruled. If she was dead, there was no sense risking other lives.

He himself was threatened with arrest when he attempted to set out on his own. He had to calm down; wouldn't do anybody any good under lock and key—not Tiffany, not his mom. Nor would he be able to go after the bastard who did this the second he was free to do so. Mitch raged privately, railing against perverts, twisted minds, drugs, and his own failings, too. He paced long stretches of parking lot as they waited, unable to remain still, fearing the worst. Still, he couldn't help but hope that his sister somehow miraculously still breathed—and yet that tortured him further, as he was unable to go to her when she could be lying there, broken and bleeding in the dark, dewy chill...

As pink tinged the horizon, the team came alive, hauling packs and setting out over uneven ground. Their high-powered flashlight beams crisscrossed now and then in the distance, the artificial light still helpful in the shadowed basin. They'd hiked at least thirty minutes when a shout went up. Mitch turned abruptly toward the sound and tried to discern the words behind the voices he heard. He ran as fast as the uneven terrain would allow, fell once, then again, his own beam of light bouncing.

As soon as Mitch saw the spotlights pop on one by one without any shouts for medics, he knew.

Dear God. How could it have come to this?

He stopped in his tracks, hidden in the shadows, bowed his head, and his fisted hands crossed over his heart. Tears welled, and Mitch let them come, but only for a few moments.

He no longer had a suspect to find. He had a killer to trap. The faster Mitch caught him, the better.

He pulled up the bottom of his T-shirt, wiped his face, and straightened his shoulders. As he traversed the hard earth, sliding now and then on gravel, he began to steel himself mentally for seeing Tiffany.

By the time he reached the already busy technicians, he wore a poker face. He looked up, surveying the walls of the quarry here, his trained mind noting the length of the drop—probably two hundred-plus feet. Inside, however, his stomach churned, his ears rushed with white noise, and he fought hard to keep a grip on himself.

The woman clicking photos stopped first, and then everyone else noticed him, too. The man kneeling stood, moved aside, and Mitch suddenly had a clear view of Tiffany.

His breath stalled in his lungs and he shut his eyes to block it out. But he still saw the scene of his mangled sister as if it were imprinted on the inside of his eyelids. Her torso and one leg looked bizarre, unnatural in their twisted pose. Blood seeped from under her head, turning her hair dark. She faced the sky with skin as white as the moon, but, thank God, her eyes were shut.

"I'm so sorry," somebody said.

"We'll give you some time," somebody else said, and they scooted aside.

Mitch swallowed and forced himself to move. He'd seen so many dead bodies over the years, even people he'd been close to, but he couldn't remain detached now. He knelt beside Tiff, just under her arm that was thrown up and out beside her, and bent from the waist, hanging over her. But the ingrained training to keep a crime scene free of contaminants kept him from hugging or holding her.

"Detective, it's okay," he heard from one of the techs, as if from far away. "In this case, it's okay. We can eliminate your DNA."

Except it wasn't. If there was any evidence to be found on her body after a fall like that, he couldn't risk disturbing it. The witness had said Weihle—for in his mind there was zero doubt that the man with Tiffany had been him—hadn't touched her. But he'd gotten her here somehow, possibly driven her, possibly dragged her. There had to be traceable evidence to find somewhere.

He choked off a sob, wishing for all the world that he could gather her in his arms and cradle her one last time. Instead, he allowed himself only to smooth his fingertips over her forehead.

"Baby girl, I am so sorry. So, so, so sorry that I didn't get to you in time." Then he lost it, and wailed for her, for him, and most of all for his mother, whose heart would rip in two.

When he could speak again, his voice was a rough, halting whisper. "Be an angel and watch over Mom, okay? And don't worry. I know who did this to you." Mitch felt resolve harden like steel and fury boil like magma as he spoke. "I won't rest until the bastard pays with his life."

———

Mitch sat in his truck, hands locked hard on the steering wheel. He looked out at the parking lot, just beginning to come to life under the early morning rays of sun, but didn't see it. A cool breeze floated in the window, along with the hum of crickets in the underbrush surrounding the base of the trail and parking lot. The beautiful spring weather mocked him on the worst dawn of his life.

Horror at the situation, fury at the sick bastard who'd so wronged his sister and Charlie and who knew who else, guilt and impotence at his failure, and a mushrooming grief all warred for first place inside him. Then there were the questions. What if he'd clued in sooner? What if he'd exposed Charlie and her story the minute he'd discovered her? What if and what if?

He worked hard to push it all aside. He didn't have time. He needed to dig deep within for some courage. Mom had to know, immediately, and from him. He couldn't imagine a worse task. And yet he would never allow anyone else to tell her. As God-awful as he felt, he wanted to be with her, be there for her.

He pressed the heels of his hands into his eyes hard, and reached for the key in the ignition. No courage was going to help him now. He just had to drive.

After Mom's—he couldn't bear to imagine it, better to think of something else—he'd let anger boil up and out and go after Weihle with all he had.

At his mother's small Cape-style house, he stood for a moment on the back stoop. The house he'd grown up in, the same one that had seen them through loss too many times before—first his brother, then his dad, now this... He wished she'd move. For him, at least, the bad had now officially squeezed out any good memories he might have been able to dig up.

He reached for the metal handle of the old screen door, but as his hand touched the cool metal he halted. He tried to take a deep breath, but it forced out a sob. He clamped his lips shut and breathed as shallowly as possible through his nose. When he felt he could speak, he pushed the lever down and pulled the door open, then he stepped in, shutting it as quietly as possible behind him.

She was waiting—just inside, tears already sliding down her soft cheeks. Her hands were clasped tight at her chest and her eyes, bigger than ever—so much like Tiffany's—searched his.

"Mom. I'm sorry—" He broke off, sobbing and heaving. He bowed his head, and bent at the waist, both unable to face her and trying to hold it all inside.

Her toes—tiny and painted, sporting yellow flip-flops with bright plastic flowers—entered his line of sight and she wrapped her arms around him sideways. He raised up, to make it easier for her, and held on tight to her tiny frame, tucking her into him as if she were a child. Her chest heaved against him, his tears soaked her hair…They grieved like that for a long time.

Eventually, when they'd both quieted a bit, she slipped away for a box of tissues. She yanked out the flimsy sheets over and over until she had a big wad for herself and one for him.

Mitch mopped his face and blew his nose, then shuddered as he took a breath.

"I need you to tell me exactly what happened, Mitch." She pinned him with her swollen eyes. "Don't sugarcoat it. I am so sick and tired of all the not knowing, you understand?"

He nodded.

Instead of the kitchen table, where they'd had most of their more serious talks over the years, she grabbed a mug and the pot of coffee and moved toward the living room.

His chief, Dominic Marcone, stood stiffly by the recliner. Had he been here most of the night? Or had he arrived at an ungodly hour this morning? Either way, Mitch shouldn't have been surprised, but he was. He'd paid so little attention for too long.

Mitch reached out a hand as if to shake, but Marcone pulled him into his embrace.

"I am so sorry, son," he said, his voice catching. They slapped each other's backs, and Mitch found himself once again unable to speak for the grief that kept welling up.

He nodded his thanks as they pulled apart. His mom filled the mug for him, then topped off her own and the chief's. She didn't return it to the kitchen, simply plunked it down on the side table. No hot pad, not even a coaster.

They sat, Mitch on the sofa next to his mom, turned

slightly toward her with his back to Marcone, who perched in his dad's old La-Z-Boy.

Deirdre reached for his hands, closed her eyes, and said, "Tell me how she died."

Mitch gulped. "From a fall, out at Stone Hill."

Her fingers clenched and he saw a shudder go through her. After a few seconds, she opened her eyes. "Was it suicide? Or she was so high that she just lost her balance and fell?" She shook her head. "But if she was that out of it, how did she manage to climb up there, and why?"

"We won't have the tox screen back until after the autopsy—and Mom, it's important we autopsy, okay?"

She nodded.

"Yes, I'm sure she was intoxicated, I just don't know on what. And it's likely that rather than taking something on her own, she was given or forced to take something."

Her expression turned fierce. "The man you told me about, the one Tiffany knew from the nursing home that had abused the Macnamara girl?"

He sucked in a good breath. "Yes, Thomas Weihle—he was there with her at the top of the quarry. We have a witness. I can't prove yet that it was him, but I will."

He glanced briefly at Marcone, who he knew must have heard the dispatch report and likely most of the other details from Carson. Surely that was why the man had wanted to be here with Deirdre, for when she was told. But he'd likely been holding out hope for her, so he wouldn't have shared all the details.

"Go on, Mitch," Deirdre said.

"He didn't push her, or even touch her, and didn't try to stop her or act shocked. According to the witness, they just looked like they were talking, and after she'd jumped, he simply walked away." He shook his head. Still incredulous. "Either she was so totally high on her own or he'd given her a hallucinogen. A team is going through Weihle's house now. If whatever's in her system matches something he's got in that house—it's done. If not, still, a person doesn't go to commit suicide with someone else along for the ride. She was coerced into it. Charlie—Laura Macnamara, I mean—says this is how he gets off. Making people do what they don't want to do, making it somehow their choice to come to him or do his bidding—without physically forcing them."

"That's…sick." Deirdre's face had turned hard, lips compressed and eyes glinting. "And it doesn't absolve him of guilt."

"Hell no."

Deirdre didn't respond, and Mitch watched as her eyes glazed over with thoughts she kept private. Marcone's face was pained—Mitch felt the same distress. He reached over and grasped his mom's hands. He needed her touch, and surely she could use any measure of comfort.

Unexpectedly, she said, "I saw her, Laura, on the news."

Mitch grimaced. "Yeah. That was my doing. It was the only way I could speed up the hunt for Weihle on this end." His fists contracted into hard rocks. "But I was too late."

"Will she help you prove all this?"

"No. I tried. She refused. She's terrified of Weihle, will feel I've betrayed her, and likely has already run for the hills. She's good at disappearing." Anger surged anew. How could Charlie hide, keeping silent? How could she run, leaving Weihle free and clear to torment other girls? She wasn't sixteen anymore.

Marcone spoke up. "Then we'll track her and subpoena her."

Mitch nodded. Hell, yes. Charlie would be easier to trace

this time. Her trail would be hot, and his personal knowledge of her invaluable. And the case against Weihle had wheels this time—witnesses, evidence, and his unique pedophile's signature.

Putting Weihle away wouldn't do Tiffany any good here on earth. But he would make damn sure she could rest in peace knowing that his particular brand of evil would stop.

CHAPTER 31

CHARLIE APPROACHED the automatic doors at Rolling Meadows, body tense, brain whirling. She couldn't believe she was actually, finally, here. The red-eye flight had gone off okay, but the rain delay in Washington, DC had prevented her connecting flight from boarding for several hours, making her want to climb out of her skin. She'd considered ditching the second half of the flight and driving instead, but she'd never driven on a highway and was terrified to learn at such a high rate of speed. Add in her agitated state, and she'd likely have a recipe for disaster. She'd made the right choice. Her first experience behind the wheel, from the Allentown airport's car rental agency to Blakes Ridge, had been hairy.

Now, with the car crookedly tucked into a parking spot, she took a deep breath and prayed she'd find her mom, right where she'd left her, right where she'd been picturing her for the last six years. She'd warred with checking on Mackenzie first, but suspected Thomas would be watching the child. Lying in wait for her. Once he'd found her, she might never know if her mom was still okay. Thomas had claimed Mackenzie would remain safe as long as Charlie came home. In the past, he'd never lied to her, even took perverse pleasure in only speaking the truth. She prayed that was still the case—otherwise, all bets were off.

Charlie had already decided that if the receptionist gave

her—Joanne Strinner—any trouble about visiting a patient who'd previously had no visitors, she'd confess who she really was—for could it matter at this point? Her name and face were plastered all over the news—national news, apparently, for she'd seen the footage herself in DC. She'd had to hide behind a magazine in a corner the whole layover. Surely Rolling Meadows would be glad to have Ellen's daughter finally paying a visit, and considering the media coverage, they'd understand why she'd attempt to enter under a false name.

However, she was conscious of the fact that Thomas paid regular visits to her mother. Accidentally bumping into him would be—she shuddered—horrid. She'd do better if she were prepared. More important, she did not want him alerted any earlier than necessary that she'd come home.

Oh, he'd know soon enough, she was sure. She planned to visit the Hudsons next to see if he left her any instructions and to find out—exactly—what he'd threatened, what he intended.

So first she needed assurance that her mother remained safe and sound, tucked away in her hospital bed, with a full staff of good people looking after her. She didn't think he needed the leverage of threatening her mother—not while he had Mackenzie dangling like a carrot. But then again, she never had been able to grasp the twisted cunning of Thomas Hadfield Weihle's mind. She had to be sure of the stakes, however, before she sacrificed herself, before she lost the little power and freedom that she'd gained. She had to know who she had to watch out for, who to protect—her mom? And Tiffany? Or was only the child in danger?

As it turned out, the reception desk sat unoccupied, and the foyer was quiet. Noise and activity buzzed through the open dining room doors past the lobby. That made sense. Her watch read 5:30 p.m., and seniors did live here. Charlie hustled into the hallway on the left, hoping that they hadn't switched Ellen's room or reorganized the layout.

A nurse approached from the other direction, hands full with a tray and a sheaf of papers tucked under her arm, but she just smiled and nodded, causing her big earrings to swing. Charlie forced her lips to curl upward in a greeting as the woman walked right past.

Charlie aimed for a room on the left toward the end of the corridor. Her chest felt tight, and her nerves were on edge. Please, please, let her mother be here, safe and sound.

She hugged the wall to her right, and peered into what she believed was her mother's room. Instead of entering, she strolled slowly past it, noting that the chair at the foot of the bed was empty—thank you, God. She looked over her shoulder— the hall remained quiet. Without further hesitation, she turned back and poked her head around the doorframe.

And let out a sigh of relief.

No one stood tucked into the deeper corners of the room, and this was indeed Ellen Macnamara's room. The framed photo she'd packed for her mom sat on the dresser. It was from the day they'd moved into the house on Dale Drive. Her mom wore a kerchief and a wide smile, her Dad was alive and well, and she was no more than two, wrapped around her mom's leg.

And this was how she loved her mother still—with a little girl's heart holding tight to memories made before she was old enough to appreciate them. She hadn't known her woman to woman. They hadn't had time to become friends.

Charlie moved to the head of the bed. She stayed to the right—less visible from the doorway—and sucked in a ragged breath. Her mom lay peacefully, covered by a lightweight blanket, hands over her middle, knobby and frail. And her hair had gone almost entirely gray. Yet her beautiful face looked just the same, lines no deeper on her face.

"Mom, I'm here," Charlie whispered, her voice cracking with emotion. She put her hands over her mouth and sobbed as quietly as she could manage.

She swiped at her cheeks, breathed deep, then grasped her mother's hands in her own.

"Mom, it's me…Laura…I'm sorry I've been gone so long. I wish I could tell you everything that's happened so you'd understand why I had to go, and why I chose to come back now."

What to say?

"I don't know how things are going to turn out. I'm here to…well, to fight evil, like a superhero. Unfortunately, I don't have any superpowers. Just maybe this time around, a friend or two in my corner, a few more years of wisdom, and a little more fortitude…I hope that somehow, this will all turn out okay, but if it doesn't, I won't be able to come back and see you."

She'd swear her mom's hands squeezed her own just slightly—she wished she'd open her eyes, too.

"Mom, I know he—Thomas Weihle—visits you. Don't trust him. Don't believe him. If you have any ounce of will left…" She'd spent some time cursing her mother's illness, her weakness, and had worked hard to come to terms with the reality of the situation. She shook her head at herself. Her mother had been powerless for so long, though Charlie always found a tiny nugget of hope to hold on to. "Well, just know he's bad news."

She could feel time ticking away, and took a deep breath.

"I have to go now, Mom. But please know, I love you, so much, and always will."

She squeezed her mom's hands once more, as hard as she dared, and tears welled up again. Then she slid free, stroked her mother's long gray hair once, and forced herself to leave her mother's room. It was time to face Thomas Hadfield Weihle.

Charlie ducked her head, swinging the red mane of hair forward, as she slipped into the lobby of Rolling Meadows. Before she'd reached the double doors, they slid open and a man barreled through them as if on a mission.

Holy shit. Not just any man. Mitch. Charlie's heart leapt, then faltered as she recalled their last argument.

Still, she'd done a lot of thinking since then. She'd forgiven him for exposing her. She herself had done everything in her power to protect her loved ones—of course, Mitch would have been compelled to do the same. And she had so many questions. Had he found Tiffany? Weihle? Was Mitch himself okay? What about his mom?

His eyes skimmed past her as he visually swept the room and angled toward the reception desk. Charlie took a step toward him, noting the haggard, yet wild look about him. Suddenly, his gaze swung back to her, tracing the bright hair and layers of clothes. He zeroed in on her face, and all rational thought deserted her.

"Mitch," she said, wanting to run to him and hold on tight.

"Charlie." He crossed the floor fast, and grasped her upper arms hard. "What the hell are you doing here?"

"I—I had to check on my mom."

"I've been checking on your mom. She's fine," he growled.

Charlie didn't understand his anger. "Listen, I understand why you did what you did with the media, and I forgive you."

He laughed—a mean, awful sound. Was Tiffany still missing, then?

"Did you get my letter? I'm ready to tell you the rest."

He shook her and shouted, "You're too late!" He let go abruptly.

Charlie scrambled to make sense of his anger. Tension emanated from him in waves. There wasn't a shred of softness in his eyes for her.

"Tiffany's dead."

Dead? Tiffany? No. It couldn't be. Her soul shrieked. She searched his eyes, saw the despair, the fury, and the—

"He killed her," Mitch spat. "You refused to help, and now it's way too fucking late."

That was it, what she saw on his face—blame. He broadcasted disgust and loathing, too, before he turned his shoulders and stalked off.

Charlie shrank inside, horrified. Sickened at this news. Wounded by his feelings. Humiliated at her selfishness, her shortsightedness. She deserved his venom and more.

As if through a block of ice—feet frozen in place, mind sluggish, hearing foggy—she realized Mitch was speaking to a shocked receptionist.

"Thomas Weihle visits Ellen Macnamara on Wednesdays." A murmur of assent from the woman, whose eyes grew even wider. "I doubt he'll show today, but we're not taking any chances. There's a warrant for his arrest, and there'll be an officer posted nearby. Notify me *immediately* if you see him or hear anything."

Charlie fought to breathe. Mitch was right, of course. If she'd come forward, spoken up, accused Weihle when Mitch had pleaded with her to do so...That letter was too little, too late. She'd failed Mitch and his sister. Tiffany was dead, and

Mackenzie was at even greater risk now that Weihle had escalated to murder.

Oh my God, her little girl. The ice shattered, freeing her. Charlie charged the doors, squeezed through sideways the second the gap was wide enough, and took off at a run. She had to find Mackenzie—now.

CHAPTER 32

CHARLIE RANG the Hudsons' bell once more, this time holding it hard. She pushed her cheap glasses—which fit exactly like you'd expect for five bucks—back up on her face. A car sat in the driveway, although she supposed the threesome could all be out somewhere together in another vehicle.

She jiggled her legs, finding it difficult to stand still while so exposed on the stoop. She ran her hands through the long red hair she wore, smoothing it forward to conceal her face.

This was a cookie-cutter-type neighborhood—the homes modern, with two- and three-car garages. Unless you were visiting, there was ample room to park on your own property. And Charlie could see no cars other than hers parked on the street. Still, she couldn't shake the worry that Thomas could be watching her right now.

The rental car from the airport sat at the curb on the opposite side of the street, as if a different family had a visitor. She driven a car only a handful of times in driver's ed on a simulator in school before she'd run. Now she could count an hour's drive from the airport to Rolling Meadows, and half an hour's drive from the nursing facility to here. She still couldn't profess to being comfortable behind the wheel. And, if she had to guess, she imagined she'd completely bomb a test. However, her Nevada driver's license suggested otherwise, securing her the rental.

Charlie looked up and down the street once more. She heard squeals of delight from some kids playing in one of the backyards a few houses down. It was feasible, she supposed, that Mackenzie could be there too, playing with friends, Pam chatting with the other moms.

Surely, if Thomas had threatened the Hudsons—and he had, because they wouldn't have sent that letter otherwise—they wouldn't be out enjoying the spring evening? They'd be in lockdown, or better yet, they'd have packed up and left.

Probably not, though. Charlie bit her bottom lip. Thomas could be so charming when a person first met him. Maybe the Hudsons didn't realize, or couldn't fathom, just what level of threat they faced. She'd tried to impart to them—way back when—how important it was that her own whereabouts—and Mackenzie's very existence—remain a secret.

"You don't understand," she'd said at age sixteen, gripping the receiver of the phone. She'd snuck into New Beginnings' office to call, but frustration made it a challenge to keep her voice to a whisper. "The father is dangerous. He beat me, and he'll do worse someday if he ever finds out I'm still alive!" she hissed.

"Okay, okay," Pamela said. "I saw the news reports, Laura. I believe you." She had transferred the call—their second conversation—from the floor of Macy's to the manager's office, but even still, her voice, too, was hushed. "Laura, we want the baby, so badly. But I have to say, even though I don't know exactly what the situation is, you should get help. The police are looking for you. Surely they can protect you."

"No, that's not an option." Laura knew without doubt. "This is the only way."

Pamela sighed. "All right, then. We have what you asked for."

Laura shut her eyes, torn between relief and heartbreak. "Then the baby is yours, if you promise me a few things."

"What?" Pamela had asked.

"I can't be part of the baby's life, but I…I'd really like pictures now and then. You know, like updates."

"Of course," Pamela had said, relief evident in her voice.

"But when I send you an address you have to keep it secret, hidden. If mail ever gets returned to you, just wait for another address."

"Okay."

"If ever anyone comes looking for me—*anyone*—you say I stopped showing up for work, and you've had zero contact with me since. You know absolutely nothing about what happened to me now, or ever."

"Laura, you have my word. And I speak for my husband, too."

"Okay." She exhaled hard. "Okay," she said again, calmer. "Thank you." Then she looked down at the bulge of her belly and smoothed her hand over the loaner maternity top. "I'll call you when the baby is born. You'll have to come to me, in secret, because I can't come back there."

Charlie hadn't imagined then that she'd ever be standing one day on Pamela Hudson's stoop—bursting to meet Mackenzie just once, while simultaneously fearing the worst.

Charlie frowned and clanked the knocker a few times. Unfortunately, all she had was this address. Because she'd always been on the move and didn't own a phone, she'd never exchanged numbers with Mackenzie's parents.

Thomas simply would not have allowed them to leave. No matter what. And what really had her gut clenching was that line from the letter: *the child's safety depends on you.* Had they believed him? She'd taken the words at face value herself, at first. But knowing about Tiffany changed everything. What Thomas might consider "safe" should terrify anyone in their right mind.

And how long would Thomas have waited for her return? She'd checked the post box only days before she found the letter, so she knew it couldn't have been there more than a few days. Still...

Envelopes stuck out of the Hudsons' mailbox mounted to the bricks at her right shoulder. She looked around again. All the blinds were closed tight. The thumping of her pulse gained momentum.

Charlie hustled down the steps and headed for the garage. She raised up on tiptoes to peek in. Another car. The bad feeling she'd been bracing for grew like the stain from a bottle of wine tipped over onto one of Cleo's white tablecloths. She yanked with two hands on the oversized garage door handle, felt the strain across her shoulders. Locked, probably automatic.

She sprinted back up the front stoop and pounded frantically with the knocker, then tried the knob. No luck. Charlie placed both hands on the red paint of the front door to calm herself. *Think, think,* she ordered. *What next?*

A faint noise registered through her panic. Charlie froze, listening.

There it was again. She looked around, but saw nothing. The sound was indistinct and almost rhythmic, but not quite. A muffled pounding? From inside the house?

"Oh, no," Charlie said, and moved to the windows. All the shades were drawn; she couldn't see a thing.

"Pamela? Ray!" she yelled, and pounded on the glass, then stood still to listen. The noise from inside picked up tempo.

In vain, she jiggled the door handle again, pushed at win-

dows. She ran around the back of the house and up onto the
deck, her satchel bumping her hip awkwardly. Another locked
door. A window fastened tight.

Her breathing came hard and fast. If Thomas was inside,
he'd have opened the door wide and escorted her in with a
cat-who-ate-the-canary grin. So it must be one, or both, of
the Hudsons. Could they be locked in a closet? Wounded and
bleeding somewhere and unable to walk or yell?

Horrible possibilities—each worse than the last—flew
through her mind and drove her to action.

She yanked her fashionable scarf off and wrapped it
around and around her hand. It wasn't thick, but like this, she
hoped, thick enough to do the trick.

"I'm coming in!" she yelled, and then, as hard as she could,
hit the glass panes of the door with her fist. "Owww!" she cra-
dled her hand. The glass was too thick.

She tried kicking it with the heel of her sturdy boot, but
the panes were too high for her to get good leverage.

Charlie spun frantically, looking for something she could
use.

She lunged for the heavy wooden brush peeking out from
under a covered grill. She lined up as if she had a bat, and
swung hard.

Crash! The glass smashed. She used the wire brush to
knock out a larger hole, her hand still wrapped with the scarf.
She reached in, fumbled for the doorknob, and managed
to unlock it. Although the handle twisted easily, the door
wouldn't budge.

A deadbolt. *Damn.* Again she swung, smashed a pane
higher up, reached in, and felt around.

"Finally!" she cried as her fingers found metal. She flipped
the toggle, turned the handle, and the door gave.

Charlie rushed in, grill brush held high like a weapon. Wildly she spun, looking around the kitchen, but the room was clean and quiet.

"Where are you?" she yelled.

Pounding resumed, much louder now, and close. Charlie followed her ears through the kitchen to the hallway. It was coming from a door. She put her hand on the knob, clutched the grill tool in the other, thought, *Please, no blood*, and yanked.

Pamela sat just a few feet below her on the wooden stairs leading to the basement. Her hands were bound to the wooden railing with duct tape. Her mouth was taped, and her ankles, too. She wore capri pajamas, a matching top and pants. Ray, Charlie realized, was secured the same way near the bottom step, clad in only his boxers.

Pam sobbed, the muffled noise snorting through her nose as tears filled her eyes.

"Is he here—in the house?" Charlie asked. Pam sobbed again, but shook her head vigorously.

The grill brush clattered to the floor as Charlie exhaled hard. She went down a few steps, squatted, and yanked the tape off Pamela's mouth.

"He's got her! He's got her!" sobbed Pamela.

No shit, Charlie thought, but kept her mouth shut as she clambered down the steps and did the same for Ray.

"You got the letter, but he didn't give you enough time," he said.

"I'm getting a knife," she said, and took the stairs two at a time to the kitchen.

Charlie yanked open drawers, her heart beating fast. They were all alive, at least.

Ray's wrists were red and swollen from struggling, and she

could see that he'd nearly loosened the banister from the wall. The moment he was free, he climbed up to Pamela and held her, while Charlie sawed at the heavy wrap of tape binding her wrists.

"How long since he left?" she asked.

Ray shook his head. "I'm not sure. He came in the middle of the night." His face contorted. "I never heard him until he held a cloth over my face. I tried to throw him off, but I lost consciousness so fast."

"It was after three a.m., but still dark out," Pamela said, her voice rusty. "I made it to the doorway. He got me, too, and then there was nothing I could do." She flexed her fingers, as Charlie worked on her ankles.

Both of them started talking at once.

"Where did he take her?"

"Who is he?"

"What do we do?"

"We have to call the police."

"Stop." Charlie held up her hands. "Let's get off the stairs, and I'll tell you what I can."

She ushered them up and herded them toward the kitchen. There was a cup on the counter. She filled it with tap water and handed it to Pamela.

The woman's hand shook, yet she took it and gulped before passing it to her husband.

"His name is Thomas Hadfield Weihle. He is Mackenzie's biological father." She took a deep breath. "I don't think he'll hurt her."

"How can you say that?" Pamela's voice rose to a screech. "You ran away and gave her to us because he was so dangerous!"

And they didn't even know about Tiffany, Charlie thought.

"Yes. But hurting her right away is not his way. He'll need

to get to know her first. And it's possible that he won't hurt her ever, because she's his flesh and blood." God, how she prayed she was right.

"You can't know what he'll do. He's insane!" Ray slammed the cup on the counter—luckily it was plastic.

"You don't know him like I do. He's got his own screwed up moral code."

"I'm calling the cops, now!" Ray said, and moved toward the phone.

"Wait—" Charlie said.

"Wait? No! There's no more protecting you! All I care about is getting our daughter back safe!" he roared.

"There's no protecting me, or any of us, now," Charlie said. "I want her safe as much as you. I didn't mean don't call—just don't call 911. There's a detective who'll be more help, and faster." Charlie flipped open her satchel and dug through it. "It'll take too long to explain to somebody else. This guy, Mitch Saunders, knows all about Weihle, and about me. He just doesn't know about Mackenzie or you." She gave Ray the paper.

She looked them both in the eye. "It's me Thomas wants, so he'll be at his house, right where I can find him. I'm going after her. I'll bargain with him. Mackenzie for me. Tell the detective."

"I'm coming with you," Ray insisted, and shoved the paper at Pamela.

"No. That will only make it more dangerous for both of us. One way or another, no matter what I have to do, I swear to you I will keep Mackenzie safe." She smiled grimly and clasped Ray's shoulder. "I need you alive and well to raise her when this is all over."

"You can't win against him by yourself."

"I won't be alone for long," she said, praying she was right. "Detective Saunders will help, except I can't wait around." Charlie squeezed closed the fissure of doubt that threatened. Mitch was bigger than anger or blame—she knew that when she used her head instead of her broken heart. Besides, this would deliver him Weihle wrapped up with proof of kidnapping in one tidy bow.

She changed gears. "Now, did Thomas give you any messages for me?"

"No, he was gone before we came to," Ray said.

"What about before? When you wrote the letter? Anything I should know?"

They looked at each other. Came up with nothing.

"Okay," she said as she blew out the breath she'd been holding.

"What if they aren't there?" Pamela asked, hands twisting. "What if he disappeared with her?"

Charlie shook her head and dug into her bag. "I'm telling you, he's not going anywhere." She grimaced. "At least not until I've *come home where I belong*." She slapped the letter they'd written her on the kitchen counter.

Then she turned, crunching on shattered glass, stepped out the back door—which was still wide open—and hustled down the deck stairs.

Charlie yelled over her shoulder, "Give Saunders the whole truth. He knows where Weihle's house is. Tell him he'll find us there."

———

Thomas padded briskly along the carpeted hallway, torn between anticipation and worry. Although he'd calculated her weight correctly, the sleeping beauty pill he'd given Mackenzie had yet to wear off. She must have a sensitivity to one of the elements—a fact he must remember in future. He'd checked on her dozens of times today, but she hadn't once come to—and it was now early evening. The cotton candy room—as he'd begun thinking of the pink and yellow concoction—sat at the end of the hallway.

The little-girl décor had turned out so sweet—such a shame that Mackenzie would only be able to enjoy it briefly. Pinks and yellows, all soft and fuzzy…he sighed. To some degree, decorating had been a waste of time and effort, yet he'd wanted things to be just so for her, and even for conniving Laura. The way they should have been all along.

Excitement built within him as he took the key from his pocket for the small padlock he'd put on the door. Oh, how he longed to speak with Mackenzie, face to face, as father and daughter for the first time.

He pushed the door open gently and looked toward the bed. Mackenzie no longer lay there. Neither did the ratty lovey—a small bunny—she'd clenched when he'd rescued her. He bent—not under the four-poster, either. When Thomas stepped toward the closet, he realized the room wasn't quite as he'd left it. A giant pink bear and a fuzzy yellow chair had been pushed together in the corner. His smart girl hid behind them. Only her toes and part of her face were visible. Her eyes were wide and frozen, fixed on him.

"Ah, there you are, sweet girl." He smiled.

She scowled and tried to scoot back further, her bare toes curling under.

"You are quite good at hide-and-seek." Thomas approached slowly, bent down on one knee, then sat back on his heel, giving her a bit more space.

"And I see you've made friends with Miss Sugarpie. I got her just for you." He rubbed the bear's belly.

"You're from the grocery store," Mackenzie said.

"Yes, and, you know, I do have some of that Frosty Cake ice cream in the freezer downstairs." Thomas was pleased she'd remembered him. "When you decide to come out, I could bring you a bowl. A special treat, ice cream *before* dinner." He winked and flashed his most non-threatening smile.

She frowned. "I want my mommy and daddy."

Thomas cocked his head.

"You and I need to have a serious talk. Those people that you call Mommy and Daddy weren't really your parents."

"That's not true!" she said, her face mottling between the stuffed guards.

Logically, he knew that she'd need a lot of time to come to terms with the falsehoods she'd been led to believe. Irritation prickled anyway.

"It is true, darling. They stole you from your real daddy—me."

Mackenzie lunged out from behind the animals and pummeled at his chest with her small fists. Thomas was so shocked at her vehemence that at first, he just accepted the pounding. Wide-eyed, he felt his heart swell with admiration for her spunk and fire. Shortly, however, he'd had enough.

He grabbed her upper arms, turned her back to him, and penned her in tight in a bear hug. He murmured soothing words, shifting left and right, rocking as rhythmically as he could manage as she fought. Mackenzie thrashed and screamed like an Amazon-sized banshee lived inside her small form.

Thomas began to panic—he couldn't have the cops next door investigating this noise. He shoved her off his lap and onto the floor. Surprised, she quieted for a moment. He scrambled backward, held up his hands to show he wouldn't touch her, then stood and moved toward the door.

She took a big breath—aiming to scream again, he was sure. "I'll leave!" he said. "I'll leave if you stop screaming. Okay?"

Her brows lowered and her eyes narrowed while she determined if she believed him.

Thomas didn't wait. "I'll be back in a little while to leave you some food. I'll bring the ice cream just as I said I would, but you must eat some dinner, too. I'll set it up like a picnic for you and the animals."

Mackenzie pressed her lips into a thin line but didn't move or speak.

He cracked open the door. "Why don't you hide again until then, okay?"

He slipped out, shut the door fast, and snapped the padlock until he heard a metallic click. Listening to the blessed silence that followed, he heaved a sigh of relief.

Screaming simply would not do. Not here.

Surely, when Laura arrived, he could use them—mother and child—to keep the other in line.

CHAPTER 33

CHARLIE'S NERVES had been jamming on high since Mitch had left California. The fight with him, the shock of the media showing up, the horror she'd felt upon receiving Thomas's letter, the fear of returning to that nightmare, the worry for her mother, the realization that she could likely have saved Tiffany's life, the release of the Hudsons, and the subsequent terror knowing Mackenzie was in his clutches...

But the scene that awaited her on Dale Drive sent her into a new realm of panic. She braked too hard in the little rental, her body surging toward the steering wheel, as she absorbed the chaos ahead through the early dusk of evening. Patrol cars lined the street; flashing lights bounced like a carnival on hyper-speed; cops zigzagged all over Thomas's yard.

The sun had nearly set, yet here everything seemed too bright as her mind rushed with terrible images. Had Weihle killed Mackenzie? Was he holding her hostage? Had the Hudsons reached Mitch already? Was he in there—facing off against Thomas?

A blockade was set up. She jerked the vehicle—she hadn't gotten any better at driving during the mad trek from the Hudsons' to here—to the curb on the left side of the street. Then she jumped out and ran to the cop guarding the road.

"What happened?"

"I'm sorry, ma'am."

Her hand flew to her mouth, and her eyes filled instantly. "Oh my God," she said, as her brain worked overtime. "Did someone die?"

"No, no. It's all right." He held both hands up. He had a young face with kind eyes. "Nobody died."

Charlie's breath whooshed from her lungs, and she shifted her hand to her stomach.

The officer added, "We have a warrant for this house and the resident who lives here. Do you know him?"

"Sorry, all this…" She waved a hand at the scene behind the officer. "It looked really awful." She took a breath, gathered her wits, and took a calculated guess. "No, I don't know who even lives there. My grandparents' house is over there. I came to check on them. I worry about them so much. Can I pass?"

He looked from her to the house she'd pointed at. She held her breath. Did the Rogers still live there? Or, God willing, some other elderly couple? He checked his clipboard, and then nodded.

"Should I just leave the car here?"

"Yes, that's best. Just stay out of the fray on your way through, okay?" He gave her a stern look, then shifted his belt on his hips.

"Of course," she said, and hustled back to her car to grab her bag. At the last minute, she thought better of it and stuffed the satchel beneath the seat. She couldn't stomach her few remaining valuables sitting in plain sight as if they were up for grabs. However, if Mitch was looking and saw the contents, he'd know for certain that she was here.

Charlie stepped around the patrolman and his blockade. If she kept on past Weihle's, she'd pass her old house, one more, and then the elderly couple's home. Except she had no intention of going that far.

She'd hug the left side of the road where nobody had ever ended up building houses, although the lots had always been for sale. Oh how she'd wished as a young child that playmates would move in. Later, when it had become clear that her neighbor was a real-life monster, she'd prayed that no other little girls would ever, ever come to Dale Drive. A couple of trees remained, and somebody'd planted a few bushes. Not much in the way of cover, though with all the focus on Weihle's property, she thought she could step a few yards into the empty lots, just out of the ricocheting lights, without anybody noticing her.

She crunched through weeds, checking over her shoulder, but nobody even glanced in her direction.

Alone for a moment, leaning against a tree, she took a deep breath and raised her eyes above the activity on the ground. A shudder skidded over her, leaving goose bumps in its wake.

Thomas's house hadn't changed at all. Tan siding, black shutters, a perfectly landscaped yard. And always, the candles in the windows. Only she knew that the quaint colonial touch—Christmas all year round—spoke of evil intent.

It had been her job to watch his house, check his windows every night. Whenever a light had been left off, one would assume a burnt-out bulb or a room missed. In actuality, it was a signal. Thomas required her presence.

Sometimes, he'd already given her instructions for the next visit—to build the anticipation, he said. Sometimes, she'd find a box or gift bag on her stoop—lingerie or a mask. Sometimes, her stomach would plunge upon opening an item she didn't even know the use for…yet.

Old feelings of hatred, and fear, and powerlessness swamped her. Yet this time, she didn't suffer only for herself. She thought of the Hudsons' panic and the confusion and terror their—her—beautiful Mackenzie must be feeling. Her heart squeezed in agony.

She ground her teeth. She didn't have time to give in to the maelstrom of crippling feelings.

There was no way in hell that she'd let Thomas Weihle get away with this. She'd never allow him to ruin Mackenzie's life like he had hers. She'd do everything in her power to return the little girl to her parents. Furthermore, some way, somehow, after she got Mackenzie and herself free of the pervert, she'd make sure he'd never hurt another child again. She owed that and more to Tiffany. Like Henrietta had said—sometimes you have to face your demons. Stand and fight.

She wasn't the same stuck girl she'd been, always struggling under the yoke of so much responsibility, always bargaining for her and her mother's welfare, and trying—unsuccessfully, in the end—to keep the two of them together. Her mother was safe, and she herself had come a long way, baby. This was the time, her turn, to fight back, and win.

She scanned the crowd for Mitch's tall form. Could he ever forgive her? She ached with the need to lean on him, to bury her head in the crook of his shoulder and let him keep her safe, keep them all safe, as he'd once promised. Would he comfort her—or push her away?

No matter. She was on her own anyway. The cop at the barricade hadn't mentioned a missing child, only the search for the resident. Which meant the Hudsons hadn't yet reached Mitch.

For Mackenzie's sake, she had to figure out her next move

quickly. The sky was nearly full dark now. The sun hadn't quite set, but neither had the moon risen.

Tonight, all the candles in Thomas's house were lit. Good thing, because she couldn't have gotten past that many cops when his property was lit up like the aisles of a grocery store. She had only the letter from him, and next to no useful information from Pamela and Ray.

Frustrated, she gripped the bark of the tree with her fingers, as her brain darted around dead ends. She'd never even considered that she wouldn't find Thomas here in his house, with Mackenzie, waiting patiently for her arrival. She was sure he'd meant for her to come to Blakes Ridge, to Dale Drive, and right into his bed to do his bidding. He'd have been here if it wasn't for the cops looking for him.

Charlie dug for the letter in her blazer pocket and then remembered that she'd left it with the Hudsons. Proof of some sort, if she didn't make it out of this. She'd read the cryptic message over and over on the plane. Now, the words replayed like a sick mantra in her head.

Mackenzie's true father.

The child's safety depends on you.

Return home where you belong.

Home: she'd never thought she'd see it again, never dreamed—

Her gaze shifted reluctantly to the home that had been hers. Like everyone else, she'd been so focused on Thomas's house, she'd paid no attention to her own.

Blinds and curtains were drawn, but a golden glow seeped through the seams.

All the lights were on—save one.

Charlie stared at the dark window. Fingers wrapped

around fabric and the edge of a curtain pulled to the side. A figure stood still, a black silhouette against murky dark. She couldn't see his face, but knew in her soul—he watched and he smiled.

She felt his sinister gaze grip her, like a giant black fist, squeezing out her breath, and causing her vision to swim.

She gasped for air and clutched the tree, leaning into the solid, scratchy trunk. The helter-skelter feeling receded just enough.

Every molecule in her body fought against it. Nonetheless, Charlie forced her feet to move—toward Thomas Weihle, rather than running far, far away.

She didn't dare go to the front door where the light over the stoop blazed. She may as well borrow a spotlight and a bullhorn from the police and announce her presence. Surely that didn't fit into Thomas's plans.

So she clenched her fists, skittered across the street, and then slowed in the shadows as she moved along the driveway that had once been hers. The cops appeared to be focused on Weihle's house. She saw numerous men with broad shoulders, all of them facing away from her, some in uniform, some in plainclothes, yet still no sign of Mitch. She felt a crazed urge to run, alert them to the danger lurking next door, and beg them to call him, but she feared Thomas's retaliation. If he hurt Mackenzie…

No, she couldn't risk it. Thomas might harm the child or escape with her. He'd have a backup plan, or two, or three. Oh, how she wished she knew what she'd find inside, but as always, wishing was pointless. She simply had to pray that Mackenzie was okay, and that he held her here, and not at another location.

Charlie's only hope was to go inside, play his game, and

bide her time until she could somehow free them both. That, or Mitch would eventually come for them. If only she could let him know to go to her old house—not Thomas's. Deep inside, she knew he wouldn't rest until he'd found them—the trick would be staying alive until then.

She hesitated at the corner of the house, peeked around first with her head. The garage doors were closed, and there were no lights. Did she dare take a moment to leave Mitch a clue? Yes, she must, but what? She'd love to hang the wig on a branch like a beacon even in the dark of night, but Thomas had spotted her; he'd expect to see her wearing the long red mane. In her panic, she'd left her bag in the car, so she dug through her pockets. Her boarding pass. Mitch wouldn't know the name, but the departure city read San Francisco. She left it folded in quarters—less chance it'd blow away—and watched it sink to the ground, a flat white rectangle—near the size of a playing card—against black pavement. Charlie's brain registered that with an oddly normal thought—someone had finally paved over the gravel.

Mitch would connect the dots, if—big if—they extended their search just thirty feet. Then she took a deep breath and stepped forward past the cover of the house and into the rear section of the driveway.

Charlie's breath stalled in her throat. She'd been focused on the house itself before, but she saw now that a swing set stood at the far end of the yard—not the old metal one she'd played on that had rocked up out of the ground with a suck and a thump when you got high enough. This was new— wooden and colorful with a slide, climbing equipment, and a tented top. If it hadn't been for all the artificial light generated by the authorities next door, she might have missed the play area entirely.

Did children live here now? Had Thomas become close
to them? Where were they now? My God, what had he done?

And just what on earth was she going to find inside this
house?

Charlie's breath came suddenly in pants. She talked herself out of losing it. Thomas wasn't the mass-murdering type.
He preferred to act behind the scenes like a puppet master,
controlling every soul, twisting the show and the players at
his whim.

Maybe the family was away. Maybe he'd blackmailed them
somehow and forced them to leave. Mitch had told her the
house had eventually gone into foreclosure. Maybe Thomas
had bought it himself—that would be just like him to plan
for her eventual return. That wouldn't explain the play set,
though. Unless he had other girls—children—he aimed to
entice.

No, she couldn't go there. Right now, she could only help
this one—Mackenzie, her own child. She moved with leaden
legs toward the door next to the garage. The utility room.
There was no light behind the thick squares of block glass, but
she knew she'd find it unlocked.

The time had come. *Mitch*, she thought, *don't make me do
this alone. Hurry!*

———

"Uh, Officers," said Harvey Ballas, Weihle's managing director at Novatru Pharmaceuticals, after surveying the warrant
Mitch produced, "you'll want to leave your cell phones and
wallets here in the lobby, or better yet, in your cars."

The director functioned more as a group leader than a
boss—as Ballas himself was quick to point out—and headed

up Weihle's research and development group, which targeted specific types of breast cancer. Weihle's career choice appeared saint-like, just as visiting Ellen Macnamara religiously at Rolling Meadows had, but Mitch knew well that appearances, especially Thomas Weihle's, could be deceiving.

"Care to explain?" Mitch asked.

Ballas was a scarecrow type through and through. Six foot three and stoop-shouldered, with stringy hair and wrists that snuck out of a fleece marked over the heart with the Novatru logo. He shrugged. "The NMR instrument in the lab is essentially four thousand megahertz of magnet. It can wipe all your electronic data within ten feet."

After stashing their valuables in their vehicles, Ballas led them to Weihle's workspace—both a lab and an office—flipping on lights as he went. At eight p.m., they had the place to themselves.

Mitch took a look at the office. Standard fare consisting of a built-in desk in an L-shape with a computer monitor front and center, a file cabinet, and a row of plants on the windowsill. The desktop was neat and tidy. Mitch would bet money the insides of the drawers were as well. Framed diplomas lined the wall—bachelor's, master's, and even a Ph.D. for the sick perp. Just went to show you that education couldn't eradicate evil.

"Ryder. You take the office."

"Boring," the officer quipped.

"You never know. We'll take the computer in," Mitch responded, but he suspected Ryder was right. Paydirt would be in the lab. They had various suspicious-looking pills and tablets from Weihle's house. In no time, they'd have Tiff's tox screen back as well. Mitch had a good feeling for once—something would match. If they scored here at his workplace too, even proved the possibility that he could have manufactured drugs here? Then—bam. Slam dunk.

Mitch and Amenilo followed Ballas past a few more offices, until they reached a large rectangular room with a long workstation in the middle. Refrigeration units filled a corner, and rows upon rows of drawers lined the walls with open shelves mounted like stairs above them. Mitch could see boxes of gloves and syringes, stacks of petri dishes—apparently he remembered something from high school—and beakers in more sizes than he ever imagined existed.

Amenilo pointed to a big, sealed glass box with gloves you could reach your hands into. She asked, "Is that the NMR machine?"

"No. That's the Glove Box. It's filled with nitrogen gas to conduct certain tests without moisture. The NMR is that one." He pointed to a cylindrical contraption. "It helps us read our various test results through a series of peaks that show up on the computer screen there."

Mitch could tell Ballas was dumbing things down for them—just as well; the scientific details weren't exactly what he was after here. Plus, he fought distraction, constantly squashing down images of Tiffany's broken body. Even the shock and hurt on Charlie's face haunted him. How could he want to crush her to him, soothe the hurt he'd dealt her, then send her packing far away from Weihle—and still want to lash out for her part in the mess? And Weihle—Mitch worked overtime to keep a tight lid on his rage toward that sicko. Not easy. He had to focus. He believed evidence in this lab would seal the case against the bastard.

"Give us an idea of how the chemists work in the space," Amenilo suggested, yanking his attention back to the conversation.

"Okay, well." Ballas pushed his glasses up on his nose. "The bench there, with all the flasks and solvents, burners and whatnot, is where the team would do most of their work. The hood there"—he pointed out an oversized glass box— shatterproof, Mitch guessed—built into the bench with a handle on the front—"is where anything potentially toxic would be done. There are showers there, and the eye wash too..." After a rundown of the space, Ballas twisted his hands together. "I'm not sure exactly what you mean to find, but there won't be any fingerprints. We gear up when we enter— always a lab coat, safety goggles, and latex gloves, of course."

"It's a given that Weihle works here, so fingerprints aren't that important," Mitch said. "You saw the warrant, so you've likely gathered that we suspect he's been making drugs. Could be heroine or meth, maybe roofies or ecstasy. We're not sure, but that's what I'm looking to confirm."

"Weihle's a little off...I've never warmed to him." Ballas shifted on the balls of his feet. "But he's so...snobby, really, that I just can't imagine him selling street drugs, risking his job, his whole career."

"We don't believe he sold any drugs, Mr. Ballas. We're just looking for proof that he made them." The man nodded, and Mitch continued, "I'm going to need a list and contact numbers of all the other scientists that work here with Weihle. But first, tell me what kind of checks and balances you have here in the lab. For instance, would Weihle have been able to log time alone here, maybe after hours?"

"Lots of us work late—it's practically a job requirement these days, but no, because of toxic accidents, you must have at least two people in the lab at all times." Ballas crossed to the bench and grabbed a notebook. He handed it to Mitch, and raised somber gray eyes to look directly at him. "I'm embarrassed to even admit this, but it is possible—even easy—to do what you are asking."

Mitch raised his eyebrows and glanced at Amenilo, who wore the same expression. "How?" he asked.

Ballas cleared his throat. "Everything a chemist does is noted in his logbook. Unfortunately, that's not to say that he couldn't log in one compound, but actually add another."

Mitch smiled for the first time in ages. *Bam*, he thought.

Now he just had to find the fucker—something he was more than happy to do.

CHAPTER 34

CHARLIE GRASPED the knob with a shaking hand and twisted until the mechanism slid free. She pushed the door open.

The space that greeted her had her mind reeling backward through time. Although the open door barely illuminated the room, she could see that no one had touched this space. Her body remembered just how to slide past the support post in the middle of the space—a pass-through between the tiny laundry room and the rest of the house—without clonking her elbow or hip. Surely she could even still manage it with a laundry basket under one arm.

Charlie paused at the threshold to the short hallway. Would she find that the rest of the house was exactly the same? The thought gave her the willies.

"Laura."

She jumped. Thomas stood mere feet to her left, leaning against the doorframe to the kitchen. She stood stock still with fright, although her pulse broke speed records.

"I was hoping you'd call out, 'Honey, I'm home,'" he cooed.

Charlie couldn't quite see his eyes, but his voice vibrated with excitement.

"I'm not playing your games anymore," she said, although if she had no other choice, she'd do just that.

"Oh, but you are, my sweet." Thomas stepped forward, and

she moved back a pace before she caught herself. She wasn't as well trained as she used to be.

He grasped her chin in his hand and yanked it up. She felt the anger in the movement, and knew she'd better tread carefully. In the past, he'd been gentlemanly during their encounters—almost always. The cops outside must have him on edge. Or maybe his simmering fury over her leaving had a boiling point—and they'd reached it.

He hadn't aged much, but his face was harder, and his eyes glinted with a scary mix of hatred and wanting. His arm flew up. She flinched, her eyes snapping shut, and instinctively turned away.

Her head was yanked to one side, and then snapped back again—but he'd only pulled off her wig.

"Disgusting," he snarled, "what you've done to yourself." He eyed up her blond hair, which surely must be matted to her scalp by now. "Please tell me I won't find a tattoo somewhere as well." *No*, she thought, *I've spent years avoiding identifying marks.* The hand that still held her chin squeezed the bones of her jaw hard, then he traced his thumb along her lower lip.

She refrained from biting him, and instead twisted out of his grasp.

"You've gained some fight." His smile was pure malice. "You know how a challenge increases my enjoyment."

"Where's Mackenzie?"

"Ah, finally—a little motherly concern."

She narrowed her eyes. "If you've hurt her—"

"You know me better than that, my dear. I haven't hurt her—in fact, I've saved her. Those imbeciles you left her with don't even know how to keep her safe." His eyes glinted. "How could you, Laura? Give away our child?"

Charlie blinked. Anything she said would be wrong in his eyes.

"You abandoned her. Left me. Tore apart what could have been a beautiful nuclear family." He shook his head in disgust. "And your poor mother. Six years have passed, and I remain astounded at the callousness of your actions."

He leaned back against the wall and crossed his arms.

Did he think they had all the time in the world? Maybe they did, since letting him talk was buying time for Mitch to catch up. Still, she ached to lay eyes on Mackenzie and assure herself that she was—at least physically, if Thomas spoke the truth—unharmed.

"Poor choices on your part, and gravely miscalculated, too," Thomas said. "I've gone round and round about how you should be punished."

She couldn't help it—she flinched.

"Ah, perhaps you, too, have some ideas." A grin showed perfect white teeth. "Oh, my Laura, how I've missed you." Then he laughed.

Charlie gritted her teeth. He always was a sick fuck. Maybe she could work that toward her purpose.

"Since you are so looking forward to…spending time with me, I offer myself to you—in exchange for Mackenzie."

Thomas merely smiled. "Besides the fact that I hold all the cards here, I want her as much as I want you."

Charlie's stomach plummeted. "You can't—"

"We are meant to be a family."

"Thomas." She kept her voice soft, trying another tack. "I really would like to see Mackenzie. I've waited a long time. Does she…" Charlie ducked her head.

"Does she remember you?" he asked.

"No, there's no chance of that. I wondered"—she paused for effect—"if she looks like me at all?"

Thomas reached for her face, tracing a finger along her cheekbone. "Just like you as a child." His face lit up. "Utterly captivating."

Then, without warning, he knelt before her. Charlie tensed, but he grasped her hips and pulled her toward him. His fingers dug in hard, bruising the skin over her hipbones, she was sure. One hand let go, to spread her jacket and lift up the hem of her top. He smoothed his hand over her skin, then nuzzled his face against her belly.

Charlie's skin crawled, but she held her ground. If they hadn't been in a hallway, if there'd been something to grab to clobber him over the head with…but so far, she'd discovered squat about Mackenzie…and if she wasn't here, she had to find out where she was.

"I would have loved to see my child growing within you. To think of my seed, making you round with life," he murmured. "You robbed me, Laura." His voice turned hard, his words clipped. Abruptly, he stood to look her in the eye.

"We'll remedy that," he said. "In fact, we'll start working on another child this very night."

Dread slid over Laura. The thought of him inside her, his aim to impregnate her, the possibility—no matter how small—that he'd succeed and see her swell months from now, holding her captive somehow all that time… She fought hard not to shudder, and she succeeded. But she couldn't hold his eyes, because inside she trembled with horror.

He chuckled. "Darling, don't worry. You'll feel so much more maternal when you see our little girl. She's an absolute angel, and, although you've made regrettable choices in the past, I'll be here to keep you in line."

"Can I see her now?"

"Soon." He tilted his head and looked her up and down. "As soon as you are presentable."

————

The warm water sluicing down Charlie's back was no relief from the tension. Thomas had pulled off the decorative curtain, and now he leaned against the wall—watching her shower through the clear liner. The water was tepid only—he didn't want steam to impede his view.

"Please," he said, "that hair." He handed her a bottle from the end of the tub. She squeezed it into her palm, passed it back, and raised her arms to her head.

She saw his small smile as he feasted his eyes on her breasts.

"You've filled out nicely, darling. Less coltish, more curvy, with maturity. Or perhaps from pregnancy?" He raised an eyebrow.

She closed her eyes and tried to breathe. She soaped and rinsed her hair, as quickly as possible, trying to block him out and focus only on the routine task. When she opened her eyes, she discovered that he held out a bar of soap.

"Your breasts need attention."

Woodenly, she accepted the soap and spun the oval between her hands. When it was slippery, she set it aside and placed her right hand over her heart. The other fell to her side.

He cocked his head to the side. "Both hands, I think." Charlie did as he said. She knew what was expected of her, but God, how she wanted to fast forward. She lowered her lids, once again attempting to shut him out.

"Slowly now, my pet. Hmmn, yes, that feels good, doesn't it?"

Tears squeezed from under her lashes. So that he wouldn't see, she leaned further under the spray.

"Ah, the way the water winds around your nipples, it's divine. But I ache to see you spread the soap lower."

Charlie did as he said, but a sob escaped.

He smiled. "You were aching for this, weren't you, darling?"

She didn't speak. He could pretend whatever he wanted. She was dying inside—certainly not from desire, not even from fear—but from the past, rising up, swamping her.

No! She refused to let this happen all over again. She'd do whatever she had to until he produced Mackenzie. Once he'd taken her to the child—wherever she was—this sick game was over. Weak, terrified, little girl Laura would quit playing along and would disappear forever. She—Charlie—would fight with everything she had to put an end to Weihle's power, with or without Mitch's help.

———

By the time Mitch exited Novatru's pharma building, the tally of missed calls on his cell totaled forty-three from three different local numbers. Fifteen messages. With Marcone looking after his mom, he was free to hunt down Thomas Weihle. Beyond that, he didn't much care who was trying to reach him. But, being a cop, he checked anyway. He peeled out, anxious to get over to Dale Drive, and hit speed dial to voicemail as soon as the hands-free device connected.

He frowned at the first message coming through his speaker—a loud, incoherent mess of blubbering from a woman about a missing child. The second message was more of the same. He thought he caught the names Laura and Mackenzie. Mitch sat up straighter, as if he'd hear better that way. The third from a man, also frantic, but clear. Their child had been abducted by Thomas Weihle. Laura—*Beep!*—had told them to—*Beep!* Mitch tore his eyes from the road to look at the number of the call coming in, while his mind spun through a series of cusses.

Another girl in Weihle's clutches? Right now? Could the man possibly mean Laura Macnamara? Charlie?

The beep of the call waiting was them, one of the three missed numbers. He jabbed the green button on the truck's display with his thumb.

"This is Saunders."

"Thank God!" a female voice screeched. "You have to help us. Our daughter—oh my God."

"Who is this?" Mitch gripped the wheel hard. The voice was the same as on the message.

"Pamela Hudson! My baby's been taken. Please help!"

"Ma'am, I've only just gotten your message—"

"So much time has passed already!"

"Ma'am—"

"You have to hurry!"

"Pamela!" Mitch barked. "Stay calm! Tell me the details."

He heard a sob, a scuffle, and a muffled, yet still overwrought, "Here, you talk." A male voice came through the line. "Detective?"

"Yes, Detective Mitch Saunders. Who's this?"

"Ray Hudson."

"The husband of Pamela and father of the missing child?"

"Yes."

"All right, Ray. I've only just gotten to my phone and your

call interrupted me while I was attempting to sort through your messages. I need you to stay calm and explain to me, from the beginning, what's happened. Can you do that?"

"Yes."

"Shoot."

"About a week and a half ago, we got a scary visit from a man with a gun who claimed to be the biological father of our daughter—she's adopted. He said that she was taken from him without his consent and that he didn't know about her until recently."

"Thomas Weihle?"

"Yes, but we didn't know his name at the time."

"Who was the officer on the case?"

There was a pause. "We didn't report it. He threatened us, threatened Mackenzie. He said if we gave him what he wanted, he wouldn't harm her." A choking noise. "We believed him."

Mitch wanted to shut his eyes, but refrained—he was still driving, even faster now. "What did he want?"

"He wanted to reach the biological mother. We only had a PO box, so he made us write her a letter."

"The mother's name?" Mitch's fingers clenched the steering wheel, for he already knew.

"Laura Macnamara."

Everything fell perfectly into place. Why she ran, whom she was protecting, and what she must have feared most— shit!—had happened. Jesus—he'd been too hard on her. She'd been trying to keep a little girl—her own little girl—out of Weihle's perverted clutches.

"Okay, so what did the letter to Laura say?"

"I have it right here. He wanted her to come home where she belongs. But he didn't wait for her." Ray's words gained speed. "He broke in last night, knocked us out with some chemical, tied us up, and took Mackenzie! We don't know where she is—Laura wouldn't let me go with her. She went herself to find them."

But he'd just seen her—how many hours ago had that been?

"When?"

"Today. She found us and cut us loose. She gave us your number—said you'll know where to look for them."

Mitch's mind was reeling. Weihle's house, except half the force was over there. He'd have heard if they found Weihle or hostages. Where things so hairy that O'Dell couldn't call? Or had Weihle adapted his plans?

"Do you know where they are?" The urgency in Ray's voice was palpable.

"I know where they should be." He didn't want to give Ray false hope. "What time did Ch—Laura leave you in search of Weihle and Mackenzie?"

"I don't know. Feels like forever." Mitch could hear the man's frustration.

"You called me right away, right?"

"Yeah."

"Then I'll check the time of the call." Damn. Too long, regardless. "Anything else, Ray, that you think I should know?"

Mitch heard Ray's breath blow out, then the man spoke. "Laura doesn't think he'll hurt Mackenzie right away. She said something about him needing to get to know her first, but Detective? She's wrong. The guy's deranged—seriously scary. I—"

Mitch waited.

"You should count on him being very, very dangerous."

"Noted." He paused. What else? "Okay—Mackenzie, she's what, six years old?"

"Yes." His voice was quiet. "Six this coming September."

"Tough kid?"

"Yeah. Spunky." Mitch could hear the pride in the one-word description.

"Good. I don't expect I'll find another child with Weihle, but just in case, describe her to me."

"Brown hair, to her shoulders or so. Brown eyes. Birthmark on her neck—Weihle's got one, too. The same shape." A pause. "Detective? It doesn't matter who she came from. She's ours and she's beautiful."

Mitch's heart, stiff with worry, gave a lurch. If the child was anywhere near as gorgeous as her mother, he could imagine. Yet this experience—assuming he got her out of it alive—would leave a deep scar.

CHAPTER 35

CHARLIE STOOD OUTSIDE the door to her old bedroom—no longer scratched-up brown hollow-board, but a pristine, quality white door, with an indented panel both top and bottom. Unlike the laundry area, the rest of the rooms she'd passed through seemed to have been updated.

Mackenzie had been right here, in the house, next door, all along. If only she had known—but it was too late now. She couldn't attack Weihle in front of the child.

Even still, she pictured her childhood room exactly as it had been, as if the door and time didn't exist. She felt queasy and feverish. Between the residual chill from the shower, Thomas's hand resting possessively on her lower back, his cologne slinking up her nostrils, and the thought of coming face to face with her—surely terrified—child, the buzzing in her head was near to causing her to pass out.

But then, after he had wiggled a key into a padlock and pushed open the door, the disturbed air hit her exposed collarbone area. She cooled down as goose bumps erupted under silk, the lightheaded feeling fading some.

After he had deemed her clean—everywhere—Thomas had presented her with a wrapped gift. A nightgown, white and demure, except for the sheer parts. Suitable for a bride on her wedding night, he'd said, and added that the matching wrap was solely for Mackenzie's benefit, for Laura wouldn't be needing it for long.

She stepped forward, her bare feet silent on a fuzzy carpet. The curtains were closed, but a night light showed pastel colors, oversized stuffed animals, and a four-poster bed. Every little girl's dream room. In this case, a nightmare.

A spread of food was arrayed on the floor like a child's tea party—a sandwich, a bowl of syrupy peaches, some Goldfish, and a soupy-looking white liquid with colorful polka dots that might have been melted ice cream. The silverware lay on top of the napkin, neat and precise, as if never touched.

The bed was made perfectly, minus one pillow, but no child.

Charlie raised an eyebrow at Thomas.

He smiled and whispered, "She enjoys hiding. She's quite intelligent."

"Mackenzie?" she called softly, and knelt to check under the bed. She saw a movement at the far side, opposite the avoided meal.

She walked around the edge and found the little girl, nearly covered by a pillow, lying prone against the baseboard of the wall, knees and feet hidden under the head of the bed.

"Mackenzie?" Charlie sank to her knees. "Are you all right?"

The girl didn't speak, didn't move. Only the top of her dark head was visible, with a part still as straight as a knife. The hair around it, however, was fuzzed up, as if she had slept, or struggled hard.

"Please tell me you aren't hurt."

The child shook her head. Then a mumble through the pillow: "Who are you?"

"My name is Charlie."

Charlie felt rather than heard Thomas behind her.

"Her name"—he squatted and wrapped his hand around Charlie's neck from behind, squeezing for emphasis—"is Laura. She's your mother."

The shaking of Mackenzie's head sped up.

"Your *real* mother, Mackenzie," he insisted.

"She's not my mommy! And you're not my daddy!" came the muffled yell.

"Now, sweetheart, we've talked about this, and if you'll remove that pillow, you'll see the resemblance you two share."

Mackenzie's arms snaked out, and she gripped the pillow in a fierce hug.

"Thomas"—Charlie looked up at him—"may I have a moment with her? Please?"

He considered, then nodded once. He dropped his hand from her neck, then pressed a kiss there. Charlie repressed a shudder.

She watched him move to the doorway, propping an arm up on the frame so that he faced them. Of course he wouldn't leave them alone.

Charlie unclenched her fists and concentrated on drawing a full breath. The pillow, and the girl behind it, had stilled.

She gulped. "Could you lower that pillow just a little so you and I can see each other's eyes?"

She squeezed the pillow tighter.

"I won't hurt you. I won't do anything. I just want you to see my eyes, so you can see what I feel inside. I would never, never hurt you. And I'm not going to lie to you. I'm scared, too, but I'm going to try and help you get through this strange situation…"

Charlie shook her head. She couldn't speak freely with Thomas in the room, and yet she had to reach the girl.

"Mackenzie, I've seen your...Pamela and Ray. They're okay. They're safe—just worried about you."

"Then why haven't they come for me?" she sobbed.

Charlie's heart broke on the spot. "They don't know where you are."

"Daddy always says he'd move heaven and earth for me. He should know where I am!"

Brown eyes, big and shimmering with tears, peeked over the pillow.

"Well, I bet he's doing his best with heaven and earth, but since he's not God, it's probably harder than it sounds."

Mackenzie stared at her for a few seconds, and Charlie realized that from her angle, the girl probably couldn't see Thomas through the bed.

"Mommy said..."

Charlie winced, but Thomas held his tongue.

"What did she say?"

"She said never to go with a stranger." Her voice hiccuped around all the tears. "She must be so mad. But I didn't go, I just woke up here!"

Charlie's own eyes filled, and she reached out slowly to stroke the little girl's hair, getting a good look at the sweet, tear-stained face now that the pillow had drooped.

"She's not mad at you. I promise you, she knows it's not your fault."

"How do you know?"

"Because I'm kind of a mommy, too. And mommies know these things."

"I'm still scared," Mackenzie whispered, her lower lip trembling.

"You know what? I am, too." Charlie's held back a sob of

her own. "But no matter how scared I might get, I'm going to keep you safe."

Mackenzie whimpered and held out her hands. Charlie pulled her onto her lap, wrapped her and the pillow in her arms, tucked the little head on her shoulder, and scooted her back toward the bed.

"I promise to keep you safe. It's okay. It really will be okay in the end." She began to rock side to side, repeating the phrases over and over, dropping her voice to a murmur as Mackenzie sobbed her heart out. "That's it, let it all out."

Now or never, she thought, while Mackenzie still made noise. "Sweet girl, listen to me," she crooned, dropping her cheek against Mackenzie's head, her lips just inches from her ear. She felt the girl nod against her chest. "Keep crying, but listen. In the back of the closet, there's a tiny door. A storage space—very dark, but good for hiding. When you get the chance, go in and close the door behind you. Crawl as far as you can and there'll be a tiny bit of light at the end. Hide yourself really well, okay? I'm going to get us out of this. I promise."

She returned to the mantra of reassuring phrases, as much for herself as for her child.

Thomas's presence hovered like a threatening storm, yet he let them be until Mackenzie quieted.

Then the back of Charlie's neck prickled and she saw him approach out of the corner of her eye. Italian loafers and high-end slacks, perfectly creased. She didn't raise her eyes.

"Mackenzie," he said, and Charlie saw him draw something from his pocket. "It's time for some medicine to help you sleep."

Charlie dug her fingernails into the child's shoulder in

warning. Mitch had likely been right about the synthetic drugs. Poor Tiffany.

"I'm sleepy already," the child whined.

"I'll just tuck her in," Charlie said, and struggled up, hauling Mackenzie against her.

"No fussing from either of you," he said in a firm voice.

Charlie yanked at the covers. Thomas leaned over to help, drawing down the comforter.

"On the floor, on the floor," Mackenzie cried.

"I forbid it!" Thomas barked. "You'll sleep in the bed."

She scrambled out of Charlie's arms and under the covers.

"Open up," he demanded. She did. He placed a little yellow tablet on her tongue, then bent to kiss her forehead. She turned away, burying her face in the pillows.

Charlie saw his face darken and his eyes narrow.

"She just needs some time," she said, then leaned down, her backside presented to Thomas, to kiss Mackenzie. Her lips rested on her ear. "Spit it out," she whispered as softly as possible. A kiss, then, in a regular timbre, "Sleep tight."

The girl didn't flinch, likely hadn't even heard her instruction, or perhaps, she couldn't comply. Surely the drug—whatever it was—dissolved quickly. Thomas hadn't offered her water. It might be too late.

He put his hand on Charlie's shoulder and ushered her out of the room. Just before he shut the door, he spoke softly, with love and reverence in his voice. "Goodnight, my child."

The key was still in the padlock. Thomas secured the door and pocketed the key.

"That can't be safe," Charlie said. "What if there's a fire?"

He stood watching her, his face inscrutable.

"Surely," she said, "with the pill you gave her she'll sleep soundly without the danger of being locked in?"

He smiled and shepherded her into the master bedroom, which shared a wall with Mackenzie's. They'd passed the doorway of it earlier.

"Although that was a fine display of motherly affection in there, *Laura*, I don't believe you are qualified to offer parenting advice. If there's a fire, or other calamity, I assure you that Mackenzie's well-being will be foremost in my mind."

Another smile, this one tinged with something darker. "Furthermore, I'm not taking any chances. I don't care to be interrupted on our wedding night. We may not have as much time as I'd prefer, but"—he glanced at the window—"then again, we may be holed up here for quite a long time."

She shivered, cold anew at the thought of being imprisoned with Thomas all night or—God, no—for days. Surely Mitch would find them, or she herself could figure out a signal—or better yet, an escape.

"Take off the wrap," Thomas demanded.

Charlie shrugged out of it, playing along for now, and let it fall to the floor. "How do you plan to accomplish this wedding, without someone to do the ceremony?"

She scanned the room with her peripheral vision. Lamps, a squat jewelry box, framed artwork on the walls. There, on the nightstand on this side of the bed only a few feet away, a decorative, but heavy-looking, beer stein with a pointy lid, probably from a trip. She envisioned that point slamming into Weihle's temple. Braced herself.

"Ah, well, tonight is more a matter of celebrating our reunion and honoring our private commitment toward our future together, just the two of us," he said. "Tomorrow, or as soon as the street is clear, we'll make it legal, and include Mackenzie. I've got your birth certificate, you know, and applied for our marriage license."

Could he do that? Was he bluffing? No matter. She wouldn't wait around to find out.

Thomas went on: "Now that you've seen what—or who—is at stake, I imagine you'll manage not to create a scene." He smirked. "Climb onto the bed, darling."

Charlie moved forward as if complying, then turned to face him. Behind her back she wrapped her fingers around the handle of the fancy mug. "I'm not the same girl I was. You can't control me so easily anymore."

Now!

Charlie swung hard, but her shoulder strained. Heavy—too heavy!

She saw the surprise register on his face, yet Thomas blocked her arm easily. Coins flew out of the stein and pelted his torso before falling to shower their feet and the carpet.

She lashed out with her left, connecting with his head, just above his ear. No real impact—he'd shifted, and her fist slid off his hair.

"Bitch!" he shouted, and pushed her hard. She stumbled into the nightstand. The lamp tipped over, the clock hit the wall under her weight. She twisted to her right, rolling away. He slammed her into the closet doors. His hands grasped her throat. Hard, punishing. Thomas's face was red, his grimace twisted, his eyes thrilled.

Charlie panicked, gasping and flailing, pulling at his shoulders, scratching his neck.

No! she thought, as she began to see spots, her arms became weak, and the hollow pounding of her elbows against the doors ceased.

Then suddenly, release—and air! He'd let go. Her knees buckled and she crumpled to the floor. She gulped for breath, lungs burning, fingers digging into the nap of the carpet.

"You conniving bitch," Thomas spat, breathing heavily himself. "Look at me."

Charlie raised her head—let all the venom she felt show on her face.

"Don't ever try that again," he said between clenched teeth.

"Why not?" she rasped. "Afraid you'll accidentally kill your favorite toy?"

His eyes flared. Charlie felt fear spike again, braced for a kick or punch.

Instead, Thomas used both hands to smooth back his hair and tuck in his dress shirt. "I never do anything accidentally," he said with a voice that was smooth and polished, as if the struggle that had almost killed her hadn't even occurred.

He reached out a hand to help her up. When she didn't move, he laced his voice with warning. "Laura."

Charlie shifted, gritted her teeth, put her hand in his, and rose on shaking limbs to a standing position. Inside, she swore she'd never give up.

Thomas straightened her nightgown, inspected her sore neck with his fingertips.

She glared at him.

He cocked his head to the side.

"You've matured, Laura. The daring alone—infuriating, but sexy. Providing me the challenge I so enjoy." He chuckled. "As for controlling you—I can, and I will. One word: Macken-zie." He watched her eyes, must have seen the fear she felt for the girl, and nodded with a smug twist of his lips.

"You forget how well I know you. Our relationship was such a success only because I admired how protective you were of your mother. And I've just witnessed how much you already care for the child." He shook his head, a small smile playing on his lips. "Although I'd prefer to keep Mackenzie safe from harm, safe from *me*, even, it's ultimately *you* who will determine her well-being."

Charlie's bravado plummeted. If she couldn't find a way to get them out, she would, if he threatened Mackenzie, do anything he demanded. And they both knew it.

Thomas's grin stretched his face when he saw the defeat dogging her. So she raised her chin a notch—because there was hope yet, in the form of a yard full of law enforcement just next door, searching specifically for him. There were also the Hudsons and Mitch—neither of whom would rest until she and Mackenzie were found.

"How do you expect to get away with it all?" She waved her hand at her gown and then out toward Mackenzie's room. It hurt her throat to speak. "Kidnapping, forced marriage, evading the police? They're already onto you."

"Yes, well, I imagine you are to blame for that, no?"

Charlie didn't move a muscle. Shit. In her attempt to keep him talking, she'd inadvertently added to his ire.

"Another item added to the list of your massive transgressions, then. Thankfully, I had the forethought to use your house, rather than my own."

"Did you buy it?"

"A delicious thought, but no. I simply borrowed it."

"The family that lives here—what did you do to them?" Charlie shut her eyes, bracing for the worst.

"You're worried?" he asked, and she heard him laugh. "Don't insult me, Laura. I still prefer brains over brawn."

Oh really, and the attempt to throttle her had been—what? A calculated move? She didn't think so. Charlie opened her eyes and stared him down. "Where are they?"

"The Silvias, gullible simpletons that they are, departed days ago for her mother's in Delaware." Thomas's eyes twinkled. "Oh, what the smell of sulfur can accomplish! Not to mention a few well-placed words about the ill effects of unknown gases on young, still-growing children. Tony Silvia didn't stand a chance against his panicked, pregnant wife."

Relief washed over Charlie. At least that family was safe.

Without warning, Thomas reached out. Instinctively, she stepped back.

"Stand still." He narrowed his eyes in warning and his voice darkened. "Time to get back on track."

He stepped forward and used the back of his knuckles to trace a path from the hollow between her collarbones to the thrust of bone at her pelvis.

"Where shall I take a pound of flesh from first?"

She forced herself not to move. He hated insolence, and she'd been pushing it.

He slid his hand back up to her chest, cupped her right breast. Charlie ignored his slimy touch and gauged the distance to the lamp. If she—

"Here?" He grabbed a nipple and twisted so hard she cried out. As her hand flew toward the pain, his landed a blow between her legs. She doubled over.

"Thomas," she gasped, tears filling her eyes. "This isn't like you."

"I told you earlier to climb onto the bed," he said in a menacing whisper.

She scrambled up, pain and all, her bottom facing him. *Crack!* He smacked her ass so hard she tumbled sideways.

She cried out and scurried backward to the headboard, attempting to put herself out of his reach.

He chuckled. "Oh, how I do enjoy a good spanking. Shall I mete out your punishment that way—perhaps a wooden paddle for my college student who's abandoned her studies?

Yes, eventually, when the mood strikes. But, I'm afraid, I'm feeling that the current punishment should meet the weight of the crime. That pound of flesh must come directly from your soul."

He eyed her. How ice-blue irises could look so fevered, she didn't know. She thought of Mitch's compassionate light brown ones, lit with warmth. *Now, Mitch, please.*

"Lie flat. Put your hands through the restraints."

Her eyes slid across the headboard rails, and then widened. He'd introduced her to bondage long ago; however, as he'd pointed out, the stakes were higher now. Plus, his control over his own actions had become tenuous and his fury had likely reached an all-time high. She shook all the way to her core. This time, he wouldn't be playing an idle game.

"They won't chafe, my dear—silk."

She stared at him, unmoving, unable to render herself powerless with Mackenzie to save.

"Tsk, tsk. Let me explain something to you," he sneered. "Our little games have reached a new level. You changed the board and upped the stakes." He reached behind him, slid open a dresser drawer, and pulled out a gun. He caressed it, then moved to the end of the bed and aimed at her torso—dead center. She held her breath, and the metallic tang of fear filled her mouth.

"Hands," he ordered.

When she was lying flat and he'd tightened both silk hand-cuffs, he moved again to the foot of the bed. He pressed the nose of the pistol snugly between her legs. Charlie squeezed her thighs together—as if that would somehow save her. He shook his head and raised an eyebrow.

She forced her legs to fall apart. But she was suffused with complete terror.

He wiggled the gun side to side, then slid it up to caress her clit, right through the flimsy nightgown.

Charlie broke out in a sweat, her breath coming fast and ragged. She didn't believe he'd kill her, at least not yet, although she had no idea if he knew how to use a gun. What if, in his excitement, he accidentally squeezed the trigger—there?

She had to *do* something.

"If you—" She had to clear her throat. "If you know me, then I know you, too. You aren't some thug who needs to rely on a gun. And you aren't a killer, Thomas." Charlie pushed away thoughts of Tiffany. She had to talk him down. "I won't believe that you'd use that."

"Actually, darling, I have killed." His eyes lit up again with passion, and Charlie suddenly understood, with ice-cold clarity, that she herself was also doomed.

CHAPTER 36

BY THE TIME Mitch disconnected Ray Hudson, he was yanking the truck into the curb on Dale Drive behind a subcompact. He couldn't believe that it was just yesterday that they'd secured a search and seize warrant based on the information he'd gotten from Laura, hoping to find evidence to put away a pedophile, hoping—in truth—to find Tiffany. Now, Weihle was wanted for Tiffany's murder, Mackenzie's abduction, and possibly Charlie's, too.

Given the phone call with Hudson, he'd expected a hostage situation. Better yet, he'd have liked to find Weihle in custody—or bleeding from a hole in his forehead—and medics giving the all-clear to Charlie and Mackenzie.

Yeah, the level of activity on site was high—uniforms swarmed, all appropriate vehicles sat at the ready—but the vibe felt off.

Mitch jumped out of the cab. This scene looked—not dull exactly, but maybe too standard, too procedural. He didn't sense that palpable air of death or defeat, nor any frenzied frustration in being duped. All good, to his mind, because it meant that both Charlie and Mackenzie were still safe.

Yet he worried, because the current buzz also lacked the adrenaline rush of danger or the giddiness accompanying success. Which meant that fucking nothing at all had changed here. And that meant Charlie was—where exactly? Carson had already checked. Weihle owned no other property, no cabin, no time-share no empty lots, nada...

He didn't need to flash his badge at the cop on patrol at the erected barrier—he knew him. Young Dennis Blank—dedicated and hardworking, but damn inexperienced.

Mitch bore down on him, covering the distance. "You seen O'Dell?"

"Not lately." Dennis tilted his head toward Weihle's residence. "Hasn't come out of the house."

Before the kid finished his sentence, Mitch had already changed directions and leapt the barrier.

He ducked under the crime scene tape hung just above the steps to the small covered porch. His gaze swept everything—a tech at the wall of shelves surrounding the TV system, another cataloging prescription bottles in a cupboard in the kitchen. Good, Mitch thought—they'd received all the details about Tiffany's death and knew anything drug-like was top priority.

Mitch turned, ready to head upstairs or down in search of O'Dell, and spotted him at the top of the basement stairs.

His legs ate up the distance.

"Saunders—" Carson started, but Mitch was already barking.

"Weihle obviously hasn't shown up?"

"No, APB is out—"

"What about a woman and child? Laura Macnamara and her daughter?"

"No." Carson raised his eyebrows. "What the hell, Mitch?"

"Damn." Mitch's gut had known, and yet he'd hoped. He'd been here earlier himself, but asked again anyway. "Nothing suspicious? You've double-checked every room, every closet, attic, basement?" All nods from Carson. He ran his hands through his hair. "Trapdoors? Fake walls? Space unaccounted for?"

"No. I was aiming for a stash of child pornography or prized sicko keepsakes, so, believe me, I was looking for hidden spaces. Didn't expect anything to be out in the open, but it was." O'Dell pointed to the tech in the living room. "Those DVD cases labeled with numbers on the outside? I checked the first few—all Laura. Filmed at a distance. Nothing sexual so far, but she was very young when he started watching her."

Mitch's stomach pitched—she hadn't stood a chance.

"Here's the deal," he said to O'Dell. "Laura got pregnant by Weihle." Damn, but every time his mind strayed to that sicko inside her, the urge to commit murder consumed him. Mitch gritted his teeth against the rage and went on: "She gave the child to this couple, Ray and Pamela Hudson. Weihle somehow found out and nabbed the kid last night. Girl, six years, Laura's look-alike. Charlie—Laura—"

He looked to O'Dell for confirmation that the man was following. Carson's brow was furrowed, eyes narrowed, but he nodded.

"—came after her, intending to trade herself for the child. You saw her on TV today?"

Another affirmative.

"She was sure she'd find them here—at his house." He slammed his palm against the hall wall. "So where the hell are they?"

Carson shook his head, his blond hair sticking up like a troll's. "No other residences came up when I was working the warrant."

"I know, I know. We're missing something." He thought aloud: "The house was empty when you arrived. Barrier set up pronto?"

"Of course. And we've been here since yesterday."

"Then we need an AMBER Alert out on the girl, Macken-zie Hudson." Mitch relayed the child's description to O'Dell. "Taken from her home in the Oak Grove subdivision some-time after three a.m. Get CSI out there." Mitch plowed through possibilities. "His vehicle?"

"Only the Volvo, still in the garage."

"Check the rental agencies, too."

"Yeah, right away," Carson said.

Mitch spun on his heel and headed for the door, O'Dell right behind him. He ducked again under the tape and then leapt the remaining steps.

"Blank!" he called.

"Yes, sir?" The uniform turned as they approached.

"I need to know exactly who's come through since you set up."

"Uh, okay. Well, I was here last night, off today, but Fischer said it was quiet on his shift," Dennis Blank said, straightening his shoulders. "Earlier, there was a woman worried about her grandparents who live there." He pointed to the last house on Dale Drive. "That's her car."

Mitch and Carson both went over to take a look. The doors of the little vehicle were unlocked. Keys in the ignition. The front seat was spotless—free of the junk most folks rode around with—but no rental papers in the glove box. Mitch moved to the back seat and yanked out a duffel, clunking it on top of the trunk. Carson peppered Officer Blank with ques-tions about the woman's age, height, hair, and dress.

"Doesn't matter," Mitch said. "She won't look anything like Laura Macnamara, or Charlie Hart, for that matter." The bag proved it. The clothing was of another style entirely. No hip-hugging cargo pants or tight black tank tops, no hair dye, no sexy earrings. Some dry food, the kind that could last months and months and still be edible, and some everyday cosmetics—all common drugstore brands.

"What time did you log?"

"Seven thirty-eight p.m., sir."

"Shit, nearly two hours." Mitch said.

Then he came up with an over-the-shoulder satchel that had been stuffed under the front seat. It wasn't the same one he'd seen Charlie use in San Francisco. He had no recall on what bag she'd carried today at the nursing facility. He found the Avis car rental papers and a slim wallet. The ID read Joanne Strinner. Red hair, glasses—with the right props, Charlie'd pass. He handed it to Carson, who said, "The news is showing one photo of her with long red hair."

"A wig," Mitch said. "I saw her earlier today at Rolling Meadows." This car had to be hers.

Mitch discovered an envelope tucked in a side pocket—

"Bingo." He fanned out photos on the roof of the car for O'Dell and Blank, who'd released his flashlight from his belt ring and directed the beam at the prints. All Mackenzie, in various stages of growth. A dead ringer for a young Laura.

"So she's here somewhere," Mitch said.

"Uh, Detectives, I think I've seen that little girl."

Mitch spun around so fast he nearly knocked Blank over. The photos whooshed off the car and fluttered to the ground.

"Last night. The only other car that came through. A man and his daughter, just getting home from Disney. Said he lives right there." He pointed to the house Laura grew up in. Dennis Blank cleared his throat before speaking again. "I let them pass." Mitch's hands clenched into fists. Deck the idiot officer or kiss him?

Mitch looked at Carson. "It's him."

Carson looked at him, eyes wide with amazement. "Prick's got serious balls."

"Was the girl agitated, scared?" Mitch asked, but Blank was already shaking his head.

"She was totally sacked out in the back seat. Big stuffed princess doll under her arm." He fidgeted with his cap. "May I ask—"

"The child, brown hair? About how old?"

"Brown hair, longish. Caucasian. Old enough to be in a booster seat, but not a big kid. I don't know, somewhere between five and seven?"

"Perp woulda been in disguise," Carson said.

"No doubt," Mitch replied.

"God," Dennis Blank murmured, "I never suspected a thing. He was cool as a cucumber, and my list says family of five, three kids, so…"

Damn his naiveté, Mitch thought, but at least he knew for sure where they were now.

"What time?"

Blank consulted his clipboard. "Three thirty a.m."

Fuck. Hours and hours too long.

"For Christ's sake, Blank, don't let another civilian past you for anything, got it? In *or* out." Mitch stalked away.

Carson was right behind him. They halted as soon as the shadows swallowed them up.

"You think the family of five is in there, too?"

"God, I hope not." Mitch ran his hands through his hair. "But get more EMS—no sirens. Keep it quiet. From that house"—he tilted his head in that direction—"things should appear status quo."

"What's your plan?" Carson asked.

His plan, he thought, was to save them. Period. Whatever it took.

Mitch exhaled hard. "I'm going in." He'd been too late for Tiffany. He refused to fail Charlie and the little girl, too. "Can't wait."

He looked at the old Macnamara house and spoke as rapidly as his thoughts fired. "Get SWAT here ASAP." He glanced at his watch. Nine fifty-two. "Fifteen for them to get here. Five more to get in behind me. I'll wait if I can. If there's shots, fuck stealth."

O'Dell nodded, and Mitch knew he could count on him to take care of everything.

"But pound it home: two confirmed hostages, five more possibles. I don't want a single scratch on anybody but Weihle."

CHAPTER 37

AS CHARLIE LAY, physically still bound at the wrists to the four-poster bed and emotionally frozen with dread, Weihle's eyes became dreamy, as if he were lost in memory as he spoke. "I helped someone end her miserable life just yesterday, in fact."

Oh no, no, no. She didn't want to hear this. But if she ever got out of here, Mitch might need the details. Her voice was a mere whisper. "Who?"

"A young girl I'd once had high hopes for," Thomas said, as he focused once again on her. "But it's so hard to find good girls these days. You, my pet, spoiled me so."

"Who?"

He cocked his head to the side, considering the repeated question. "You'd like a name?"

She nodded.

He shrugged. "Tiffany Scott."

Charlie sobbed involuntarily, somewhere between a gulp for air and a sudden exhalation of pain. She'd known, of course, but hearing this monster speak her name so casually was too much.

The evil smile stalled on Weihle's face. "You know Tiffany? Dare I ask?"

She shook her head, crying now for Tiffany, as she hadn't been able to earlier.

"Prepare to share all the details with me later—after you've been broken," Thomas said, and she knew he would tell her nothing more right now. "We need to rebuild the trust between us before I will believe a word that exits your traitorous mouth anyway.

"So"—he inclined his head in a slight bow—"as with all new games, we have new rules for playing nice." He raised his eyebrows. She barely managed a nod. "You seem to have forgotten that I don't care to repeat myself. You will do as I request the first time. It goes without saying that if I ask you a direct question, you will answer it, in full. Manners, manners." He tapped his chin. "Ah, yes. You are still, and always, my Laura, and will think of yourself as such. I don't want to hear that other name come out of your mouth again. Speaking of," he said in a more conversational tone, "Mackenzie's name is simply abominable. We must change it legally the first chance we get."

He lifted her leg—should she kick him? What next, though? Her hands were bound without room to maneuver, and that gun he held drastically lowered her chances of success. He slipped her foot through a silk tie, then moved to the other leg, caressing her calf, before cinching the noose tight. Charlie fought not to freak out.

"Perhaps we'll name her after your mother? Ellen? Or perhaps Elena?"

He circled the bed, arrived at the other nightstand, and looked down at her.

"Your poor mother. We shall be forced to leave the area, live in hiding indefinitely—did I mention that I've chosen somewhere exotic? Hot and warm, where everyone is low key, and stays out of one another's business. Needless to say, we'll be leaving the country. Anyway, what a shame that your mother will wake up and find that her only daughter has abandoned her—again!"

He laughed, and pushed the hem of the nightgown up over her thighs until her pubic bone was just exposed. But the gooseflesh hadn't risen on her flesh from the exposure or even the creepy-crawly feeling of his pedophilic digits on her bare skin—her subconscious had already realized what her rational mind fought.

"What are you saying?"

"Your mother, darling. Without my interference, she'll soon recover. Oh, not completely, perhaps, because she truly was a mess in her own right. I just helped her along to a more peaceful state."

Charlie felt the blood drain from her face as her heart splintered like shards of glass.

He smiled and came around the far side of the bed, away from the doorway, to stroke her hair with one hand while the other hung loose at his side with the gun. Bound hand and foot and stunned with horror, she was no threat to him.

"Sweet, trusting girl. Don't beat yourself up. So innocent, you couldn't have known."

Her keen started deep within and rose up like a wild, living thing.

He stroked her hair. She thrust her head violently back and forth, then snapped her teeth to bite him. He was too quick.

"I'll kill you," she snarled.

He threw his head back and laughed. "That's the spirit!"

When she'd exhausted herself struggling but had stoked her insides to an inferno of hatred, he lowered his chin and pinned her with his eyes. She watched them turn scary, but she was done cowering.

"Now," he said, his voice like steel. "To break that spirit all over again, carve out some soul." He reached over, caressed her breast and popped it out of the nightgown. She hissed, causing him to grin.

He reached the hand without the gun into his pocket and pulled out a switchblade.

Charlie held her breath, shocked. Dear Lord, first a gun, and now a knife. Years ago, he had only been playing, toying with her. Although she feared him now like never before, she promised herself she wouldn't go down without a fight. Not now that she knew the whole of his evil—oh, no, now she'd fight to the death, his death, no matter what it took.

He pressed the flat side of the blade to her nipple, then removed the knife. Her nipple had hardened, popping up, from the cool metal, and he smiled, pleased.

"Physics," she snarled. "I will *never* desire you."

He slid the knife to the plunging neckline of her gown, and yanked upward in anger. The flimsy material parted straight down her middle, from breast to belly, with only a whisper of sound. Although the garment had been sheer in parts, she was now utterly exposed.

"Ready to ante up, Laura?" He moved the knife to her nipple—involuntarily, her eyes followed. Weihle traced the areola with pressure, and she gasped at the sharp sting as blood beaded along the glinting silver.

Charlie's mind raced. There were cops outside—could they hear her if she was loud enough? How fast could they get here; how swiftly would Thomas silence her? Permanently? And would it be enough to save Mackenzie?

"Every time you disobey me, I'm going to mark you."

She opened her mouth to start screaming, but he clamped the knife hand over her mouth.

"Should you still have trouble"—he leaned to stare into

her eyes—"Mackenzie will bear matching scars. The sins of the mother, hmmn?"

———

Mitch was sure of only two things: one, he hadn't yet conclusively pinpointed Mackenzie's location, and two, the longer Weihle yapped, the more time SWAT had to catch up. His initial relief at finding the Joanne Strinner boarding pass as he'd circled the house had dissipated as he'd climbed the stairs in torturous increments. Weihle's voice had become fully audible. Not only did it sound as if Charlie had been rendered completely helpless, Weihle seemed seriously on edge. Barely holding on to his temper and overexcited. Things were going to come to a head fast.

Mitch caught the admission about Ellen Macnamara, and his soul bled along with Charlie's. The urge to simply step into the room and get trigger happy on that sicko Weihle, just so he could put his arms around her, had nearly overcome him.

Yet he'd held steady, exercising his better judgment and listening intently for some sign that backup had arrived. He remembered the layout of the house from the Macnamara investigation. Weihle held Charlie in what would be considered the master bedroom. From the sound of things, the man probably faced the doorway. No way could Mitch risk a quick look-see. Coverage from here was nil.

Mitch didn't need Ray Hudson to tell him the psycho was dangerous. Weihle had killed his sister—tossing her aside like a discard in one of his twisted little games.

The minute Mitch heard Charlie's cut-off yell and Weihle's subsequent threats about cutting her and Mackenzie, he knew he could wait no longer.

Mitch exhaled hard, spun around the doorframe and into the bedroom, gun leading.

"Police! Freeze!"

Weihle had a blade at Charlie's chest—*shit*—and held a gun. Oddly, instead of firing at the intrusion, he'd swung it wide, pointing the weapon at the far wall. Interesting.

Mitch's eyes bored into Weihle—the man was dead in point two seconds if he gave him the slightest reason to fire—but his peripheral vision encompassed nearly all of the small room. Positioning was as good as it got. Charlie—*Jesus*—virtually naked, spread-eagled, every limb tied down, and a knife at her breast—reacted with only an instant of relief and then tensed up again.

She looked at Weihle, then looked at him, and shook her head. Mitch saw no sign of the kid. What exactly was she trying to tell him?

"Detective Saunders," Thomas sneered. His torso was unprotected—the button-down shirt the man wore showed skin at the V and was tailored to fit closely. He definitely hadn't gotten his hands on any Kevlar—yet he thrust out his chest anyway. With no armor to work around, Mitch planned to fire chest first, head second—all he needed was a little push. No way in hell would Mitch let him come any closer to hurting Charlie. He refused to lose anyone else to this fucker.

"Drop the weapons, Weihle." Mitch's voice was hard.

Charlie said, "Mitch—"

"You know him?" Thomas asked, his voice dripping scorn. "That explains so much."

Charlie was doing something, motioning with her head, the slightest repetitive movement to her left. The same direction Weihle was pointing his gun. That confirmed it: Mackenzie must be in the next room.

"Drop them!" Mitch barked.

Weihle titled his head to one side, as if he were considering it, then smiled. "I think not."

"I'm only the front line. You can't win this."

"Depends on how you look at it."

Mitch said, "Two options only: life in jail or dead on the spot. Your call." Adrenaline pumped hard, but he felt steady and calm, all his focus on Weihle's eyes. The slightest flicker would telegraph his answer.

"It's too bad, Laura," Weihle said, though his fevered eyes held Mitch's, "that I can't take you with me. Don't fret, darling." A small smile curved his lips. "I won't go alone—"

That confirmed it for Mitch—Mackenzie was on the other side of that wall.

Charlie yelled, "No!" and surged up against her ties.

Weihle threw the knife at Mitch and simultaneously fired his pistol at the plaster.

Mitch had fired, too, even as he leaned right, the knife zooming past him.

Weihle's shots and Mitch's—two in the chest, one in the wrist to stop him firing—drowned out her scream.

Weihle staggered backward and fell, and the gun bounced out of his now useless hand. One shoulder, his neck, and head canted awkwardly against the wall. His eyes slid to Charlie, and a satisfied smile twisted one side of his mouth. Then her tormentor shut his eyes and his body abruptly slumped in on itself—a marionette without a master.

"Mitch!" Charlie's voice was panicked. "Mackenzie—she's in that room!"

"I know," he said, but he couldn't go yet. Mitch kept his gun trained on Weihle and went for the loose weapon, kicking it backward to the door.

"The family that lives here?" he demanded.

"Gone."

"Dead?"

"No, no. Just not here."

SWAT pounded up the steps, shots fired eliminating the need for stealth. Two officers trained their weapons on Weihle; another quickly lowered his, seeing that Charlie was no threat.

Mitch looked at Charlie. Finally—directly—at her.

"Hurry!" she pleaded.

He nodded hard, unable to speak for the relief swamping him. "Cut her loose and get her covered up. Radio EMS. Possible child down, next room."

As he rushed out, Mitch saw one of the special team kneel to check Weihle for a pulse. He and the remainder of the SWAT team sprinted down the hallway. Padlocked.

Mitch stood aside as the team moved in a well-rehearsed dance. One in position to enter, another shouting, "Police!" and swinging the battering ram back and then forward with force and precision. The door popped open as if on a spring, and SWAT rushed in, guns drawn, hugging the walls. One second, no more, and they cleared Mitch to follow.

He charged into the room, only to stop dead in his tracks when he saw—nothing. No blood, no body, no child. Three of Weihle's four bullets had ripped through the plaster wall. The fourth likely hit a stud or a metal air duct. Other than a big, fluffy bear, who lay facedown on the floor, and a few feathers still drifting down from a pillow that must have taken a hit, there was no carnage—nor any life.

He checked under the bed, took a quick survey of the closet. Nothing.

He spun to return to Charlie, only to have her burst in

behind him—wearing a thin, silky robe, tied hastily, but mostly covering her. He grasped her shoulders. "She's not here."

She blinked, craned to see past him, and then broke free. She sprinted to the closet and yanked the door open wide open with a bang. Then she fell to her knees and started throwing stuff behind her, out of her way.

"Mackenzie!" she yelled as she pushed open a tiny door. "Mackenzie, it's okay! It's over, come out!"

Before he even got the words out, the nearest SWAT guy was handing him a Maglite.

Charlie had already scrabbled into the dark.

"Here, take this!" He knelt and reached in with the high-powered flashlight. Her eyes were wide when the beam shot past her face. She grabbed it, then pivoted around in a squat, careful of the slanted beams only a foot overhead.

"Mackenzie," she called, "it's me, Charlie. Only me and some policemen. The bad man is gone. It's safe to come out." Mitch heard a soft murmur, then Charlie's voice again. "Where are you? Okay, I'm coming to you."

More clumping around, then sobbing—from both of them.

Mitch bowed his head, bracing his hands on his thighs, gun still clenched hard in his fingers. Fear dissipated like a burst balloon, as relief rushed in like a tidal wave knocking him sideways.

"Give the all-clear," he managed to tell the nearest officer.

By the time Charlie climbed out of the crawlspace with her daughter in her arms, Mitch had holstered his weapon, wiped his eyes, and—mostly—gotten a hold of himself.

"Mitch," she said, her eyes shining with tears.

He wrapped a fleece blanket that he'd snagged from the

foot of the bed around the pair, then rested his forehead against Charlie's and shut his eyes for just a second.

Then he pulled back to soak up the sight of her.

She said, "This is Mackenzie, and she must be starving."

He smiled at the girl still burrowing into Charlie's shoulder for comfort. "We can take care of that," he said, "but first, brave Mackenzie, I bet you'd like to talk to your mom and dad, wouldn't you?"

Her head popped up, and her sweet face—so much like Charlie's—sparked to life.

He pulled his cell from his back pocket. "How's right now sound?"

CHAPTER 38

Two and a half weeks later

SOMEHOW, WEIHLE had lived.

Charlie couldn't help but wish that he hadn't. For everyone's sakes: the Hudsons', Mitch and Deirdre's, and her own.

Granted, Thomas Hadfield Weihle was resting firmly in hell, the one right here on earth called federal prison. Charlie knew Thomas's fine sensibilities would find it even more horrid than most. Mitch promised it'd be an inferno: pedophiles were a special class of low, even there.

But Charlie also realized that unless that monster befell an unpleasant accident sooner rather than later, she'd be rehashing the past again, and again, courtesy of the legal system.

Not today, though.

Charlie watched Mackenzie run through the Hudsons' backyard after a wayward stomp rocket, and shook her head again. This Memorial Day was one for the record books.

First of all, she was here, in Blakes Ridge, at the Hudsons' home, with her daughter—who was, simply, a joy to behold.

"Charlie, another beer? Another dog?" Ray asked.

"No, thanks." She smiled. "I'm good—perfectly content."

Ray moved to check in with the other guests, for they'd invited numerous friends and relatives to celebrate, even Mitch's mom, Deirdre, though she'd not been up to a social gathering and had instead opted to stay home with Dominic Marcone. Mitch worried so much, for the woman's grief was always palpable and often consuming, and he felt that he'd failed her. Charlie, too, carried that weight. Deirdre would never stop grieving, but she would manage to carry on. She had strength in scores, not to mention that she had Dom, Mitch, and now Charlie, too.

"Stomp it again!" Mackenzie raced back to the rocket's stand, settled the tube of the rocket onto the base's cylinder, and pointed to the place he needed to jump to force air into the thing.

"How high this time, Mack?" Mitch grinned. "A hundred feet?"

"Two and forty hundred thousand!" she demanded.

Mitch and Charlie exchanged grins, and then they all whooped as he landed with a *pop!* sending the rocket soaring.

Pam smiled and moved beside Charlie to watch Mackenzie's antics. "You know, I am, too—perfectly content. Thank you, again, for yesterday."

The three of them, Pam, Ray, and Charlie, had finalized Mackenzie's adoption with a lawyer. The only reason they'd even waited that long was that Charlie had needed time to legally change her name. With no hesitation, she'd left Laura behind and kept Macnamara, as a tie to her mother. She was now, officially, Charlie Macnamara Hart.

Other adjustments, like settling down in a place where there were so many bad memories and where her trauma was known by what felt like everybody…well, that'd take more emotional fortitude. Mitch had suggested a good psychologist, previously with the force, who was experienced with victims of sexual abuse and trauma. Charlie was game. Besides her own well-being, she knew that facing a real relationship for the first time ever and learning to trust was going to take a lot of work.

Especially when she wasn't the only one with demons. Mitch was hurting, too. On the surface they'd each forgiven the other. And he'd begun to talk about leaving the force for private investigation, allowing him to focus on runaways and missing people, putting families back together whenever possible. Assuaging his guilt, she knew. But was it really that easy? The pain of losing Tiffany in that way...she wondered, deep down, could he truly forgive her, when she wasn't entirely sure she could forgive herself?

In the meantime, she and Mitch sought solace in each other's arms, a natural byproduct of the fact that she was currently crashing at his apartment.

And in getting to know Mitch better—from learning where he was ticklish, to how he took his coffee—she found true joy in the simplest, smallest things.

Charlie nodded now at Pam. "I wish I could have given you legal custody from the beginning."

"Believe me, we understand." Pam shuddered. "And honestly, for years, I didn't think it even mattered. Now, though, I feel like a weight of worry I didn't even know I was carrying has been lifted."

A lot of weights had been shucked recently. The intense media maelstrom that had followed Laura's reappearance, the truth about Tiffany Saunders' death, and the shootout at the residence where the Macnamaras once lived had finally subsided. The Silvia family had returned home once the crime scene tape was removed. According to Mitch, they'd had the home blessed by a priest. There was some talk of exhuming

Rowena Leonard's body to see if she'd really died of natural causes or if Thomas had caused her heart attack with some chemical. Charlie tried hard not to think about that.

And many of the bigger decisions she needed to make could wait. Like where to live and how to support herself and her mother.

Her mother—my God, she could still scarcely believe it—had woken up and begun to improve. Only this morning, Ellen had grasped Charlie's hand, tears filling her eyes, and said, "Honey, I'm so sorry."

Charlie had bawled. Her mother had been apologizing only for getting sick, in terms of not being there for her daughter. She didn't yet know the horrors her child had experienced, or what Thomas had stolen from Ellen herself. Those blows would wait until she was stronger.

"Don't cry, love. Things will be better now, I promise," Ellen had murmured.

Charlie saw Mitch extract himself from Mackenzie and her new toy. He crossed the yard, making a beeline for her with a funny quirk to his lips.

"It just came to me," Mitch said. "From chasing the rockets."

"What did?"

"A name."

Charlie cocked her head. "A name?"

He turned up both palms. "Retrieval, Inc."

She smiled. Vague consideration had apparently just shifted to real possibility.

"What do you think?"

"I think you sound serious."

He nodded slowly, but his smile grew. "Yeah. I am."

They watched as another rocket shot skyward, Mackenzie

shrieking in delight before racing off to retrieve it. She and Mitch exchanged a look, and Charlie laughed, marveling at this day, these gifts.

"Might be time for that driving lesson," he said.

She raised an eyebrow. "You don't want to stay for the fireworks?"

He tucked her into his side and whispered into her ear, "Leaning toward a more private celebration."

Charlie felt the strum of his deep voice rocket down her spine. "That'll work." She grinned. "I have a feeling you'll need some TLC after you've experienced my driving."

Charlie linked her fingers in his and let the promise of their love take root—no matter the thorny bits still to contend with.

Her mother had the right of it. Things *would* be better now.

Because for once, Charlie's possibilities were endless, and her timeline infinite.

Thank you for reading!

If you enjoyed Runaway, please consider leaving an honest review at your retailer. Besides word of mouth, reviews are the best way for others to find new reads, and all authors greatly appreciate them.

Newsletter subscribers are the first to receive news and updates! Sign up via my website:

www.jbschroederauthor.com

Turn the page for a quick preview of JB's other books!

If you enjoyed Charlie's do-gooder ways and Mitch's tough-guy heroics, you'll love the UNLIKELY *Series featuring their friends.*

Evil lurks in the most unlikely places...

UNHINGED
Unlikely Series, Book 1

Small-business owner Tori Radnor is determined to stand alone and become her own success story. Wealthy Aiden Miller aches to help her despite his own obstacles. As an unhinged villain taunts Tori and escalates to terrorizing her son, they begin to suspect that Aiden might be more involved than he can possibly imagine. When the stakes become life-threatening, they learn exactly what they are willing to risk for love.

UNCOVERED
Unlikely Series, Book 2

Marine Eddie Mackey knows his estranged wife didn't commit suicide. Videographer Miranda Hill knows more than she'll say. When she is attacked, Eddie swears to protect Miranda despite her secrets, his misgivings, and their undeniable attraction. In the end, there's only one choice: join forces to uncover evil—before anyone else winds up dead.

UNDONE
Unlikely Series, Book 3

When Maxine Ricci finds another model murdered, she can no longer deny that it's her agency being targeted. With the killer leaving messages even the police can't decipher, she has no choice but to enlist Shane O'Rourke's protection. As a former-model himself, he understands the unique demands and pitfalls of the fashion world. Unfortunately, it was Max herself who fired him. Now she's stuck up close and personal with a very serious, very sexy bodyguard, and she's falling hard.

Between temptation and fear, Max is coming undone. So, too, is the madman, whose ultimate obsession is her...

*Then, Charlie and Mitch's story continues
in the next* RETRIEVAL, INC. *story...*

Where everday meets evil...

TRAPPED
Retrieval, Inc. Series, Book 2—Coming Soon!

Charlie Hart and Mitch Saunders form a private investigation firm called Retrieval, Inc. and search for their young friend. Yes, Ian Cross is in more trouble, but this time it's not of his own making. As they race against time to save the teen from a trap he'll never escape, the tenuous trust between them is tested. Will working together make or break them?

ACKNOWLEDGMENTS

Sincerest thanks go to:

My parents, all of them, for their unwavering support and years of encouragement, in addition to more practical means of help. And my sister for always propping me up, and the many times she lent an ear.

My husband and kiddos for believing in me, humoring me, and keeping me grounded. It helps, too, that you don't really care if you eat.

My fellow critique partners, blog mates, and dear writer friends: Joanna Shupe, Michele Mannon, RoseAnn DeFranco, Diana Quincy, Jaye Marie Rome, Maria K. Alexander, Tina Gabrielle, AJ Scudiere, and Maureen Hansch. I'd be utterly lost without your invaluable feedback, advice, camaraderie, and cheerleading. Maureen and AJ: double kudos for your spot-on instincts regarding the ending of this book. It's thanks to you that Charlie and Mitch will get another story, and another...

New Jersey Romance Writers, Romance Writers of America, and the Writer's Police Academy—I'm so grateful I found you. And to the leaders and contributors of the Self Publishing

Info Swap and Crime Scene Questions for Writers loops, for providing treasure troves of practical information.

Barbara Greenberg of BJG Publishing Services for stellar proofreading, not to mention invaluable friendship. Plus Arran McNicol for lightning-fast copyediting and Erin Stoner, Excel guru, for helping me track productivity—a constant challenge.

Anne Hawkins, my first agent, who took a chance on me and gave me the confidence to continue.

Petr Vachal for the details on research labs, Bill Booth for fielding my SWAT team questions, Mark Pfeiffer and Wendy 'Piper' Rome for help with weaponry and concealed carry laws, and Kelly Deere for the early primer on custody. Also, despite the fact that the details did not work their way into this book, I must thank Mariah Stewart for sharing links on baby trafficking and Amber Leechalk for answering questions about hunting season in Pennsylvania. Those bits just might show up later...

Finally, despite all the help I enlisted, any and all mistakes are most certainly my own!

The research I did for Runaway compels me to include a note about giving.

If you've been moved by this story, you might consider donating time, money, goods, or services to your local homeless shelter, soup kitchen, or food pantry. If you don't know of one near you, Charlie's Glide is a real place in San Francisco (despite the literary license I've taken for purposes of this story). The website is www.glide.org.

Thanks to you and your generous hearts, and many blessings.

—JB

JB SCHROEDER, a graduate of Penn State University's creative writing program and a book designer by trade, now crafts thrilling romantic suspense novels. Blessed with a loving family and wonderful friends in NJ, JB has no idea why her characters keep finding evil—but she wouldn't have it any other way.

JB loves to connect with readers and can be reached through her website:

www.jbschroederauthor.com

Made in the USA
San Bernardino, CA
18 August 2018